SKIPPING STONES

a story of finding home

a novel

Gloria Koll

Skipping Stones is a work of fiction.

Words and phrases of Norwegian in this book are in Nynorsk, the language often used in Vestlandet, western Norway. Along with Bokmål, Nynorsk is the official written language standard of Norway. Any mistakes on the printed page are my own.

Sections of this book have been previously published or presented in public readings. Chapters of *Skipping Stones,* formerly titled "A Valentine's Day Story" and "Lost in Libby," were first published as short stories. "Another Kid in Minneapolis" and "Libby Town Team" were selected to be read by the author at Seattle Writers Association's Artists in Performance. A shortened version of "Lykke and Moon" entitled "Anders" was selected for public readings by Whidbey Island Writers Association. These and other writings have appeared in national magazines *The Lutheran* and *Lutheran Woman Today* and in regional publications *Montana Journal* and *In the Spirit of Writing.*

SKIPPING STONES. Copyright 2013 by Gloria Koll. All rights reserved.
ISBN: 1499230923
ISBN 13: 9781499230925
Library of Congress Control Number: 2014907726
CreateSpace Independent Publishing Platform
North Charleston, South Carolina

for my father,
Ludvik,
the storyteller

CONTENTS

SKIPPING STONES

Part One

I Will Make Myself Lucky

1

KARI

She was six years old, hair the color of barley, arms and legs thin and wiry as river reeds. She crawled up the ladder into the loft of the hay barn, a place forbidden to her, and stood there towering over the cows shuffling below. From the edge of this high platform, little Kari could view the farmhouse where she lived—just Kari with her mother and father. Beyond the yellow house, she saw newly-sprouted green fields that sloped down to the stream. "Mine!" she whispered, her eyes bright with certainty. One month later, on the 4th day of July, her brother Rasmus was born. With his baby hand wrapped around her finger, he stole her heart; and with his birthright as oldest son under Norwegian law, he made off with her inheritance.

One child followed another on the little farm, until there were eight in all, Kari, the oldest, and Inga, the youngest—two girls bracketing half a dozen brothers. Inga's round cheeks dimpled each time Kari bent down to pick her up. Their brothers said it was no wonder that Inga's sturdy legs creased at the knees; why would she not be chubby, with Kari forever carrying her up and down the farmhouse stairs? But as year after year the fields produced only meager harvests, Kari silently praised

God that at least one child could be well fed and pampered on this poor farm with more children than crops.

Even as a young girl, Kari understood she would some day have to leave the farm. But each child born exacted a cost to her mother's health and strength, so Kari stayed on to help with the little ones. Still, by her mid-twenties it became clear to Kari that she could remain on the farm no longer. Her choices were these: to marry the oldest son of another farm, to hire herself out as a serving girl in a more prosperous household, or to go to America. Brainard, who would inherit the neighboring farm, was strong as an ox, and just as stupid and stubborn; Mrs. Lillquist, wife on the biggest farm in the valley, bullied and starved every girl she hired. America—now there was her chance. "Land of the free," some said; and even better, to her mind, a place of free land for those who would work it.

Kari sat down on the flat mossy rock very near the fjord—Nordfjord, one of the longest of the fjords, its fingers reaching deep into Norway's western mountains. She let her own fingers probe the beach pebbles until they found the right rock, and then she looked at it. A perfect circle, fitting smooth and flat into the palm of her left hand. She stood and took three strides to the edge of the water, the movement of her shoulders and hips strong from milking the goats and walking them to mountain pasture. Her arm swung back and to the side as her fingers clasped the edge of the stone. Like a slingshot, her arm whipped forward in a horizontal arc, and she released the stone. It skimmed the surface of the gleaming fjord waters, and then broke through and flew on, to skip lightly as she counted: *en, to, tre, fire, fem, seks, sju.* Seven skips before it sank into the fjord. Seven—that lucky number. In America, I will be lucky, she thought. I will make myself lucky.

The silken fabric of the fjord wrinkled slightly, caught the last beams of sunlight and scattered them. The reflected light shimmered across in wavelets as the breeze nudged the water. It was the season of sunlight, mid-summer, and she watched as the sun dipped below the horizon just before midnight. Even then the sky stayed in half-light, so that she could see the moon above Eggenipa, the pointed mountain, but not the stars. They were invisible, yet present, God's kind eyes watching her.

She reached down again to the rocky beach and chose another stone—flat, round, and smooth. She pushed it deep into the pocket of her skirt. Silver light trembled above the water, in the sky, and over the land. Kari looked for a moment at the iridescent footpath that led away from the fjord; then she turned to walk the mile back to the family farmhouse.

Just behind the farmhouse a well-worn pathway led to the outhouse, its wood painted and repainted the same shade of mustard yellow as the main house. Inside, the bare wood of the walls and bench were smooth from scrubbing. Kari stepped onto the fragrant fir branches, changed every day by her mother. She let the door remain slightly open to the field of yellow rye reflecting midsummer twilight mingled with moonbeams.

Then Kari retraced the path to her farmhouse—her brother's house when *far* and *mor* died, perhaps not many years from now. She turned and looked back at the cow barn, her place of milking and cleaning for the last fifteen years, her playhouse before that.

She pushed open the door of the farmhouse and moved quietly down the darkened hallway. She knew the five steps to the stairway, the eleven risers up the stairs, the six steps to her bedroom. She slipped inside and looked into Inga's crib. Baby sister's hair, blond and damp, lay curled against her forehead.

No child of my own will hold my heart as this one does, thought Kari. She brushed Inga's cheek with her fingers and pulled the blanket down a bit on this warm night. *"Sove godt, litle Inga."* Sleep well.

Kari crossed the room to a narrow bed and sat on it as she removed her clothes and shoes. She lay back on her pillow, pulled the covers across her legs, and whispered into the silence her favorite English words: "work" and "land" and "lucky."

The sun slid behind the mountains for only a few hours before angling up again. Kari heard first her mother in the kitchen, rattling copper kettles, and then the bell of the clock striking six. Yes, an early start this day, with *lefse* and *rømmegraut* to make for the meeting tonight. She rose and splashed water from the basin onto her face. She breathed in cool air from the open window and felt it lift her shoulders and chest.

There would be no stinking smoke to breathe this night, for sure—just the smell of brewed coffee and fresh-baked bread as her mother Hannah and her father Johan hosted the ten-year anniversary party for the anti-tobacco society of Byrkjelo. The party might also be somewhat in her honor, the last party to be held in the farmhouse before her journey to America, though she would not be so proud as to ask about that.

By 7:00 in the bright sunlight of early evening, folks began to gather. Some from neighboring farms walked briskly, carrying flowers or cakes. Others from Jølster, Myklebust, and Sandane arrived in wagons pulled by a horse or two. Hannah and Johan welcomed each arrival, and Kari took the flowers and cakes with proper words of praise and thanks for the gifts. *"Takk for sist,"* said each guest. Thank you for our last visit. Then the meeting began.

The society president preached fervently against the poison called nicotine, and then urged all present to make this a real party. So the socializing started, with Johan leading in the harmonizing of favorite old songs, and then everyone talking at once over coffee and the sweet rolls they dipped into coffee before popping them into their mouths. Coffee cups refilled, the neighbors settled onto benches and chairs and turned their attention to the local schoolteacher, Mr. Hegge, who lectured about the serious threat of tobacco and ways to fight against it. "Ladies have enough to do," he said with a courteous nod to the women, "without cleaning up the ashes of smokers."

Mr. Hegge urged all those in the farmhouse to their feet for a rousing *"tre ganger tre hurra"* for the anti-tobacco cause. And so they did, shouting three-times-three "hurrah!" in support of the society.

And perhaps they cried out even more joyfully because the speech was over and the party could begin. They filled the house with hearty singing and lively dancing to the accompaniment of the fiddle, losing all sense of time on this rare night of celebration. At 4:00 in the morning, with weary feet and merry hearts, the guests left the farmhouse for their own homes, soon trudging wearily into their barns to care for the animals.

Each guest paused at the door to shake Kari's hand and each wished her God's protection on her journey. "You may see my son there," said one woman, her jaw tight. She pressed a paper with his name and address into Kari's hand.

Kari left on a Tuesday with her wooden-staved steamer trunk, filigreed in tin and painted in shades of red, yellow, and green. In the weeks leading to this day, Uncle Gunnar soaked and bent the staves that held the curved lid in place, and Dorte, Kari's godmother, painted the trunk with the intricate and decorative swirls of rosemaling.

The family did not shed tears as she left, for that would be unseemly and perhaps make the parting too difficult for her. Rather, they shook Kari's hand and wished her a safe journey and a godly life. And her mother held both of her hands and whispered to her, *"I himmelen skal vi møtast igjen."* In heaven we will meet again.

Kari lifted sturdy little Inga into her arms. "And you, little one, will you come to join me some day in America?" Inga, thinking this was another of her big sister's silly games, answered with a laugh and a kiss.

Brother Rasmus and her father took Kari and the trunk to Sandane where the local ferry waited. Her father pressed coins into her hand, held her tightly to his chest for a moment, and then turned quickly away. The ferry took her to Bergen where she boarded a ship bound for the English port of Hull.

The ship's whistle groaned as the vessel pulled away from the Bergen dock, and Kari heard its low pitch matched by the first note of an accordion tune. Strolling the deck was a Norwegian lad, playing the squeeze-box and singing out in his clear, true tenor voice the words of pain and hope held in the heart of every emigrant.

> *Farvel du moder Norge nå reiser jeg fra deg,*
> *og sier deg så mange takk fordi du fostret meg.*
> *Du ble for knapp i kosten i mot din arbeidsflokk,*
> *men dine lærde sønner du giver mer enn nok.*

Farewell, Mother Norway, I must sail away from you
and offer words of thanks for raising me from childhood.
You are stingy with food for your poor, hard-working folks;
but to your rich, educated sons you give more than enough.

2

SEA AND LAND

A sharp sea carried the ship between Bergen and Hull. Brisk wind broke the water into quick waves, and the ship cut cleanly through. Kari felt her skirt pushed aside by two boys threading their way around the legs of the other passengers. "My sons, Steinar and Kristian," said their mother, Sofie, her left hand grasping the arm of a tiny girl. "They are wild as rabbits here on the ship. I cannot catch them, so I no longer try." Kari nodded in sympathy, remembering her own boisterous brothers.

"Their father, when he meets us in New York City, he will capture them and put them right." Sofie shook her head in defeat, her right palm settling onto a belly expanding with a fourth child. Still, Kari envied this family who had a father to meet them when they walked down the gangplank in New York.

Little nine-year-old Steinar and his brother Kristian, husky and strong for his twelve years, knew ships and the sea from their toddler days; they were born to the smell of it, lived near enough to Bergen harbor to feel every spanking breeze. The excitement that snapped between them came not from this ship ride over the familiar North Sea but from anticipation of what their father in America had promised them in a letter that arrived just before they sailed. They were to ride a train! A train across England, and after that, a truly big ship to America.

And so it happened. In Hull Kari and the family found the train station and settled into a compartment of the evening train to Liverpool. The train clicked along the tracks until the sound and sway of the train car rocked Steinar and Kristian to sleep. When they arrived in Liverpool the next morning, Sofie scrubbed their faces with a rough cloth. *"Raska på!"* she said. "Quick!"

Finally, Kari, with flowered trunk and knitted wool handbag, joined Sofie, her children, and the other third-class passengers on the ship that would take them to America. The ship first made a stop in Ireland to take on Irish families also heading for the Promised Land. Kari peered over the rail as the Irish came aboard, but the crew divided the ship's passengers by nationalities, so she could watch these smallish, sandy-haired people only from a distance. She turned back to the Scandinavian deck just as Steinar and Kristian scooted by.

The ship moved into the Atlantic, with its long, rolling waves. A strong wind blasted the waves higher, pushing the spray from the top of one wave to the next and splashing saltwater across the deck. Kari, Sofie, and her boys knew the motion of the sea, but these others, the inland people, moaned as the ocean shook them about. A big Swede stumbled by Kari and her new friends, barely making his way to the rail before he vomited. Steinar silently mimicked the Swede's trembling and retching as Kristian collapsed with laughter. "Land crabs," they whispered to each other, using the fishermen's insult for landlocked farm folk.

"Up on deck! Up on deck!" The sailors ordered all the passengers still down below into the fresh air, hoping the cold breeze would calm their seasickness. In the commotion, Steinar slipped onto the Irish deck, with Kristian right after him. A young woman, pale as death, lay motionless on the deck with the ship's doctor bent over her. "Only seasick," he said, and turned to others who whimpered that they might soon die—that they wanted to die—and to please let them die. Steinar and Kristian snickered at these pathetic inlanders. "*Land-krabbar!*" To waste time being seasick, when there was so much to do on board!

The seamen had closed off a large part of the deck with chains and rope. Now the waves came rolling in, high as their house in Bergen. When the ship set her nose into the valley and cut the next wave in two, the spray blew high overhead and came down like a waterfall onto the deck. The two boys screamed with delight. They rushed forward to the bow of the ship and held onto the anchor chain, riding each wave, diving straight down, and then soaring up again, shrieking and laughing at each other's saltwater-streaked faces. Then, shouting at them, came the ship's master.

"*Raska på!*" said Kristian. The two boys dashed for the ship's mast, and they scampered up it as they had done so many times in Bergen harbor. Steinar taunted the sailors, like a chipmunk in a tree, chattering at the upraised faces of the seamen gathered below. But the sailors could climb, too, and soon enough the boys were captured and carried down. Kristian righted himself and stood the scolding like the young man he nearly was, but not Steinar, who wriggled away, trying to escape back to the slippery, heaving deck. The sailors, laughing by this time, finally tied the irrepressible Steinar to a bed until he promised to behave himself. "So boys," a sailor said. "Now that you have come to your senses and decided to stay alive for the length of this sailing, you had better come eat with the rest of the seamen." And so Kari and Sofie found the boys eating raisin pudding at the seamen's table.

Finally, the sea settled into wide, smooth swells, and Kari and Sofie walked the deck as easily as walking to church in Bergen. Steinar and Kristian ran freely again around the deck, as the ship passed near the Newfoundland coast, tacked around icebergs, and ran alongside gray whales. Then the fog closed in, and the boys could not see beyond the rail. The ships horn blew and its bell rang, warning small fishing boats. "Lest we send them to the bottom," intoned a sailor, pointing downward and rolling his eyes at the lads. The fog lay cold across the deck, hovering around the boys' feet and crawling, it seemed to them, right up their pant legs, numbing their skin and chilling their bones.

Yet, a few days later, the ship sailed into New York harbor where the sun was so hot it melted the tar on the deck. Drifting up from the fog of sleep, Kari opened her eyes and watched transfixed as the family who had been sleeping next to her snatched up their bedding and dragged it up the stairway to the deck. In a panic, she grabbed her satchel and ran for the steps. Is the boat sinking? She almost called out the question, then shook the sleep out of her head. This is it, she thought. We are coming into New York City. We are coming to America.

Kari pulled her trunk from beneath the bunk, opened it, and carefully lifted out her one good wool dress. She unwrapped it, laying aside the covering sheet, and slipped the dress on over her head. Her fingers fumbled against the buttons, and the heavy fabric scratched against her skin.

On deck, Kari watched as many of the immigrants dumped their bedding, crawling with lice, into the harbor. She shook her own feather *dyne* into the fresh air and hoped it was not infested with the crawly things, though she was suspicious of a peculiar itching just at the base of her neck where her hair lay wrapped in a tightly braided bun.

Officials in uniforms guided Kari and the other passengers onto shore and toward a huge building called Castle Garden, though it was neither a castle nor a garden as far as she could see. The structure began with a lower wall of bricks stacked to form a wide oval base. Plunked onto the brick oval, a rectangular middle layer rested, itself topped by a round cupola. On a pole stuck into the top waved an American flag, as if celebrating this festive cake of a building and its arriving guests.

The immigrants were ushered through the two columns flanking the doorway and into the crowded building. There they stood or sat and waited. Some read newspapers, but Kari couldn't make out the print, all English words. A Swedish family next to her pulled out a small kettle, poured water into it, and placed it on the radiator. Soon the water bubbled and steamed, and the mother sprinkled grounds into the water. *"Kaffe?"* she asked, smiling at Kari. Kari nodded and gratefully took a cup from the woman's hand. Weak it was for sure, but at least hot water with the flavor of coffee.

Kari watched those ahead of her as the doctors and nurses examined them for sicknesses. Most passed on through, but a few were shunted off to one side, chalk marks on their clothing. She knew her own body to be strong and sound, but she straightened her spine and pulled in her stomach as she approached the medical team.

"Name?" asked the scribe at the next table. "Kari Johansdotter," she replied. The man at the desk looked puzzled and then said, "Well, I heard of some odd names with 'son' at the end, but I never heard of one ending up with 'daughter.' So, my girl, we'll put you down for 'Kari Johanson.' Now that's your American name, so don't you forget it." Kari couldn't understand most of what he said, but she took the paper he handed her and looked down at the name that was now hers. "Son," she whispered. "They think I am a son. Maybe in America, a son, a daughter—it's all the same—and in this strange and lucky place, a daughter can own land as easily as a son."

She looked ahead at the line of immigrants pushing out of the gate and onto the street. She glimpsed Sofie, Steinar, Kristian, and their baby sister running to a tall, thin man in a suit. The boys pulled back, but Sofie and her little girl rushed into his arms. Kari lost sight of them in the swarm of people meeting relatives arriving on this immigrant ship. Other people she could see jostling their way along the street were real Americans. What funny habits might she see in them? And what might they think peculiar as they looked at her?

Her hair, thick strands of brown and blond twisted tightly into braids, pressed against the back of her head. A russet fringe curled across her high, even forehead, a few wisps escaping heavenward above her smooth, wide face. Her eyebrows created a faint horizontal line above her astonishing eyes. Beneath fringed lids, glacier blue irises circled the polished onyx of her pupils. She seemed to be looking beyond, her eyes not quite centered on what was directly in front of her, but fixed rather on some distant point.

The startling, single-minded focus of her eyes made those standing in her pathway step aside as she strode from the dim Castle Garden immigration building onto the streets of New York City. As she passed, they turned to look again at her square shoulders and high bosom lifting the wool fabric of her dress. Narrow white stripes woven into black formed a pattern, first one stripe, then two, then one again. A black lace collar floated around her neck, just under her chin, and capped sleeves gathered in twin mounds over her shoulders.

Kari waved at the driver of a horse-drawn cab and pointed him to her trunk—distinctly hers, covered with rosemaling, yellow, green, and red. As she rode to the train station, Kari looked at the dresses of women walking in the streets. Fashions were different here, she could see that. The dress she wore, carefully tailored by her own hand, was in no way inferior in quality to those on these New York women, but its style already seemed old fashioned to her. She lifted her chin. They will see that I am from the Old Country, but I will walk like a queen, and they may think I am Norwegian royalty. With that, she descended from the cab and paid the driver extra to follow behind her with her trunk as she advanced toward the train.

The train to Chicago bustled with businessmen in suits, parents with children, women in pairs or small groups, and individuals on their own, as she was. Kari looked around the crowded car. A woman sitting alone smiled at her and motioned to an empty seat. Kari nodded to her and settled in, pushing her handbag under the folds of her dress. They sat side by side, mile after mile, exchanging names and the few pleasantries Kari could manage in English. After the first day, exhaustion dried up even that conversation, and they both slept. When, in the middle of the night, Kari felt the women's head on her shoulder, she let it be.

During the daylight hours, vendors offered food and drink, pushing their carts down the aisle. Kari took the water, which cost nothing, and a small bread roll. She regretted now paying the cab driver to carry her trunk. Her seat partner drew out a heavy basket of fruit, sausages, and cake. With nods and gestures, she urged Kari to take some. Kari shook her head several times, as anyone with manners would do, and then allowed herself to be persuaded to take a sausage, an apple, and later on, sweet vanilla cake. The two ate in companionable silence. The train rattled on and on until finally they were shaking hands and waving as they parted in the Chicago station. Kari found a cart to haul her own trunk to the connecting train, the train to Dakota.

From Chicago westward, train cars and stations were wreathed in tobacco smoke and stained with brown juice where a chaw of tobacco had missed the spittoon. Was there no campaign against this dirty habit, as there was in Norway? Kari lifted her skirt as the train jerked into motion, and she made her way down the aisle to her seat. The tracks led through bleak warehouses and onto the prairie. Outside her train car window, the flat, pale plains slipped by. It seemed to Kari that this prairie country was empty, not just of people, but of shape and texture. Her gaze moved to the sky, a bright blue bowl over the land. Her weary eyes found faces in the billowing clouds. God in heaven, I count only on you now. My people are far behind me. Lead me, you must, for if you do not, who will? Kari looked down at her open hands, and whether from sleepless nights or from the release of prayer, she felt light, unencumbered, and ready to close her eyes.

3

FLAT

The train squealed to a stop at the Brem station on this eastern edge of Dakota. Kari hefted her cloth bag down the aisle of her train car and handed it to the porter on the platform. She saw that passenger luggage lay in a jumble beside the train. Her own trunk, painted with rosemaling flowers, now seemed overly bright, even gaudy, as it sat surrounded by the sedate black and brown leather cases of the other passengers. She hurried to her trunk and pulled it off to one side, sitting on it and spreading her dark skirt over its lid. Then she looked up to see an inquiring face peering down at her.

"*Er du Kari?*" said the woman. In Norwegian! After a week of English words in New York and on the train, mixed with smatterings of other unintelligible foreign languages, Kari felt these three Norwegian words lift her to her feet.

"*Ja, og er du tante Margrete?*" Kari answered with a question. The woman nodded, yes, she was Margrete, very dear friend of Kari's mother and so glad to welcome Kari to Dakota.

As the porter lifted the trunk onto the horse-drawn buggy, Margrete's lilting Norwegian continued. Kari would stay in town with a family that needed a cleaning girl. A lowly job in the beginning must not discourage Kari for this is how all immigrants must start in America, until they learn English. If she worked hard, soon she would have land or a business of her own. Kari was silent and kept the disappointment from her face as Margrete introduced her to her new employers and settled her into a small, cheerless bedroom.

"Flat." Mrs. Schultz said the word to her in English, and although the word is the same in Norwegian, Mrs. Schultz had to say it three times and demonstrate with her hand on the ironing board by sliding her stretched palm across the sheet that Kari was to iron. "Flat!" she said, with a harsh, wide "a" sound that does not exist in Norwegian. Kari perceived that this sound fit the meaning of the word better than the Norwegian "ah" vowel, so soft that the word flutters on the tongue, "flaht." It was the sound in her own name, a gentle sound, "Kahri." The English strident "a" pushed against the throat, sending to her ear a squeezed, pressed down sound—indeed, flattened.

Kari lifted the iron from the top of the cookstove to the ironing board. She looked down at the wrinkled stack of sheets, tablecloths, shirts, and dresses. So many linens and clothes, even for a well-to-do family with five children.

Here I am—in service to a merchant family, as I might have been back in Norway. Kari hung a white, starched and ironed shirt on the back of a chair and reached for a heavy, black, wool dress in the laundry basket. But this is only for a little while. This is my beginning in America. In Norway it would have been all the years of my life.

Every day Kari cleaned and washed for the Schultz family. And every day she listened to the English spoken in this home. Helmet and Gunda Schultz spoke only English to their children, except in times of great excitement or anger when Kari would hear explosions of German. The German swear words sounded close enough to the words of Norwegian profanity to make Kari keep her eyes down and her hands busy with her task whenever Helmet shouted these words, and Gunda clucked her disapproval.

Kari savored the family's English words as she did her nightly stew and dumplings, chewing on the words' strange flavors, rolling odd bits of sentences around in her mouth. "Flaht," she pronounced it, "No! Flaat." She forced her tongue down, wide across her lower teeth.

On a warm, midsummer evening, Kari placed the last blue bowl into its proper spot on the shelf and hung the dishrag to dry on the edge of the sink. She slipped through the kitchen door and walked along the dirt road that ran in a straight line from the Schultz house into the prairie. Her eyes drifted up from the seed-tops of the waving prairie grass, searching for a place to focus. There was none: not a mountain, not a waterfall, not a hill, not a tree. "Flat," she said aloud. She felt her spirit shrink and tighten, so that it, too, seemed pushed down to the ground.

Her eyes followed the undulating grass back to her hands and she gestured, palms down, hands circling in opposite directions. "Flat." At her feet lay a small stone, white as sugar and sparkling in the slanting sunlight. Kari picked up the stone and pressed it to her lips, feeling the burning heat of it. She grasped the stone in her hand, strong with scrubbing and ironing, and flung it as far as she could, a great distance across the prairie. Then she tilted her head skyward and noticed for the first time a thousand little clouds, white flecks against the blue sky. Up and to the right a sparrow flitted over her, dipping into the grass. Kari heard notes from the bird hidden in the grass, its song rising into the Dakota evening.

"So—you have made your life here, too, *liten fugl*. I must learn from you to use the heavens as my escape from all this flatness. Sadly for me, I cannot fly." But like the song sparrow, she could sing, and she sang to herself all the way back to her little room.

"Den store hvide flok vi se, som tusen bjerge fuld' av sne."

The words of the hymn, with its dazzling vision of the saints, stayed in her mind through the night. In her dreams she saw snowy mountains and trees, and in the midst of them, her parents and grandparents, their grandparents, and the grandparents before them, generation upon generation of her people, row upon row, standing behind her, blessing her on her way.

4

LOG CABIN QUILT

Within the month, her mother's dear friend Margrete located a busy seamstress who needed Kari's tailoring skills and could provide her with a clean bed in a pleasant room.

"Well, now, that's done." Margrete seemed to jump about from task to task like a grasshopper in summer. "You now have a good workplace, but you are too much with old people. A woman new to Dakota must make younger friends." Margrete smiled brightly. "And I know just the group for you, with your quick sewing fingers."

The next Sunday after Norwegian Lutheran service, a young woman named Anna stepped in front of Kari. "I hope you will come to our quilting circle," she said. "We've heard about your sewing."

How could Margrete make this happen so fast? But Kari had come from a village in Norway, and she knew that news in a small town blows in the wind, the words drifting from mouth to ear, on and on. She smiled at Anna.

"Well, yes I will be pleased to come."

Scraps of bright cotton fabric lay scattered on the rug next to Matilda's quilting frame. Around the frame women settled themselves, two on each side of the rectangle. A ninth woman bustled around the edges, like a sparrow trying to flutter her way into the flock.

"Today we are making the old log cabin pattern." Anna placed Kari at one end, where she could observe the craft of American quilting. Anna explained the meaning of the log cabin pattern. A red piece centers each square: red, for the flames of the hearth at the center of every home. Strips printed of many colors build up the logs around the red hearth. Dark pieces stay separate from pastels, so that the eye sees a repeated diagonal stripe in the over-all pattern, first a dark band and then a light one.

"My grandmother made me a dress of this, just before I took the boat to America." Anna lifted up a sizable scrap of blue flow-ered print, her eyes soft upon it before her scissors sliced it into useful lengths.

"This was baby's christening gown." All eyes focused on the small white robe held against Marta's cheek.

"It may be you would like to keep..." Anna's words were interrupted.

"No," said Marta. "I have mourned long enough. And God has granted me others." With this she clipped lace from the baby dress, and cut the fabric into strips. The other women low-ered their eyes. For several minutes, only the click of scissors punctuated the silence.

Kari cut fabric, arranged patterns, and sewed with tiny stitches, along with the others. She was no doubt the most expert of all the sewers, but as an unmarried woman and, even at twenty-nine, younger than many around the quilt, she was careful neither to look overlong at awkward stitching nor to correct pieces imperfectly arranged. Still, others noticed her expertise.

"Is it true, Kari, as we have heard, that you were trained in tailoring back in Norway?"

"Well, perhaps a bit, from the seamstress in Byrkjelo. I was, I think, her worst apprentice."

"I would like to see her best then." Matilda approved of Kari's modesty and her sewing skills. One day soon, this Kari-girl would make a fine wife. Matilda's mind wandered over the selection of young farmers and craftsmen settling on the prairie. Perhaps something could be arranged.

The women stopped midday for coffee, bread, and soup, a simple meal on this day dedicated to quilts. Some of the quilts had been assembled and stitched at home, needing only to be tied by the gathering of women. The log cabin quilt would be saved for the next wedding, though as far as they could tell, no wedding would be happening soon.

Katta, the fat white housecat, wandered among the legs of the eating women, hoping for a crumb. "No, don't feed her." Matilda picked up the cat and closed her into a bedroom. "Anyway, she has not earned her food today. Maybe we can put her to use when the log cabin quilt is done."

Kari watched glances telegraph around the circle. She had not been here long enough to understand all the new customs, even those created by the local Scandinavians. This new world, it seemed, grew its own tales and tricks.

Stitched and tied by many hands, the log cabin quilt soon stretched across the frame. Narrow rectangles of cloth, like stacks of logs, guarded the sides of each red hearth square. Light fabrics contrasted with dark, perfectly arranged to form shadows in wide swaths across the quilt, corner to corner. Wool batting lifted the pattern, and the quilters imagined its warmth blessing the next marriage bed.

"Time for the cat!" Anna's strong voice enlivened the others, who unhooked the quilt from the frame and lifted it to the center of the room. Before Kari could question, she was pushed into place at the top end of the quilt, as the others gathered around and pulled the quilt out flat, all nine of them grasping its edges.

"Hang on tight!" ordered Anna, and Matilda tossed Katta in the middle of the quilt. The laughing women tossed the poor animal around and about, up and down on the surface of the quilt. Fluffy white and flailing, the cat frantically tried to find a foothold on the multicolored patches of the quilt. Then the quilt tilted, as if at a signal, and the cat rose directly in front of Kari. They were face to face for a moment; Katta's yellow eyes locked onto Kari's, seeming to beg for mercy. As the cat thrashed hopelessly at the air, its claws caught the cuff of Kari's sleeve. It was enough. Kari felt the cat attach itself to her bodice, and in pity, she held it close, petting its ears and head.

She sank into a chair with the cat. "What in heaven's name..."

The other women seemed delighted at the game. "Don't you know? The one the cat jumps to is the next bride!"

Kari and the cat settled down into the chair together as the confusion subsided. "I think the idea is not so bad, my friends, but I see no one knocking at my door just now."

"Don't worry, our dear Kari." Matilda stood behind the chair and placed her hands gently on Kari's shoulders. "Men never know their own minds, and neither does a young woman, who might too easily fall in love with a good-for-nothing, sweet-talking boy. We will be on the lookout for you, never you mind." The other women smiled and nodded.

Kari smiled back, for she knew they meant well and that in this world, women must always gather to protect each other. But she also believed that, at a time of her own choosing, she would join herself to a just and gentle man. She stroked the cat's silky fur. And if that man could make her laugh—and if he had eyes that begged her as this cat's eyes had—he would find himself resting his head in her lap with her fingers stroking his bottlebrush beard and thistledown hair.

In Norway, mountains reach up from the sea, green cliffs pushing high above blue fjords. The sky in Norway is suspended as a backdrop to the drama of ocean and earth. In high summer pastures, girls watching the sheep and goats have trees, crags, salty inlets, and gleaming lakes to catch their eyes. A farmer stepping outside late in the evening might look directly overhead to a small patch of starlit sky, but only on a winter night—for in Norway's summer, true darkness never comes.

"Flat," thought Kari, when she first arrived in Dakota. Flat and brown, dusty and featureless. She arrived in August. The summer sun had singed the crops. Horses hooves and wagon wheels ground clods and manure into sand and grime. The air lay humid and hot as a heavy wool blanket, pressing all life earthward.

It was in autumn that she began to hear men talk of the sky. Lightning overhead brought down rain or hail. A rare, dreaded funnel cloud sent families running to the cellar. Then winter covered the land with snow and a cold crispness that Kari understood. Again the men turned to the sky. A certain darkness on the horizon in the evening told of tomorrow's blizzard. Cloud cover at night might protect crops against plunging temperatures.

Next came springtime, and women looked to the heavens. "It's a buttermilk sky," said Marta as she strolled with Kari through a wheat field on the edge of town. Kari looked up, and she saw the upside-down blue bowl of the sky clotted with tiny clouds, like buttermilk after churning. She saw the sky over the prairie, immense, arched over the earth and stretched smoothly to the ground in every direction, so that she stood at the center of a spacious circle.

In midsummer as she walked on the prairie, the green wheat waved in the wind and grazed her hips. "Thigh high by the 4th of July!" said a farmer driving by in his wagon. Seeing her puzzled look, he repeated the phrase in Norwegian. She smiled, waved, and nodded that she understood. He tipped his hat to her and drove on. Kari turned again to the wheat. "So, you are growing right on schedule this year." She ran her hand over the plump heads of the wheat as she walked. A bird fluttered up and away, chirping madly. Kari stepped carefully and peered down into a grassy patch in the field. Hidden under the long green strands of grass, she spied a nest woven of straw. In the nest lay four brown-speckled eggs. The mother bird scolded and flapped her wings. Kari stepped away. She stood for a moment and considered the land she had called flat.

Now she saw that the land gently rolled into the distance, that the lines of the field edges moved upwards for some acres and then down again, undulating like swells in a slowly shifting sea. Eyes used to mountains and fjords needed only to adjust to the light and slant of this place to search for and find this new, subtle beauty.

Jens looked at her across the room through a jumble of farmers and their wives. There she stood, the young woman he had seen in the wheat field. His eyes moved over the skin of her face. Eggshell smooth and white, it looked cool to the touch. Her light brown hair was pulled back from her face, well behind her ears and flat against her head. With only a curly fringe high across her forehead, her face presented itself fully: determined chin curving into a continuous arc, which moved up and across her high cheekbones and disappeared behind the wisps of shiny, sable curls framing her brow. Her eyebrows formed a pale shadow above dark lashes. Her nose was straight as a plumb line, though not overly long. He saw that her mouth rested easily in this company, neither smiling artificially nor frowning with the tension he suffered in crowds.

He felt her pale blue eyes catch his for a moment, clicking against his stare. His gaze turned down to his worn, polished shoes. I am too bold, looking at her like this, without any introduction.

The fiddler began with an old dance tune from Norway's west country. Jens glanced up again and saw a little smile lift the corners of her mouth. Perhaps she is from the western fjords, he thought. Couples danced around the floor to the lively folk melody. Jens crossed the floor and stood before her. *"Vil du danse polka med meg?"* She gave a nod, and he took her right hand in his left hand, and he placed his right hand on her waist. It was as simple as that. He held her in his arms and whirled her around the room, lifting her high off the floor and setting her gently down. All this they could do, because of the music and dancing, all this they could do even before he said, *"Eg heiter Jens Nilsen fra Bergen,"* and before she said, *"Eg heiter Kari Johanson fra Nordfjord."*

He knew enough, gazing at her face, holding her dancing body in his arms, to commit his life to her. When he later
learned that she was thirty years old, it didn't matter. He saw
her as fresh, virginal, and innocent as a confirmand. And if she
was not quite that, who was he to judge, and who else was there
to judge, this far from Norway's church laws and chattering
gossips. In this new country, with her, he would make his rocky
farm pay, though he cared nothing for farming. With her, he
would make a good life on this prairie for them and for a family.
He knew this, without a single doubt, as he danced her around
the floor.

As she stepped and hopped to the polka, Kari tossed a smile
at this man Jens because he could dance very well—and, though
she had seen him only once before, driving by in a wagon as she
walked in a field of wheat, she knew almost everything about
him and about every one of the other single men in the room. A
conspiracy of married women made it their business to inform
single young women arriving from Norway about the bachelors
of the town and countryside.

And so Kari knew this about Jens: that he smoked but did
not drink alcohol; that he did not gamble; that he attended
church most Sundays; that he owned a modest farm from his
father's homesteading; that the old father lived with him in
the farmhouse. This last was a mark against him, said the farm
wives, but the father was near eighty and in poor health, so that
problem would, in God's own time, be solved. Another fact, they
told Kari, was more worrisome. Jens was a reader. He read not
just for practical purposes, like checking the newspaper for hog
prices, but also for foolishness—for learning about history and
theology. Leave that nonsense to the teachers and preachers,
was the opinion of the housewives.

Kari smiled at this, too, as she danced. She herself partook of foolishness, decorating her dresses with gathers and lace, singing songs to herself out in the meadow, and growing flowers inside the house in winter. A bit of foolishness in this man intrigued her, as long as she had first checked off the practical aspects of his livelihood and character.

5

JENS

She tailored the dress of black taffeta, nipped in at the waist and wrists with wide satin ribbon. The same satin, dark and shiny as a raven's wing, marked a deep V at the bodice, filled with rows of black satin smocking. Covering the puffed sleeves and long skirt, textured taffeta drew the light into its blackness, while satin at the bodice, waist, and cuffs reflected the glow of the kerosene lantern. Enough. The light was too dim for sewing. Kari slipped the needle into the high collar of the garment and folded the dark fabric into her cedar-lined trunk. The clean scent of the cedar surrounded Kari's wedding dress, permeating the fabric. Each stitch in the garment was a mark of deep joy.

Kari, at age thirty, had all but released dreams of marriage. That her heart could be filled with a splendid man, and that he could hold her in love as well—this came to her as an unexpected and magnificent gift. She reached deep into the trunk, rustling under the fabric for godmother Dorte's gold bracelet and for the *sølje* pin, worn by her mother just under the chin on the blouse of her Nordfjord *bunad,* the folk dress of her region, at every wedding and holiday. Kari had no *bunad* to wear as a bride, but she would have a fine dress, useful after the wedding for special occasions, and she would wear the gold bracelet and the shiny silver *sølje* pin, its eight tiny disks dangling like irresistible fishing lures, drawing her beloved Jens to her.

On their wedding day, Jens arrived at the church in a plain buckboard wagon pulled by a team of horses, one gray and one white. Jens' black suit and vest was borrowed, but fit well enough, the high lapels framing the white collar and tie of his shirt. Only the most careful eyes in the congregation would notice that the sleeves, reaching to the tips of his fingers, and the pants cuffs, gathered around the ankles of his black boots, were not tailored to his frame.

Kari stepped into the church fifteen minutes later, queenly in her dress, hair caught up in lace flowers. Ribbons of white rosettes defined the contours of her placid face, and a long white gossamer veil cascaded down over the back of her black dress to the church floor. The bride and groom each wore a rose and a sprig of white coral bells, tied together by a bow. Pins held the groom's flower spray firmly to his right lapel. The bride's corsage lay comfortably on her ample bosom, as if it might rest there securely even without fasteners. Each looked at the other with deep admiration and recognized in the eyes of the beloved a reflection of complete devotion. They echoed the pastor's reading of Lutheran marriage vows, using familiar Norwegian phrases. These formal vows felt important but stiff to Kari. The words she held in her heart were those Jens said on their wedding night, the words whispered in the silence of their farmhouse: *"Du er den eneste kvinne jeg noen gang har elsket."* You are the only woman I have ever loved.

"God's blessing on you and your marriage and the children to come!" Pastor Ott shouted his benediction to them in his well-trained minister's voice. Its resonance filled the little country church each Sunday, but on this morning, the prairie wind carried his words away. Beaming women passed the log cabin quilt up to Kari as Jens snapped the reins over the horses and the buckboard clattered along toward the Nilsen farm. The two rode side by side in silence until they reached a forlorn graveyard. Jens jumped down and took Kari's hand to help her off the wagon. Jens' hand felt changed to her. Her husband's hand. Somehow her hand. They walked to the graveside of his mother and looked at the name on the stone: Stina Frostad Nilsen.

Kari had been told—and further imagined—the life of Jens' mother. At the age of forty-eight, Stina had traveled with her husband and children by ship and train from Norway to a stump-filled farm in Minnesota and then, a decade later, to the rock-filled farm in Dakota. As the years passed, Stina wrapped quietness around her like a skein of wool that muffled both the few words she said and the noise she heard around her. She lived inside herself in a memory world of choral concerts, fiddle-led dances, and the slap of waves against wooden piers on Norway's westerly coast. Though her body survived in the scorching heat of the prairie sun and the bitter cold of the Dakota blizzard, her mind wandered the misty streets of old town Bergen. Bits of her heart and mind were buried in the graveyard of Bergen's Korskirken, the Cross Church, along with four of the twelve children born to her. Her own body descended into a Dakota prairie grave when she died, a shriveled, bent woman of sixty-four years.

Jens removed the boutonniere from his borrowed suit coat and placed the flower on his mother's grave. Kari laid her bridal corsage alongside.

"I was her youngest child," he said.

They drove then to the farm. Their farm—and yet, not quite theirs.

Jens' father, Nils, a trained architect and builder in Norway, had chosen farming in America over other occupations. He pictured himself a lord of the land, as others had been in Norway, with a manor house for his wife, Stina, and eight children; perhaps a house located on a high hill overlooking a rushing river. But there were no hills in this part of Dakota and no rushing river near the stony acreage he filed for, sight unseen. He knew nothing of farming, and his sons and daughters soon scattered across the Midwest, three boys enrolling in the Lutheran seminary for pastors and the girls marrying preachers or farmers. Only one son, young Jens, remained on the farm, and by the age of sixteen he had gathered up enough farming know-how from sympathetic neighbors to turn out wheat for market, hay for the cattle, and corn to feed pigs.

When Stina died, old Nils retreated to an upper bedroom of the modest, sturdy farmhouse he had designed. Surrounded by his books in Norwegian about cabinet making and boat building, he shut himself up in his room, a bitter, cantankerous old man. Now, twelve years later, as Kari rode beside Jens to her new home, she considered this—that she had acquired not only a loving husband and his productive farm—but also his father, Nils.

In the weeks that followed their wedding, Kari cleaned and organized the household. She moved quickly and expertly from task to task, cooking, sewing, and knitting as well as milking and churning. Jens soon saw the value of marrying a woman rather than a girl.

"Kari," said her husband, "you are truly my helpmate, even as the Bible says." Kari only lifted her chin a bit, for she knew her own worth.

But her father-in-law did not. Nils sequestered himself in his bedroom, coming downstairs only for meals. If she did not empty his chamber pot promptly every morning, he dumped it out of his second-story bedroom window. Almost blind, he pounded on the floor with his cane and pounded harder and louder if she did not climb the stairs quickly to attend to him.

In truth, there were many nights when Kari turned from side to side, first staring at the blackness of the ceiling, then pressing her cheek against the rumpled feather pillow, and finally pushing her entire face into the mattress, barely allowing space for one nostril to breathe. In the dark of the night, she thought of this farm, still in disrepair from years of her father-in-law's ignorance and neglect. Whenever it rained, she feared the crops would drown. Equally, when the sun beat down, she worried for the tiny, new shoots of corn and wheat. She fretted over her age, now beyond thirty, and some said too old for bearing and raising children. She created ugly pictures in her head of her mother and father, frail bones bending with age in the little farmhouse so far away in Nordfjord, with an indifferent daughter-in-law to care for them.

Only when Jens, sensing her restless tugging at the quilts, moved his half-sleeping body next to her back, drew her against his chest, and wrapped his arm snugly around her, could she sleep. In some miraculous way, the heat of his skin banished the coldness of her fears. By merely touching her, he had the power to cast out the demons—the *djevler*—that tormented her in the darkness.

Each morning, as the sun beamed into their bedroom window, Kari opened her eyes to the new day and at first blink felt energetic and hopeful. The aroma of coffee led her to the kitchen and her first cup of the dark brew left boiling in a pot over the cookstove fire by Jens, perhaps an hour earlier. She cracked eggs into sizzling butter and lifted her eyes as her husband pulled open the door nearest the barn, stomped dirt from his boots, and sat down at the kitchen table.

"Morn, min Kari," he smiled, still a bit shy with her. She looked out the window behind him and felt the prairie grass, bending in the wind, sweep away the doubts that plagued her by night.

"Some eggs then and coffee?" It was not really a question. As Kari said the words, she placed the plate of eggs and fried potatoes in front of her husband with one hand, and with her other hand she poured coffee into his waiting cup. *"Takk,"* he nodded and used his knife to push the sizzling potatoes through the egg yolk and onto his fork. Kari paused to watch as Jens closed his mouth around the forkful of steaming food. It was good to see a hungry man eat.

Soon he was out again in the barn, and Kari filled her own cup with hot, black coffee. She stepped out on the porch of the farmhouse and glimpsed a pair of quail, running down the dirt pathway, heads down, like uninvited guests making a quick exit. She almost called out to them—come back, you are most welcome here—when she saw the chicks, a covey of ten perhaps, as still as small gray stones scattered in the stubble and grass. She stood silent for a time and watched the chicks. Not a flutter. Not a cheep.

A cloud, lumpy as curdled cream, passed in front of the sun. She heard a sound, or thought she heard it, a faint whistle. Three of the chicks dashed for the brush beyond the path. The others stood their ground. Then, at a second whistle, four more skittered up the path. Finally, on the third call, the rest ran with tiny, frantic steps to the hen and cock hidden in the shrubby prairie bush. Ah! Reunited and safe. Kari could not see, but could almost feel soft feathers against her cheek, as chicks nestled into downy breasts and under sheltering wings.

6

First Snow

The first snow fell on Tuesday, dusting the fields with fine, sugary flakes. "Have a good sleep," Kari whispered to the wheat and barley stubble. "Rest well, land of ours, and wake up in the spring to grow a good crop for us."

With the snow, stillness settled over the farm. The days were bright, sun shimmering off the snow, but dark nights came early. By 5:00 the sun sank below the straight line of the horizon. With less to do on their homesteads, unmarried farmers sometimes gathered in the evenings around the kitchen table of Jens and Kari, knowing they would not leave without coffee and cake—*den beste kaka,* the men declared, raising their coffee cups to her in salute. Kari listened to the tales told around the table, many of the stories turning the hardships of farming into humor.

Then as the men leaned in to speak almost in whispers, Kari heard fear in their voices. They spoke of Indians—the native people of Dakota. The farmers described them as more animal than human. They lived, these Indians, by eating off the land, picking berries and killing wild beasts and birds for meat. They didn't have houses or farms, like proper Christian folk, but wandered from place to place, depending on the season.

"They got a new religion now, I hear, dancing with ghosts, calling on their dead to kill us all, to get this land back again."

"Do you mean they owned this land, before us?" asked Kari.

"Well, not own it with a legal deed, you know, like we got. They roamed over it, you might say, like the buffalo and rabbits. Didn't know how to farm or make use of the land." Cousin Arnie put down his pipe and frowned. "And now they got this ghost dancing. But the army will stop that heathen nonsense, soon enough."

Kari tried to picture these beings, half human and half animal, dancing around a fire. Childhood pictures appeared in her head of hair-covered monsters, troll-like and menacing. Then December came with Christmas cooking and church celebrations, driving from her mind the dark stories of gnomish folk.

After Christmas, winter darkness closed in. Kari left holiday candles in place on the table, and she lit them in the morning to push back the gloom. Surrounding the house, furrows of plowed prairie lay silent and scarred, marked with black earth and swirling snow. Kari looked through the kitchen window and imagined she saw a strange form lurking in the grassy stubble. Then movement: a distant ragged line snaked through the snowy field.

Kari placed the Christmas candle back on the white tablecloth and watched through the window as dark creatures moved slowly toward her house. Jens was out in a distant field, looking for stray cattle, too far away to call. She placed her right hand on the rifle, held steady to the wall in the wooden gun case.

The little band drew nearer still, and now she began to see their faces. Women and children, they were, and one old man. Their clothes hung in tatters, leaving patches of skin to the wind. A woman held a bundle, a baby perhaps, under her coat and wrapped her arms around the bunched cloth. The faces were expressionless and their eyes as flat and black as river stones. The old man, first in the line, walked directly toward her door. The others stumbled after him. The door swung open. Kari stood unable to move, as if caught in a strange dream.

"Cold," said the old man. "We will sleep and eat. Then we will go."

Kari said nothing and still could not move. The women brought their children near the stove. It was seeing the children that jarred Kari into action. She strode to the kitchen and grasped a knife. The old man stepped behind her and took firm hold of her wrist. She turned her head to see his face inches from her own. "No," she said. "I won't hurt them." With her other hand, Kari reached for the loaf of bread and nodded toward the knife. The old man released her arm.

Kari sliced off thick hunks of bread and placed them on a platter. She spread butter on the bread and added slices of pheasant and dried fish. She turned, placed the platter on the table, and stepped away. "Here," she said to the old man. He spoke to the women, and one by one they took the food, fed it to their children, and ate of it themselves. Kari watched a mother chew a piece of meat into tiny shreds and then carefully, like a mother bird, feed it to her little one.

For an hour or more, the four women, three children, and the old man lay on the floor by the stove and slept. Then with a few words the old man roused the others, and they filed quietly through the door. Again Kari felt spellbound, as if ghosts had visited her house. When Jens stomped the snow off his feet and pushed open the door, she looked at him in solemn silence.

"What is it," he said.

"I can scarcely tell you. But sit down here by the stove, and I will try."

On February evenings, Kari lit kerosene lamps in the kitchen and in the sitting room. The lamplight warmed the farmhouse with pale, luminescent circles near the rocking chair and the reading table. Reading, that was Jens' winter occupation. Books lined the sitting room wall—books of geography, history, and architecture. Every evening, Jens took a book in his rough hands, looked at the cover, carried it to his reading chair, and opened it. If the wind outside howled or Kari asked him a question, Jens did not hear, so absorbed was he in his book.

Kari settled in her chair as well, very near a table with the strongest light. From under the table she pulled a wooden sewing box painted with rosemaling, a design of flowers in slate blue and mustard yellow. On another night she might spin wool or knit a sweater, mittens, or stockings, but this night she had finer work to do. Her hands grasped linen and thread sent from Norway for the making of Hardanger lace. She laid the fabric on the table near the lamp and caught it firmly in a wooden hoop. On the white cloth, with white thread slipped through the eye of a silver needle, Kari stitched a small, precise pattern. Her eyes examined each stitch; her lips moved with silent counting. Still, the willful cloth and cantankerous thread conspired, and Kari detected disorder in the pattern. *"Uffda,"* she muttered, biting off the thread and pulling free, one by one, the stray stitches. Again she threaded the silver needle and pushed it through the weave of the hoop-stretched cloth. Down from above and up from underneath, again and again.

Night following night, the pattern emerged, a pattern of stars and squares, hearts and fleurs-de-lys. In a final act of courage, Kari grasped tiny, gleaming scissors and cut into the cloth, removing with surgical precision, thread by thread, bits of fabric between her stitches. She lifted the finished piece to the light. White on white, stitched pattern and clipped spaces, the Hardanger lace gleamed, linen snowflakes against the soft lantern light.

Kari found no flaw in her work, and finding none, smiled and looked across at Jens, bent over his book. Useless to speak to him, his head a thousand miles away. Kari slipped the needle back into its flannel case, placed the sewing box under the table, and stepped across the room to her husband. She spread the perfect lacework over the pages of his book. He looked up at her, and then down at the Hardanger lace. When he lifted his eyes again to meet hers, they were warm with approval. He held her eyes with his and nodded.

It was in this moment of his silent admiration that Kari found the words. She removed her Hardanger lace from Jens' book, took the book from his hands and placed it on the table. She knelt beside his chair and held his face between her palms. She turned his head until they were almost nose to nose.

"I am glad you like this little thing I have created. It is time to tell you that you and I together are creating some small thing." She took her left hand from his cheek and clasped his big, rough fingers, drawing them to her belly. She pressed his hand into her stomach, never releasing his eyes from hers.

"*Nei*," he breathed the word softly, turning his head slowly from side to side.

"*Jau*," she answered. "It is true."

Jens rose from his chair and drew her up against him, pressing her head against his chest.

She woke before dawn the next morning with this thought: life is growing inside me. Not yet a baby, but the promise of a baby. How can this be? Kari wrapped a quilt around her shoulders and stepped out onto the porch. She watched the sun rise, half-hidden behind a wooly cloud, its edges stretched in a ragged skein along the horizon.

The cloud shielded her vision from the bright eye of the sun. Kari gazed at the beams of light that streamed upward and away from the morning mist in streaks of gold and orange against the pale blue sky.

She felt herself both infused with life and initiating life. Both earthen vessel and potter shaping the clay. Both linen fabric and the hands embroidering the cloth. Overshadowed by light and shining from within. Chosen and choosing. Co-creating with the Creator.

Baby Johan arrived in June on Kari's thirty-second birthday. The prairie wind lifted the scent of lilac into Kari's bedroom window as she nursed him. His face, ruddy against her white breast, seemed already masculine and determined. He was the image of his father. Jens denied this, saying the boy had his mother's eyes, but Kari saw without resentment that he did not. When her husband held the baby, their faces side by side, Kari mused, did I carry that child within me for nine months? She watched them together and knew that the boy would become a man very like his father, and she was glad of it.

Two years later Rolf was born, howling his way into the world.

Next came baby Serianna, beautiful even at birth. She lay in the cradle, content and observant. "She looks so carefully at us, at the wind blowing the trees, at the birds flying by the window. What must she be thinking?" Jens picked her up and held her gently, turning her face to the open door and the sunny barn-yard. Serianna stared at the rooster strutting by and at the hens running this way and that. Six-year-old Johan tiptoed near and touched her baby leg.

"*Ja*, Johan," said his father. "You are the big boy now. You must protect your little brother and baby sister."

Dagny was born in winter, weak and fuzzy as a runty kitten. The midwife baptized her with water pumped into a coffee cup. The baby wheezed and mewed, squirming away from the breast. She died on the third day. It seemed to her neighbors that Kari grieved longer than necessary. "She has two sons and a daughter," they said. "'The Lord giveth and the Lord taketh away.'"

Kari stayed in bed, her head turned to the wall, for two weeks. She refused solid food and spoke only to her friend Marta. They whispered quietly together, and Marta held Kari's head against her soft bosom. "It will always be with you, dear Kari, but you will survive. No matter what they say, we do not die of a broken heart."

The next year, Kari gave birth to another girl. She had her christened with the same name, Dagny, and imagined that the new baby held the spirit of the one who had died. Kari told no one that she thought this, and she supposed it might be sinful to believe that the first Dagny was now within the second one. But her need to believe it overcame her fear of the church or even of God.

And finally in 1911, the year her father-in-law Nils died, a son Anders was born, the last of Kari's children. They filled up her life, a procession of unanticipated blessings: Johan, Rolf, Serianna, Dagny, and little Anders.

7

ANDERS AND JOHAN

Kari was forty-two years old when she gave birth to Anders, and she looked on him as a last-minute gift from God, a sweet afterthought of the busy Creator. Early in infancy this little one smiled at her and laughed with delight when she so much as looked his way. As a toddler, he brought her gifts: a little wooden horse, pressed into her hand, or a bite of cake from his plate, placed gently on her tongue. Once he pulled a baby beet from the garden and presented it to her with such pride that she couldn't scold him. So it was from the beginning, between this mother and her son.

A traveling photographer visited the farm when Anders was four, but the photographer's black and white picture did not capture her youngest son's face. Perhaps a painter could do it better. Pigment was needed. What made people look again and smile was his coloring. His eyelashes were black, thick and long. Eyes opened or closed, the lashes lay like tiny raven feathers against his white skin. On face and body, his skin was perfectly smooth and clear with never an unhealthy mark or blemish, so that even when he scraped himself, the scratch healed quickly and left no mark on the silky surface.

His mouth was almost red, and his cheeks pinked when he was mad or embarrassed. When he was very angry, he cried, and the black lashes bunched together, wet against his skin. He did not cry often.

Anders' smile and laughter came so easily that his father claimed he was born laughing. His mother knew this was untrue. He was born on Good Friday with the agony that portends, and he almost died. For five days, longer than the suffering of Our Lord, his tiny body fought to live, grunting with each gutsy breath, pushing death off with tiny gasps. It was somewhere in the mystery of that struggle that he gained his giggle, which for these childhood years had shown him how to laugh every day, as if to say, I can conquer life! I have overcome that nasty devil called death!

Anders grew from baby into boyhood as his older brothers and sisters made the little farmhouse shudder and shake with clattering feet and chattering tongues. Spiteful *farfar* Nils, who liked to trip his racing grandchildren with his cane, had gone on to whatever heavenly reward awaited him. Still, the house felt cramped with five young children rattling around in it, and it seemed old-fashioned without the household conveniences available in 1915.

Jens drew plans for a new farmhouse, with a battery-powered generator for electric lights and a coal furnace for heat, to be built on acreage purchased to the east of the homestead. Crops had been good for a few years with decent prices, so Kari and Jens had cash in the bank for the entire cost of the house, materials and labor. The town banker said they were foolish to pay the workers at the end of every day and to shell out for the lumber each time they bought a load. "Keep your money in the bank. Earn the interest yourself and pay up when everything's done. Just good business," said the banker.

"I think he may be right, you know," said Jens. "But it just doesn't seem fair to keep folks waiting to be paid." Kari gave a quick nod, and it was decided. Each week they watched their new farmhouse go up and their savings go down. Finally, with the money in their bank account spent, their new house stood finished, to the final nail.

Three doors led into the Nilsen farmhouse. Strangers and Pastor Ott knocked and entered through the library door. Friends and family called out as they stepped into the kitchen doorway. Hired men trudged up a steep outside stairway, shouldering open the door leading to their second-story bedrooms. Thus with these three doors, Kari and Jens sorted out the people in their life and maintained a simple order in their home.

The farmhouse rooms were arranged sensibly as well. At the front of the house was *"far's bibliotek."* The library was called this because it was here that Jens sat on snowy winter evenings to read his books. Beside the library sat the parlor, dim, draped, and seldom used.

In the back of the house, looking out on the chicken yard and garden stood the kitchen. A big wooden table hunkered down near the warmth of the coal-fired cookstove. Sixteen people could settle in, with wiggle and elbow room, around the long, sturdy table. Because neighbors and cousins stayed over for days or weeks, the table often gathered a full sixteen around it. On the far end of the room sat a wicker basket, catching shirts, trousers, and underwear tossed down the laundry chute from the upstairs bedrooms.

Kari's pride was the enormous cookstove. On its shiny clean griddle top, she flipped hotcakes for breakfast or *lefse* for holidays. To the right of the stove, the water pump gripped the counter, spout aimed into the sink. Kari grasped the pump handle, thrusting it down, pulling it up, pushing down again, urging the good cistern water into tin pitchers for drinking. To the left of the cookstove was the cozy corner where Kari sat and knitted in the dwindling light. She could knit without a glance at the yarn or at her stitching, and her eyes wandered to the window and the first fallen autumn leaves scattered against the henhouse. By the barn she saw her oldest son, Johan, kneeling beside his little brother, giving him something.

The little cast-iron bank fit nicely into Anders' hand. As Johan placed it there, the weight of the bank pushed Anders' hand down into his lap. Anders looked happily up at his big brother. "For me?" he said.

"*Ja,* for you, for saving your pennies. It's from the big Brem bank. When you have saved enough, we can take your little bank into town and put all of your pennies into the big people's bank. Look, this is how it works."

The penny bank was molded in the shape of a pot-bellied stove. It looked just like the big stove in the country schoolhouse where Serianna studied. Anders was afraid of that stove as it grumbled away, heating the schoolroom when families came to see the Christmas play. But this pot-bellied bank made him smile as Johan showed him how to press a penny into the slot on its little smoke stack.

Week after week, Anders slipped pennies into his bank. Sometimes *far* or *mor* gave him a penny, for they approved of him learning to save. Big sister Serianna gave him five pennies on his birthday. Once he found a penny on the farmhouse porch, pushed it quickly into his pocket, and ran to his bedroom and his bank. "Click," said the bank, as the penny fell to safety inside.

Finally, the bank was full of pennies. Anders knew this for sure because the bank was so heavy that he could barely lift it. He tried pushing in another penny, and it refused to go.

"Do we have to take it to the big people's bank?" Anders wrapped his fingers around his little cast-iron stove, protecting it.

"*Ja,* afraid so, little brother. The bankers have the only key to open it. That keeps you from stealing the pennies and spending it on candy."

"It wouldn't be stealing, would it? It's my money, isn't it?"

"Well, yes and no. It will be your money after some years, when you can learn to use it for something sensible." At the word "sensible" Anders fell silent. "Sensible," when said by his parents or by his older brothers or sisters, was always the last word of an argument.

At 10:00 on a chilly morning, Anders sat beside Johan in front of the wagon, a woolen blanket covering his legs. "First to the town bank with your pennies and *mor's* egg money. Then we'll get groceries for *mor.*" Johan looked at their mother's list, translating her Norwegian words into English: "*sukker*" into "sugar" and "*eddik*" into "vinegar."

As the wagon rolled down main street, Johan noticed a crowd in front of the bank. He reined in the horses and jumped off the wagon. "Stay right there," he said, "and hang onto your bank." Anders pressed the bank down between his legs and covered it with the lap blanket. He watched his brother elbow his way into the crowd. The voices of the men at the bank's door sounded loud and angry. One man pounded on the door with his fists. A woman turned away from the crowd with her hands over her face. Johan jumped back onto the wagon and turned the team of horses, so that the wagon began to roll back up main street toward the edge of town.

"What about my pennies for the bank? What about *mor's* sugar?" Anders still held tight to his pot-bellied bank, keeping it under the blanket until he could figure out what was wrong. But he worried about the sugar, too, because no sugar for his mother would mean no cookies for a long time.

Johan seemed not to hear his questions and snapped the reins to hurry the horses along the country road. As soon as the horses pulled the wagon to a stop in front of their new farmhouse, Johan jumped out and sprinted for the kitchen door. Anders hopped down, too, his little bank pressed against his chest, and ran after his brother. Johan's huge hand yanked the knob and opened the door with a clatter, slamming it behind them with a bang. Both Kari and Jens rose from the kitchen table.

"What is it?" said Kari. A chill went through her at the look of his furrowed brow.

"The bank is closed. The manager, Mr. Hansen, left in the middle of the night and all of the bank's money is gone."

"*Nei!*"

"Yes," said Johan. "I am afraid it is true."

"*Gudskjelov,* Kari." Jens looked stricken as he sank back into a chair. "Thank God we paid for this house as it was built, or we would be back in the old one."

Johan handed his mother a white envelope filled with coins and small bills. "Your egg money, *mor.*" Then he turned to Anders. "You come with me."

The two brothers, one big and steady, almost a man, the other a little child, walked together to the barn. Johan put his hand out for the little cast-iron, pot-bellied stove. Anders handed it over to him.

"You know that Mr. Hansen, the town banker, has stolen all the money in the bank." Anders nodded his head. "There is one more thing. The big owners of the bank, the ones from Minneapolis, are coming to take whatever is left—chairs, tables, everything. A note on the door said that all children's banks must also be turned in. If we do that, they will take your money. And that would be stealing, for sure."

Anders nodded again. "But they have the only key." His voice trembled, but he did not let himself cry.

"That is true." Johan lifted up the pickax he used in the fields to break apart boulders that were too big to move. "Can you think of a way we might open this bank without a key—to save your pennies?"

Anders looked at his little bank in his brother's left hand, and he looked at the big pickax in his brother's right hand. He looked at his brother's strong arms.

"You could break it open."

Johan placed the little pot-bellied stove on the ground. With one swing of the ax, he shattered the bank. Pennies scattered over the dirt, and the two brothers gathered them up into an impressive pile.

"We broke the bank!" Anders stuck his chest out and shined a penny against the flannel of his shirt. "Should we get another one?"

Johan considered the question. "I think it would be better for you to ask *mor* for one of her pickle jars for your pennies. A jar you could keep under your bed and count your money every day, if you want to."

"That's sensible," said Anders.

8

GYPSIES

It seemed to little Anders that the world spread out too far. By horse or buggy, it took a long time to go from his farm to the farms of friends. It took a long time to go to church or to school or to town. Still, sometimes the world came right to their own farmhouse door, and every visitor to their house that autumn brought excitement of one sort or another. Old Uncle Olav came by on Saturdays for coffee and cookies, often taking Anders along on his morning walk. Mrs. Vik and Mrs. Andersen came as a pair, chattering in Norwegian to *mor* about mishaps in the countryside, shaking their heads and sighing deeply over a sad story before plunging eagerly into another bit of gossip. But when the Gypsies came—oh, when the Gypsies came—that was the most amazing of all!

Gypsies came rolling through the countryside in canvas-covered wagons every autumn. The first year, shop owners in Brem tried to sell them a few items, reaching under the counter for chipped bowls and bent spoons, good enough for Gypsies, surely. But bargaining with these wanderers wasn't easy. Gypsy women in voluminous, gathered skirts and men in long coats with big pockets wandered here and there in the corners of a shop. Three in a tight grouping called to the clerk. In heavily accented Romany phrases, one Gypsy asked about an item—how much it cost, how it worked, who made it—while the other two gathered to form a screen between the clerk and the rest of the store. Over the chatter of the three bargaining Gypsies, the clerk could hear a sort of scurrying, a flurry of movement, and then, within minutes, an ominous silence in the empty shop, deserted of all but the clerk and the three Gypsies grouped tightly around him. No, now they did not want the item after all. Perhaps next fall, when they came through again. And the last three Gypsies, skirts and coats rustling, moved out into the warm, South Dakota sunshine. The clerk rushed from shelf to shelf, aghast at the pilferage. Shop owners moaned to each other over their losses. And the following autumn, and the ones after that, they locked their stores up tight on the day when the Gypsies came to town.

Mothers kept their children behind closed doors and forbade them to go outside, for everyone knew that Gypsies would steal a pretty blond child that caught their fancy. You could sometimes see a blue-eyed boy or girl in the midst of their onyx-eyed children, and how could that happen—unless they'd nipped away a Swedish or Norwegian child, God forbid! Anders and Dagny, playing by themselves one afternoon, saw the Gypsy wagons coming, and the two children jumped into a deep ditch until the caravan had passed them by.

But when the horse-drawn Gypsy wagons pulled onto Jens and Kari Nilsen's farm, stopping to rest in the shade of the thousand trees Jens planted so many years ago, no one chased them off or locked them out. Dagny and little Anders fixed their eyes on the Gypsy men as Jens invited them to bring their horses to drink and to settle their families under the trees to spend a night or two. With the blessing of the farming couple, the Gypsies wandered through the cornfields and plucked the waiting yellow cobs, stroking the long tassels of corn silk as they walked back to the wagons.

Kari baked them loaves of crusty bread and let her children stay up late, well after dark, when the Gypsies built a great campfire. A man lifted a violin gently from its cloth wrap and played a weeping tune of a faraway land. Then he flashed a smile at Anders, who stood watching at the farthest reach of the fire-lit circle. The Gypsy pointed his bow at the boy, lifted it to the starlight sky, and then attacked the strings of his violin. With sweeping strokes he coaxed out joy-filled songs and the Gypsies danced wildly, men flinging off their coats, women swirling layers of red and black skirts, and black-haired children prancing light-footed among the dancers like unbroken colts.

"Aren't they wonderful, *mor?*" sighed little Anders, as Kari carried him off to bed. "But people say they steal."

Kari smiled and held him close. "Well," she said, "I only know this for sure. From our farm, they have yet to steal a single thing." She slipped the bright, silky Gypsy scarf from her shoulders and wrapped it around his nodding head.

———

As he grew older, a certain adventurous spirit took hold of Anders. A physical energy pushed him to run into the wheat fields, trampling over the tender wisps of grain. When he was five, he took off through the cornfield and became lost in the tall stalks. The merciless summer sun beat down on his blond head, and he hid from the heat, crouching near the cool earth for hours. Finally, in the quiet, he heard the clanging bell of the lead cow as Lykke, the farm dog, moved the herd back to the barn. Anders followed the sound to the edge of the cornfield, dusted himself off, and walked into the barn with the cows.

"And where have you been all this afternoon, with your mother worried," said his father sternly.

"Just looking after the cows," said Anders, meeting his father's eyes, for he could tell a good lie when it was needed.

"Then I guess you are ready to milk them," said his father, moving a pail under the biggest udder.

Anders had never milked a cow, and his small hands wrapped uncomfortably around the teats. His short arms could barely reach the udder, and his nose and cheek pressed hard into the prickly coat of the cow's side. She smelled sweet, of summer air and hay, but he couldn't breathe with his face so tight against her. Still, he tried to squeeze out some milk, and a tiny trickle hit the milk pail. His father left the barn for the house, strode back to the barn, and went about his work, lifting pitchforks of hay down to the cows. After a time, he dropped the pitchfork, wrapped his strong fingers into Anders' hair and drew him away from the cow.

"I think that is enough for your first day of tending cows. Now, go and help your mother. You can carry this bucket to her. She may need this milk for supper."

Anders walked from the barn to the kitchen carrying the bucket. He felt ashamed, not so much for his absence but because there was so little milk in the bucket. Kari was at the stove when he came in, and she barely glanced in his direction.

"So," she said, "*far* says you have been milking."

"Yes, *mor.*"

He placed the bucket on the floor and stepped in front of it to hide its meager contents. Kari reached around him, lifted the bucket, and peered into it.

"Not so bad, for your first time. I had less on my first milking in Norway."

Anders kept silent, grateful for this compliment.

"But you must not wander off again without telling me. This is a farm, you know, and we count on every worker. If you want to work in the fields or with the cows, you only have to tell us that you are now a man and want to help, and we will be happy for that. But only *far* or *mor* can tell you where you are most needed."

Anders stood in silence before her and nodded his head. Their eyes met, and he saw all in that moment that she understood him completely: his need to explore, his hunger for the prairie, and even his lie about tending the cows. She understood all this, forgave him everything, and left him with his pride undamaged.

"Now," she said. "I think if you will bring me a little sugar, we will use this milk to make some rice pudding for supper."

———

Olav's chin sank into his hands, as he looked for sympathy at his little nephew. Olav's red-rimmed eyes brimmed with the memory of money lost, as he regarded little Anders from under shaggy gray eyebrows. Anders patted his great-uncle's knee, and Kari handed them a plate of cookies to share.

Old Uncle Olav lived alone on the farm just north of the Nilsen place. He was a widower whose three daughters lived out west near Seattle and whose son worked around the county as a hired man. After the fall harvest, with not much to fill his days, Olav was known to drive his wagon to Brem and get so drunk he'd climb back into the wagon, close his eyes, and let the horse find his way back to the farm. Still, he was a relative, and so Kari didn't object when he wandered in for dinner midday and sat afterward on the stoop, telling stories to little Anders. She liked that he told cautionary tales about the evils of strong drink and the chaos wild speculation had caused in his life.

"*Ja,* I really done it this last time. I shipped my cattle into Minneapolis, went along myself, and sold them for two thousand dollars—and I got it in a roll of hundred-dollar bills. That's a heck of a lot of money, don't you know?" Anders nodded his little blond head, and Kari, listening from the kitchen, tried to imagine that amount in cash. "I woke up the next morning in a cheap hotel. Couldn't remember the night before. My money was gone. Even my pants was gone. The hotel owner got something for me to wear and called the one friend I had in Minneapolis. He bought me a train ticket home—wouldn't give me the money—bought me the ticket and put me on the train. So back I come to Brem and the farm—all my money gone."

Each day after that, Olav walked his two dogs down the road and back. One Saturday morning he stopped by the Nilsen farm, sat at Kari's table for coffee, and invited little Anders to walk with him. Kari nodded, so Olav, Anders, and the dogs set off. They walked the length of the near field, looped back, and stopped at the mailbox. Olav picked up a handful of bills and letters and came to one envelope from a company called "Prairie Commodity Futures." He started to throw it away, but stopped, and then opened it. He read the letter out loud. "We wish to inform you that your investment in commodity futures has had a positive return. Enclosed is a check to your account of twenty thousand dollars."

Kari and Jens helped Olav unravel the puzzle. It seemed that when Olav was drunk in Minneapolis, he'd put all the cattle money in crop futures, betting that the price would go up. As it turned out, crop prices went up tenfold, and Olav's two thousand dollars grew to twenty thousand dollars.

Sitting with them at the kitchen table, Olav looked at the check and then looked down at Anders. He shook his head, waved the check in the air and said, "Anybody as stupid as I am is too stupid to have twenty thousand dollars!"

Olav took that money and bought three houses across the sound from Seattle for his three grown daughters and a farm in South Dakota for his son—a farm complete with tractor and combine.

After that, Olav spent most of his time making home brew and drinking it down.

———

The father on a farm to the south was also known for drunkenness—and for keeping his wife poor and pregnant. Three of his eight waifish children walked across the prairie to the one-room South Dakota schoolhouse. The other five, still too young for school, stayed at home with their mother, scurrying into her skirts at the slightest noise like a covey of skittish baby quail.

Saddled with a good-for-nothing father, it was all the more a catastrophe for this family when their shabby house burned to the ground one cold starless night. Soon enough, Mrs. Vik and Mrs. Andersen came by with the news, and as they clucked and prattled on, Kari ached for the burned-out family's little ones, a bit younger than her smallest, Dagny and Anders. She made a soup of pork and potatoes, baked two loaves of bread, gathered up clothes her own children had outgrown, and took the lot by wagon to a neighbor's house where the homeless family huddled.

The wife's eyes gave quiet thanks as her husband and children gathered around the thick, meaty soup. One little girl, about four years old, climbed into Kari's lap where she sat in a rocking chair a bit apart. Kari hugged her close and rocked back and forth, willing blessings on this small one.

The sweet face turned up to Kari's own and smiled. She attached herself to Kari's neck and hoisted herself up to the farm woman's ear. "You don't have to feel sorry for us," she whispered. "My daddy buried all of our clothes in the back yard before the fire."

With her weaving, knitting fingers, Kari had long since learned the craft of twining sturdy cloth. She sensed that all those living on that harsh plain were threads, shuttled together by a hand they could feel but could not see. Like fibers of flax, they were laced over and under, whacked with energy into a design only partly of their own making. One day the cloth might seem near completion; on another day, the plaid was nearly pulled apart. The thing was to become one strong cord in the tightly woven fabric of that place.

"Maybe I should have reported it to the authorities," Kari said years later. "But, you see, that insurance money got those children a new house, sturdy and warm." As was her habit, she rocked evenly and hummed an old tune as she clicked her knitting needles swiftly together.

9

LYKKE AND MOON

Johan cobbled the little wagon together from a wooden apple box and bits of lumber left over from building the picket fence around his mother's garden. The wheels came from a collapsed cart that had been used to move grain sacks into the barn. Slender, sturdy willow reeds from the slough ran along each side of the wagon, attached to leather traces that Johan fashioned from worn-down horse bridles. With these bindings, Johan harnessed their dog, Lykke.

Lykke didn't object to pulling the cart around the barnyard. In fact, he wiggled with delight every time Johan dragged the apple-box cart into the open area between the barn and the house. One whistle was enough to bring the Airedale racing his black and white spots into a blur, prancing in front of the cart for the harness. Johan lifted up six-year-old Anders and plunked him down into the cart, where he grabbed onto the edge of the wooden box and stared transfixed at Lykke's backside and pointed ears. A word from Johan sent the dog off, trotting to the barn, circling around, and trotting back, again and again. Anders' wide smile held Johan silent for a time, though he knew Lykke shouldn't go on forever pulling the wagon and boy around the barnyard. Finally, Johan whistled and brought the one-cart parade to a halt. Anders climbed out and staggered a bit before he recovered his land legs.

"I did it! I drived the cart," he beamed.

"So you did."

"Could we paint it red, do you think?"

"The cart or Lykke?"

"The cart!" Anders giggled at his big brother's joke.

"I think we might find some red paint somewhere about." Johan knew that the barns for miles around were painted red, not out of the farmers' love of bright colors, but because a natural paint sink had been found in the hills. The source for red paint was bottomless.

All that summer, the summer of 1917, Anders rode in his little red cart, pulled by his willing steed, Lykke. Lykke, though, had a more serious job on the farm—to bring the cows to the barn at the end of the day. The feisty Airedale nipped at the heels of the cows to round them up and point them home.

One day at feeding time, Johan watched as Lykke snapped at the hoofs of a farm mule that had wandered in among the cows. At first nip, the mule kicked Lykke well into the pasture, where he lay stunned. The dog lifted his head and looked around as if hoping no one had observed his embarrassment. Then he rose to his feet, regained his dignity, and moved with stealth and determination back to the rear quarters of the mule.

Lykke lunged for the mule's tail and locked on with his needle-like teeth. The mule bucked and shook from side to side, swinging Lykke off the ground and into the air. But the Airedale clung tight, and finally the braying mule submitted, pointing his nose toward the barn. Lykke released the mule's tail and rounded up the remaining cows, scampering back from time to time with a sharp bark as a reminder of what may happen to mules if they become too sassy.

In the days and weeks of August, Anders felt summer surround him as a time with neither a beginning nor an end. Then it was September, the month of harvest and of school.

At 4:30 on a dark, overcast morning in early autumn, Johan moved silently from his bed, down the stairway, and out the farmhouse door. Once in the barn, careless now about noise, he talked to the cows and horses as he watered and fed them. "So, Dan," he turned, feed bucket in hand, to a gentle black horse. "And are you ready to haul those wild *ugagnskråker* kids to school? Poor old Dan, with such a rowdy burden on his back every day." Johan touched the horse on its rough-coated head and ran a wide finger down to its wet, warm nostrils.

It was cold in the barn at this hour, to be sure, but quiet, too. And then there was the view of the stars as Johan walked to the barn and the streaks of pink sunrise as he walked back. A man wouldn't speak of such things, but the stars and new-lit sky lifted his heart better than any pastor's Sunday sermon.

By 6:00, Johan pushed back into the kitchen, grabbed a great handful of straw kindling, and stirred up the coals in the cookstove. He set out a bowl of eggs and a slab of bacon on the long wooden table. In a large yellow mixing bowl, he broke half a dozen eggs onto a mound of flour. He added creamy top milk and stirred the batter, beating the lumps into submission with a wooden spoon. Bacon went first on the gleaming stovetop griddle, the grease of it spreading across the polished surface; then between the sputtering strips of bacon, Johan dropped soft circles of batter, soon browned to hotcakes.

The stairway rattled with the sound of feet hurrying to the warmth of the kitchen. Two young faces, red from washing in

water from ice-covered basins, popped into the kitchen together. "I won! First breakfast for me!" It was Anders. His sister
Dagny, though a year older, couldn't always beat him in a race
anymore. Anders ran wherever he went, ran in circles if there
was nowhere to go.

"Never mind him, Dagny. You need a good breakfast for all
your book reading. Here's something to make your brain sizzle
like the bacon. And you, kid, you sit there and fill your mouth
with these hotcakes and leave your sister be!"

Kari and Jens came next, Kari embarrassed but grateful that
this big bear of a son would turn his hand to feeding the family
as well as the stock. "*Ja,* the bed covers felt warmer than the air
this morning, and that's the truth. Else I would have been up by
now."

"*Nei, mor,* you work enough to be sure, and into the night
after I'm asleep. We all do our part around here."

"*Ja, riktig.* I would say that, too. And one does even more
than his part." Jens nodded at his most reliable son, Johan, and
took a chair near the fire, holding out his cup to Kari as she
poured coffee all around.

Finally came Rolf, still half asleep, and Serianna, tall and
pretty, tossing her early morning smiles around the room like
sweet, ripe lingonberries. No one in the room could resist looking at her, though her mother felt such attention might not be
good for one barely fourteen and already catching the eyes of
farm boys. Only Dagny looked down at the table as her confident and lovely older sister swept into the room. Magic, thought
Dagny, she has some kind of magic.

After breakfast, Anders rode off to school for the first time,
the rear-most of four neighborhood kids, each clinging to the
next on the back of Dan, the patient, plodding horse. With his

mother-scrubbed cleanliness and lamblike innocence, Anders entered first grade at the country one-room schoolhouse.

Iron filigree atop the pot-bellied stove gleamed like the helmet of a German soldier in the Kaiser's army. To little Anders, the metal ornament seemed so sharp at its point that if the fat stove ever came alive and bent forward, it could rush at a boy and spear him through. Anders glanced back at the stove often. It stood double the height of a six-year-old, holding its position, never moving an inch from the back left corner of the school room. Twenty isinglass eyes peered through a web of iron curved over its rounded front. The fire inside flickered and snapped behind the translucent panes, each little mica window looking fragile as an eggshell. Teacher approached the stove boldly, feeding it in the morning and patting it to sleep in the afternoon. She was very brave, and the room stayed warm because of it.

Twenty students studied in the school room at wooden desks with fold-up tops and seats. Black ironwork, bent upward in gentle curves and graceful flowers, trimmed the desks and held the wood pieces firmly in place. Names of older boys and even some girls were carved into the surface of the desks, though teacher warned the children on the first day of school never to do such a thing to school property. Anders ran his fingers along the top of his desk over the name of Bjorn, one of the big boys, and a heart with the name Serianna next to it. Anders moved his book over his sister's name, so teacher wouldn't see it.

He raised his hand with his pointer finger extended. At teacher's nod, he slipped from his desk and walked to the back of the school room. He wiggled around the desks in the last row and moved toward the sputtering pot-bellied stove. He pushed up against his cousin's desk, keeping a foot of distance between his body and the hot metal jacket of the stove. He ran his hand along the wainscoting of the wall onto the knob of a door, let himself into the little room, and closed the door behind. Standing on his tiptoes before the chemical toilet, he peed into the bowl. A chill prairie wind rattled the only window of this new room. Last year students had to go outside to use the outhouse—even on the cold snow days, Serianna said, and she never lied.

Anders' father was on the school board and built this room, and another one, too, with a cookstove for heating hot soup once a day. And *far* built a little barn beside the school house for the horses, with hay for them to eat. Anders liked to think about his father building on the school.

He heard a sharp rap on the toilet room door. Teacher was reminding him to hurry, so he buttoned his trousers and opened the door. She looked at him with her not-very-happy look, so he moved along the wall, scooting sideways beyond the growling iron stove to the protection of his wooden desk.

When the older students finished their lessons, the teacher often asked them to help the little ones with reading, spelling, and arithmetic. Anders liked it when his big sister Serianna, who was very smart and pretty, moved over to his desk and read to him. The words that jumped around the page for him seemed to sit quietly for her. She whispered their sounds into his ear.

Recess was Anders' favorite part of school. He could run fast and throw the ball right to anybody who wanted to play. He played most with Lars, a boy whose big brother Bjorn sat near Serianna and talked to her during class, making the teacher frown at him.

Lars had a dog, Moon, who followed him to school some days. The dog was shorter than Lykke but looked very strong with muscles bulging from his shoulders and chest.

"What kind?" asked Anders.

"Moon's a pit bull," said Lars.

Anders liked Moon's mouth because the corners turned up in a sort of smile. He reached his fingers out to stroke the dog's nose. With a growl, the dog lunged at Anders, knocking him down. Lars screamed, "Moon!" and then "Bjorn!" but before his big brother could get to them, Moon sank his teeth into Anders' leg. Blood darkened his pant leg, and he heard himself crying, more from the shock of what had happened than from the pain. Bjorn grabbed a stick, wedged it into the dog's mouth, and pried its teeth apart. As the teacher wrapped Anders' leg in a towel and lifted him into the classroom, Bjorn slipped a rope around Moon's neck and jerked him along a pathway toward their farm.

Anders stayed home for a day, though *far* determined that the bleeding had cleansed the wound. *Mor* swabbed it with carbolic solution and told him he was as strong as a Viking. A white bandage kept the gash clean and its edges together.

When Anders went back to school, Lars wouldn't look at him.

"It's all right about your dog biting me. My mother fixed it and it only hurts a little now." Lars looked at the ground and walked away. Serianna sat down beside Anders on the schoolhouse steps.

"Why is Lars mad at me? Moon bit me for no reason. I didn't pinch him or anything."

Serianna reached her arm around his shoulder and leaned her face close to his.

"It's like this. Dogs should help on the farm, like our Lykke. A dog should work and play and be good. A dog can't just bite someone like that, for no reason. A dog like Moon is dangerous to everyone. So that's why Bjorn had to take him home that day and shoot him. He had to."

Anders looked into Serianna's eyes in disbelief, but he saw she wasn't lying. She never lied. He pushed his face down into her skirt to think: My leg will have a bandage on it just until it heals, with only a little scar, *mor* said. But Bjorn had to do a very bad thing. Had to, Serianna said. Now Lars doesn't have his dog anymore. And I don't have my friend.

10

Tonight, Christmas!

"Tonight!" Dagny grabbed Anders by his little shoulders and pulled, so that his face was inches from her own.

"What?" he said, trying to wriggle out of her grip.

"Christmas!" Dagny would not let go of him until he understood. Anders stopped wiggling, his eyes now wide.

"Yes," said Dagny. "It's true. Tonight Christmas begins. And today we make cookies and decorate. So come on. We need to string the cranberries and popcorn." Not waiting for his reply, Dagny snatched Anders' hand, and the two children careened down the stairway to the big, warm kitchen.

"So," said their mother Kari, smiling. "Do I have some helpers here?"

"Yes, *mor,* we'll help." Dagny pushed Anders into one kitchen chair and plunked down into the other.

"Is it really Christmas, *mor?*" Anders' eyes searched his mother's face.

"*Ja, litle gut,* my little boy, Christmas is coming now very soon. So—we must be ready. Your father says on Christmas Eve there is no work after 4:00, just as in Norway, so hurry—we have much to do." Kari placed two big bowls, one filled with cranberries and one with popcorn, on the kitchen table.

"Here now," she said. "You can do this if you are careful. Hold the needle between your fingers and push it through the berry. When the berry is on the string, do it all over again to the next berry."

She watched as Dagny carefully threaded the cranberries onto the string. Anders fumbled a bit with his needle and then placed it between the thumb and forefinger of his left hand. Kari frowned. He did this often, using his left hand instead of his right. The school teachers didn't like it, but she had no time to correct him today. Kari turned back to the cookie dough, first rolling out the *fattigmand* dough and cutting it into little diamond shapes. Then she twisted the sweet *kringle* dough into pretzels and slid the cookie sheets into the oven of the cookstove. Her cheeks glowed with the heat of the stove as she turned back to the children.

Anders looked up at her. "Just one cookie, *mor?*"

"*Nei, nei,* you know better. These are all for Christmas!"

Kari rolled out the pie dough next, lifting the dough into a pan, filling the crust with sliced apples. Again and again she pushed her rolling pin over a ball of dough, making mince pies and apple pies, one after another. The cookies were out of the oven now and the pies went in. Kari poured a cup of black coffee and sat for a moment.

Her eyes passed over the open pine shelf of yesterday's baking: *krumkake* with its pretty pattern; *julekake*, popping over with raisins, nuts, and fragrant, crushed cardamom seeds; rye bread, sturdy and brown; and the *lefse* she had rolled out into thin rounds, cooked quickly on the hot stovetop, spread with butter, sprinkled with cinnamon-sugar, and rolled and cut up into finger-length tubes. With Serianna's help, she had baked more than enough for all the relatives and neighbors who would be stopping by on Christmas Day.

She looked back at Anders, still earnestly poking each little red cranberry with the needle and pushing it onto the thread, and Dagny, who had finished threading the popcorn.

"So, *mine born,* my little children, I see you are almost finished with your work. Let's see if *far* and Johan have found us a tree."

"A tree!" shouted Dagny, then quieted herself when Kari placed a gentle finger on her lips.

"A tree," whispered Anders, his face filled with wonder. He could almost remember the tree in the parlor last Christmas, such a long time ago.

"Come now," said Kari. "Let's go into the parlor."

Opening the oak door to the parlor and stepping inside was reason enough for the children to speak softly. This was the grown-ups' room, a room for them to read and talk. Only on special occasions were the children invited into this space. Dark wood lined two of the walls, and shelves of books clung to the others. An overstuffed couch, covered with frizzy rose-colored cloth, sat heavily on thick, bowed legs, reminding Dagny of their fat Aunt Helga.

Usually cool and musty, today the room felt warm and smelled fresh and woodsy from the tall fir tree standing in the middle of the room. On the graceful, green branches were candle holders—here one, there another, a few even higher.

"Oh, I think we must have more candles." Kari walked to the tree to inspect it closely. "But it is a beautiful tree. Well done, my men, you picked out a good one." Her smile at Jens and Johan made all the struggle of hauling home this big tree worthwhile.

"The station master tells us it came all the way from the woods of Minnesota."

Johan grabbed Anders around the middle and lifted him high up, but still he couldn't reach the top of the tree. He wriggled out of his big brother's arms and ran to the kitchen and back as fast as his little legs would carry him.

"Look, Johan! Look what I made! All by myself! But how can I get them up to the top?" Anders dropped the strings of cranberries in a sad little heap on the floor.

"Well, that's why you have a big brother. Hand them to me, and they'll decorate the tree clear to the top."

And so, by 4:00 on Christmas Eve, all was in readiness for the celebration of the birth of the Christ Child, the little baby Jesus. Serianna told the story once again to Dagny and Anders. She showed them a picture in the middle of the family Bible.

"Is that really the Baby Jesus?"

"Yes, it is. And look at the angels guarding him, just as they guard you at night as you sleep." Serianna closed the Bible gently and placed it back on the shelf.

Then into the sleigh—*mor, far,* Johan, Serianna, Dagny, Anders and even Rolf, just back from town. Off they all were to have supper at Aunt Helga's house! The children sat quietly at her dinner table, but giggled to each other at the pumpkin pie, which Helga, only just from Norway, had covered with a second crust over the top. Kari gave Dagny a quick, sharp pinch, which made her sit up straight. She sighed. The main thing was to finish this endless meal and get back home to the presents.

At last back home, breathing in the scent of the Christmas tree, Dagny and Anders watched with *mor* and *far* as Johan, Rolf, and Serianna each had the honor of lighting candles on the Christmas tree. The candles flickered brighter and brighter until the whole tree shimmered with light. Jens reached out and touched Kari's hand, and together they saw the lights of the tree reflected in the eyes of their children.

"So—I think there are presents for all!" And there were—little carved animals, intricately knitted caps, and sweaters of bright wool. Finally *far* opened the box from *tante* Inga, *mor's* young sister, who lived now with her husband Mathias in Montana.

From the enormous box, Dagny lifted out a beautiful doll and held it close. Soon Anders was pushing his tiny cast-iron Model T Ford around the room, making loud motor sounds. Johan laughed. "So, little brother, you have a car to drive before anyone else in the family."

Johan held up skis made by *onkel* Mathias from barrel staves. Rolf, too, had skis, and Serianna tore wrapping paper off a handmade sled. "I'll fly down the hill by the barn with this," she said, and they knew that she would, a girl as bold as she was pretty.

"*Vel*," said *far*, "try to miss the water tank or you'll be in pieces, and, worse, we'll lose our water supply."

Dagny gazed in wonder at her doll. "Did *tante* Inga and *onkel* Mathias buy this doll in a store?"

"Yes, it seems they did. They have no children yet, you know, and I think they give you too much." But Kari said it gently, remembering that long ago in Norway her brothers had chided her for spoiling her baby sister Inga, and remembering, too, how sweet it was a few years ago to pamper and protect young Inga when she first came to America—only sixteen years old.

On Christmas Day, neighbors and relatives came—twenty of them, thirty, maybe more. Dagny lost count because the grown-ups wouldn't stay still but moved from parlor to kitchen and back, carrying the turkey, the *lefse*, nuts, candy, cakes and pies that *mor* and Serianna had baked—filling the table with food.

How insulted Kari would have been if guests had brought anything to eat! Christmas, at least, could be a time of feasting. If this was foolishness, it was the sort of foolishness dear to the hearts of Kari and Jens.

The crowd of friends, aunts, uncles, cousins, and *tremenningar*—distant cousins of some sort—ate and talked and laughed together, inside the house, safe from the cold outside. Then they formed a circle around the Christmas tree and sang the old Norwegian Christmas songs. Anders couldn't sing the words, but he bounced to the tune of *"Jeg er så glad hver Julekveld"* and knew it was about being glad at Christmas. He looked across the circle at *mor* and *far*. He saw that they were very glad and that they couldn't stop smiling. He tried to turn the corners of his own mouth down and found he could not. He understood then. No one can stop smiling at Christmastime.

11

ONE-ROOM SCHOOLHOUSE

Spring came early that year. Snow melted into enormous puddles that spilled over into murky rivulets alongside muddy roads. Low-lying sloughs, filled to overflowing, pushed out into the field stubble. Canadian geese and wood ducks heading north splashed down onto the spreading water, flapping their wings and dragging their feet for scarcely controlled crash landings. Thousands of them came to rest, eat, and then take off north again.

Anders watched, fascinated by the mix of confusion and purpose in the birds. "They know where they want to go," thought Anders. "But how do they know? How do they figure that out?"

Anders could barely see where he was going that chilly morning, clinging as he was to the waist of his sister Dagny as they straddled Dan, the faithful black horse that carried them to school. Two places ahead of Dagny on old Dan was Samuel, with his little brother Stanley tucked in between them—and sitting foremost, dinner bucket in one hand and reins in the other, was Clarence, who pretended to guide Dan to the country schoolhouse. The horse needed no guidance but plodded along with his considerable load at an even pace, never stopping along the way until he delivered the five of them to their little schoolhouse.

"Faster, Dan, faster," commanded lanky Clarence, in a voice that broke oddly as it tried to become a manly baritone.

"Fasther, fasther," echoed little Stanley, who still lisped. The horse ignored them both. Only on the return trip, after school was finished for the day, did he amble a bit faster, knowing that a warm barn and a bucket of oat and grain mash waited for him.

Five pairs of leather shoes bounced against the horse's belly as he sauntered along. The boys' black leather shoes, half covered with brown mud, were laced and tied at the ankle. Black wool stockings covered the gap between their shoe tops and pants cuffs, now far too short for Clarence, though his mother had let down the hems twice during the school year. Samuel's pants buckled at the knee. Town boys would have laughed at these old-style trousers, but the country children hardly noticed. Dagny's long skirt almost reached her high-top shoes, mostly covering her stockings, and completely hiding her wool underwear that made the cold ride bearable. Anders' shoes, handed down from his big brother, narrowed to the toe point several inches beyond the ends of his own toes. This was a problem when he tried to run fast in school games but not as he clung to Dagny's middle to keep from sliding off old Dan's rear end. Anders' shoes, along with the others, clunked in even rhythm along the horse's flanks.

"Who is that with the Miss Lillquists?" Clarence was the first to see in the bright springtime sunshine a third woman sitting on the school porch with Marit and Mandy Lillquist, the sisters who were their teachers.

"Maybe they have another sthisthter." Little Stanley felt this was a good guess, but no one else thought the skinny lady in a black wide-brimmed hat could be related to their buxom, round-cheeked teachers. Old Dan sauntered up to the school porch with his load of five. The Miss Lillquists waved to the children.

"So, you are so many on the one poor horse. But I tink he is used to it by now."

Miss Mandy Lillquist sang her sentences, the Scandinavian lilt lifting her English words up in pitch, and then settling them down again.

"You must come now and meet Miss Benson, our new school superintendent," added Miss Marit Lillquist. "She is here to observe our school today." Miss Lillquist said it cheerfully enough, but Clarence knocked Samuel in the ribs and Samuel elbowed Stanley, who nudged Dagny, who in turn gave Anders a meaningful bump. They sent this signal with their arms and hands on the right side of the horse, the side away from the women, and held their eyes steady and respectful on the faces of their teachers and this other person—this superintendent.

"Yes, Miss Lillquist," they said in unison.

Clarence flung his leg over the horse's neck and slid off, his feet sinking into the muddy ground. He stepped to the rear of the horse and caught Anders as he fell off backwards, trusting Clarence's arms to catch him. Then Clarence reached up for little Stanley and placed him on the ground. He stood back as Samuel and Dagny, too big and too proud to accept help, each jumped down. The children climbed the steps to the wide school porch and stood in front of the two Miss Lillquists.

"These are some of our children from the farms around here: Clarence, Samuel, Stanley, Dagny, and Anders. Children, this is our new superintendent, Miss Benson."

"Good morning, students."

"Good morning, Miss Benson." The children said their part all together, in the way they said the Lord's Prayer at church, slowly and respectfully. When little Stanley's "Good morning" sounded too loud, his brother tugged at his coat, so his "Misth Bensthon" came out just about right.

The day ground on slowly for these five who had arrived on old Dan's back and for the fifteen other students in the classroom. The iron stove still stood like a Prussian general in the back, pointed helmet aimed at the ceiling. The fire flickered through the glass panes pressed against the black and bulging iron framework. The heat of the stove coupled with the sun beating through the wide windows became oppressive. But the children's eyes, heavy as they were, remained on the printed pages of their books—for they knew a secret.

Days before, Clarence spread to the others what he had overheard his father, a member of the school board, say to his mother: that the Miss Lillquists were considered by some to be too young and perhaps too full of laughter and smiles to be good teachers. That a new Lady Superintendent would observe the school to see if serious learning was going on there—or only fun and games. And then the school board would decide, with the superintendent's report in hand, whether the sisters would keep their teaching positions.

All the students, from youngest to oldest, understood what this might mean. They had seen teachers come and go in this little prairie schoolhouse, and the worst of them had been cruel, whacking even the little ones with a ruler over a mistake or an answer given too slowly. Other teachers seemed bored in this one-room school with its shabby desks and ragged students. The Miss Lillquists were the best of all, encouraging the dullest pupils and stretching the minds of the brightest. The Miss

Lillquists knew songs in English, in Swedish, and in Norwegian, and they told wonderful stories.

Each student warned the next to sit up straight and act smart today, in front of this Superintendent Lady. Or else, they whispered one child to another, you know what might happen.

The stove crackled; the sun crept along; the Superintendent Lady wrote in her little notebook. Each weary bottom stayed firmly on its wooden chair. Every set of hands held its book. Eyes remained focused on the pages of the book. Paper rustled softly as pages turned. Each little mouth remained closed, unless the teacher asked a question.

"Yes, Miss Lillquist. Thank you, Miss Lillquist." These were the polite words of the little children as they gathered with Miss Marit Lillquist for reading time.

"Here is my homework; it's finished, Miss Lillquist. Thank you for pointing that out to me, Miss Lillquist. I'll correct it right away." These were the respectful words of the older students as they met with Miss Mandy Lillquist to study composition and grammar.

By 3:00, the students were exhausted from the strain and drama of the day. Clarence helped Anders and Stanley back on the horse after Samuel and Dagny climbed on. Then, grabbing old Dan's mane, he hauled himself across the horse's shoulders.

"Goodbye Miss Benson, goodbye Miss Lillquists." The children thought it was best to say the superintendent's name first, seeing as she looked so stiff and proper in her black dress and white collar. Yet, now she was smiling and suddenly didn't seem frightening at all.

"Goodbye Misth Bensthen," shouted little Stanley happily, and she answered, "Goodbye Stanley," and waved to him as old Dan walked briskly toward home.

With great relief, Anders and the other children learned that the Miss Lillquists were to keep their jobs. Without Superintendent Lady watching their every move, the boys and girls once again laughed at their teachers' funny stories and sang joyful songs they learned in English and lilting lyrics they echoed, line by line, in Norwegian. These they presented at an assembly of recitations and songs on the last day of school before summer recess. The parents smiled proudly and applauded loudly as the children bowed. During the coffee and cookie party afterward, the children heard their mothers and fathers congratulating Miss Marit Lillquist and Miss Mandy Lillquist on their excellent teaching methods.

12

CAR, ICE, POLITICS

A decade older than Anders, big brother Johan was nineteen when he scraped together enough money to buy a car—an Overland. He was the only one on the place who was allowed to drive it—the only one who knew how to drive it. Whenever he was off working on a neighbor's farm, it sat alongside the barn. If Jens or Kari wanted to go to town, they used the team of horses and the wagon. When Jens plowed a field, the team pulled the plow. But even though he had never driven a car, Jens couldn't keep his eyes off Johan's shiny black Overland, sitting there in the sunshine. He looked at it through the kitchen window. He put his hand on a fender on his way to the barn. He opened the door on the driver's side and stuck his head inside.

One day Anders asked him, "Can't you drive a car?"

He looked down at his young son, "*Vel*, I suppose I could. I suppose it couldn't be so very hard."

Anders looked up at his father with a nine-year-old's blind faith. "I bet you could."

Jens paused. His son's trusting gaze filled him with confidence. "Let's you and me drive it," he said.

He picked up Anders with his big farmer's grip and sat him down on the passenger's seat. He parked himself behind the wheel. The two of them sat there. It was very quiet.

"No water in it," Jens said finally. "Guess we'd want to drive down to the water tank." They sat again in silence.

"Johan pushes that button," Anders said, pointing to the starter. "And he pulls up on that." He touched the emergency brake.

Jens pressed the starter and released the brake, more or less at once. The car jumped forward, began a slow roll, and then gathered speed as they got to the steep part of the pasture. Jens gripped the wheel and pulled back on it hard. "Whoa!" he yelled. "Whoa!" The stubble ahead stuck up from a hilly acre, and the car slowed and then rolled faster and faster, ignoring Jens' commands. "Whoa! Whoa!" When Johan's car crashed into the eight-hundred-gallon water tank, water gushed like a waterfall onto the dusty field.

The two were very quiet again, and then Jens got out and lifted his son down to the ground. "I guess this can be our little secret," he said, as he walked around the Overland, which had, by some miracle, not a scratch on it. They walked up the hill together, hitched up the team of horses, and towed the car back up the hill to its place beside the barn. Jens spent the rest of the day making staves to repair the water tank.

It was a secret hard for Anders to keep. For weeks after, he had to press his lips together in a tight, straight line to keep the secret from slipping out. He adored his oldest brother; yet *far* said it should be their secret, and that was a grown-up honor, to be part of his father's secret. In a month's time, Anders had pushed the truth of what happened down and down into the cellar of his memory, so that perhaps it might not have happened at all; and then, once again, he could look into the eyes of his brother Johan with joy.

Winter came late and muddled along, raining, skimming the fields with ice, then thawing, then snowing, until finally in mid-November dark clouds closed in over the plains and a keen wind froze the earth's shell, all in an afternoon. The slack water of the town slough formed a skin that held it flat. Cattails along the edge, their seed-heads blown apart by the wind, leaned away from the bitter blast. Ice began in patches and spread across the pond until, one by one, the frosty scraps touched each other in a patchwork of frozen crust. As the temperature dropped, the patches hardened and united into real ice, smooth ice. Ice meant for skating.

Children and young people in Brem and on the outlying farms passed the word: the slough is frozen. Johan tied on his boots and layered on wool sweaters before driving to the pond for a final check. Yes, the look and feel of the ice as they tromped on the northern edge was solid. By Saturday morning, twenty youngsters or more sat on big rocks around the slough, pulling on and tying their ice skates. Johan was one of the older skaters, and he stopped to help the young ones with their socks, hats, and skates.

"Never mind, Lisa," he whispered to a little one on her first skating day. "You can be my partner, and we will fly around the lake." Her blue eyes went wide with excitement.

"Fly? We will fly?"

"Yes, Lisa, we will fly."

And so they did, around the lake's edge where the ice thickened, hard and safe. Lisa's red mitten fit snugly inside Johan's blue-gloved hand, and she felt her skates slide over the ice as Johan propelled her along with smooth, effortless strides. Twice, when they turned sharply to miss other skaters, she felt herself lifted and then gently returned to the ice as Johan swept her to the other side of the pond.

It was the wild boys, some from town and some from the country farms, that Johan and Lisa skated around. Already a responsible, full-time farmer, Johan watched these boys out of the corner of his eye, smiling at their bumbling attempts to impress each other and the schoolgirls. Good grief, look at Nels, he'll break his head open if he hits the ice at that speed. And Anders—Andy the kid—my own little brother in his green hat. What a clown to skate up behind Clara like that! Johan watched their fits and starts, their dashes and tumbles, meanwhile moving little Lisa smoothly around the edge of the pond.

Then in the midst of the normal confusion and noise of children skating, there came a crack, like a rifle shot, and then a shout. In the middle of the pond, two boys stumbled, fell, and sank through the ice. Johan give Lisa a little push to the lake's edge and then moved with a powerful step and stroke toward the broken ice. Across the thin middle ice stretched three young bodies, each boy grabbing the ankles of the next, so that together they made a lifeline across the fragile ice to their two sinking friends. Johan fell down on his knees, and with his strong farm-hardened hands, he anchored the legs of Lars, the boy closest to him in the rescue chain.

"Grab their hands, clothes, hair, anything!" Johan shouted to the third boy, the one farthest out and closest to the broken ice. Then he saw, by the green cap, that it was Anders out there on the thin ice, trying to reach his friends. Johan saw Anders thrust out his hand. A hand rose from the water and grabbed hold.

It was Nels, who used Anders' handgrip to pull himself out of the frigid lake and onto the ice. He scrambled on his hands and knees away from the ice hole to the arms of those who wrapped him in their jackets. Shaking with cold and fear, Nels wouldn't leave the side of the pond. He turned to see the ice crack and break again, as little Stanley, still in the water but clinging to Anders' arm, edged his upper body onto the crumbling ice. He managed to get one knee on the ice and then the other. He seemed unable to move farther but kept his fingers gripped as if frozen onto Anders' arm. Johan began pulling gently on the legs he was holding, Lars' legs. And Lars pulled on the legs of Samuel, the middle boy. And Samuel pulled on Anders' legs. In this way, and very slowly, the lifeline of friends pulled Stanley to safety, away from the pond's dark center.

Johan carried Nels and then Stanley, covered in jackets and blankets, to the back seat of his car. He jumped in front, pressed the starter, released the brake, and eased out the clutch. The Overland bounced along the road a little distance to the Wickland farmhouse, where Johan rushed the boys into a warm kitchen. "The ice broke," was all he said, and women stripped off their wet clothes, wrapped the boys in sheets and blankets, pushed them next to the stove, and poured cups of hot coffee for them to drink. Rough towels in gentle hands dried their hair. The shivering boys submitted for two hours to wrapping and rubbing and hot drinks before their shaking stopped. Then Mrs. Wickland fed them a meal of beef and potato soup with a thick slice of bread and butter. Nels and Stanley downed the soup and bread with ferocious appetites. Mrs. Wickland smiled, gave them each a slab of apple pie, and declared them recovered.

Some nights Jens read the *Tidende* from the front-page politics to the back-page harness ads. Printed in Norwegian, the newspaper aimed to give immigrants news linking them to the old country, Norway, and other news grafting them into America, their new land. Besides the Norwegian *Tidende,* Jens studied the *Minneapolis Tribune* and the local *Reporter and Farmer*. Both of these came printed in English, which Jens read quite easily but Kari only with difficulty.

"Of course, you have been here from childhood." Kari's cheeks reddened as she struggled with words of a story in the *Minneapolis Tribune*. She chose to speak to him in English, constructing her sentences carefully.

"You do quite well with English," said Jens kindly. His gentle tone made her feel like a none-too-bright child. "But why not read the *Tidende?* You'll understand everything better in Norwegian."

"The stories are not the same. Look at this picture in the *Tribune*. A woman is being dragged from the street by the police. And the word below says she is suffering. I know that word, 'suffer.' It is what Jesus did on the cross."

Jens laughed and took her hand, and again she felt like a pampered, slow-witted little girl. "The word sounds like 'suffer' but it means something quite different. 'Suffrage' is a word for voting. This woman wants to vote. She is out in the street causing trouble, and so the policeman is just doing his duty to arrest her."

Kari pulled her hand away and glared at her husband. "And do you laugh at that? Just doing his duty! Women in Norway have voted for years now—and Denmark and Iceland, too. *I himmelens navn,* even Sweden, stiff as those people are, allows women to vote!"

Jens looked at her sternly. That she would use such strong language! "In heaven's name." She might as well say, "In God's name," and such language should not come from the mouth of a woman, surely.

"I think perhaps you should read only the Norwegian newspaper," he said, as he rose from the table. "These American papers are too upsetting for you."

Yet she continued to read the English language papers. By the time Jens picked them up at the Brem train station, the papers were a week old, but for Kari they held a fascination that kept her struggling for words that made up each story. Her greatest interest was in the women fighting for the vote. She read their names, "Carrie Chapman Catt" and "Alice Paul." This Alice faced the police bravely, even going to jail.

"Listen," said Kari one evening as she read from the paper. "Alice Paul talks something like you do about farming. She says, 'When you put your hand to the plow, you can't put it down until you get to the end of the row.'"

Jens glanced up from his book. He looked down again and turned the page.

Yet, in August of 1920, when the Nineteenth Amendment became the law of the land, Jens waved the paper in the air. "Look here. You may have your way now. And I do think it's a good thing." With a little bow from the waist, he spread the newspaper before her, as if presenting her with a gift. "Women To Vote!" said the headline.

Kari lifted her eyes to Jens, raising her eyebrows in question, "And you are happy about this, too?"

"I am. This means I shall have two votes. That is to say..." He changed his tone slightly at her frown. "We, as a married couple, will have two votes, and so twice as much influence in every election." Kari's mouth formed a narrow line, and she said nothing. Jens continued. "Surely you agree that we will vote the same way. 'The two shall become one,' the Bible says so. I know we will come to agreement on this, as always, *min elskede*," and he patted her hand.

Kari poured two cups of hot coffee, and placed butter, bread, and jam on the table. She sat beside her husband, and they looked at the newspaper together. Because she was quiet by nature and upbringing, Jens did not notice her silence, nor did he guess what she was thinking: yes, you are very clever to call me *"min elskede"*—your "dear love"—as you take away the vote I have just been given.

As it happened, the next important vote in the state was for the election of South Dakota's representative to the United States Congress. Men stood around on Saturday night scraping mud and horse dung off their shoes against the boards of the town's wooden sidewalks, arguing about the two men running for office.

"Well, that Republican feller's more for us farmers, but then he took away the hard stuff, don'cha know, with that prohibition law."

"How's a man suppose'ta make do with near-beer?"

"Wouldn't feed it to the pigs."

"Fraid I'm gonna hafta vote for the Democrat. He seems to want to bring back legal liquor. Good thing Pa's not alive to see me vote for a Democrat!"

Women spoke of the election, too, at the Lutheran ladies circle meeting. One at the meeting said she thought prohibition might save the life of many a drunkard, keeping him from his gin. The others looked down at their knitting and sewing, averting their eyes from the woman's bruised arms. Kari thought of her middle son, Rolf, already wild, smoking and playing cards in spite of her warnings. Would the demon rum be his next vice?

On the day of the election, Jens instructed Kari about the voting process. They could go together, but she must give her name to the polling clerks and go into the curtained booth alone. He handed her a white piece of paper with the name of the Democratic candidate on it. "Here," he said. "In case you forget, we're voting for him."

"I'm a bit nervous." Kari put the paper into the pocket of her skirt.

Jens held her hand for a moment and said softly, "Well, this is the first time for you. There was another first time when we were both a bit nervous." He gave her a wink and helped her down from the wagon.

Kari watched as Jens entered the booth and pulled the curtain closed behind him. What a miracle this is, she thought, as she looked around at the smiling women, dressed in Sunday clothes to cast their first votes. Marta, who lived on the next farm, waved quickly and then clasped her hands in front of her skirt, as if that might be more dignified on this historic day.

Jens pushed back the curtain and placed his ballot in the box slowly, demonstrating for Kari just how it was to be done. He nodded his head in the direction of the booth and patted his thigh to remind her of the paper in her pocket.

Clutching her ballot, Kari walked into the booth and drew the curtain behind her. The brown wool fabric insulated her from the voices in the room. The booth seemed quiet and still, her private domain. She picked up the pencil on the wooden stand and placed her ballot there. She drew the paper out of her pocket and looked at the name Jens had written. He wanted her to vote for the Democrat. He wanted her to vote for liquor. She squeezed the pencil tightly between her thumb and fingers and marked a bold, black "x" beside the name of the Republican. "For my boy Rolf," she whispered.

Kari folded the ballot in two, shoved the curtain back, and with two long steps stood before the ballot box. She pushed the ballot into the slot. Then she turned toward Jens, waiting for her by the door. She took his arm, gave him a loving smile, and said, "You were right, Jens, that was easy."

13

K>I>G>Y

As winter closed in, Jens retreated to his library in the front part of the house, next to the parlor. His hand slapped along the medical and law books that lined the walls, until one leather-bound volume slowed his hand to a stop. He lifted it from the shelf, sat in the old rocker, and lowered the book to his lap. As the first snow of autumn sifted down outside the window, there came to the farm a quiet time of year. Done was the frantic harvest work; winter wheat planting was finished, too. So. A man could take an hour or longer, a whole evening after supper, and sit with books. Some called the study and pondering of these heavy volumes foolishness for a farmer. Jens called it sweat for the mind. Or said nothing about it at all. Just had a need for it. Just did it.

While she spun the yarn for knitting sweaters and stockings, Kari found a way to nourish her brain. Holding the wool for spinning in one hand, pushing the treadle on the spinning wheel with her foot, and doing it all by touch, her eyes were free to travel along the print of a book. She liked word games, too, and even some card games to wake up the mind, so long as regular playing cards were not used—the cards meant for gambling. "Those are devil's cards, do you not see?" Kari said, as she snatched a pack of kings, queens, and jacks from her son's hand and threw it into the fire, turning with conviction to face her children. And they did see, for the pack exploded with hellish flames.

The boys had no inclination to study. Johan was all farmer, up early and working late. Rolf ran for town whenever he could, to cards, wild girls, and drink. The rest of the family conspired to keep talk of that from Kari. What would be the purpose of breaking a mother's heart? And Anders, well, the youngster liked to play ball, that was all. Sports kept him happy in school, maybe reason enough for all that batting and throwing and catching. And it kept a grin on the boy's face as soft and wide as Kari's own. So who could go against that?

But Serianna and Dagny—some said they were smarter than girls should be. Jens and Kari noticed their daughters' quick minds and also observed glances of lonely bachelors on neighboring farms. Soon the girls would be old enough—Serianna almost seventeen—to be picked off, married, pregnant in the same year, old in a few more, and God forbid, in the graveyard by thirty, dead in childbirth. Jens and Kari had seen it happen often enough. The two of them talked around the problem with oblique references to this one or that one who had suffered the fate of a poor prairie farmer's wife. Kari, knitting by the stove, and Jens, sharpening his tools nearby, conversed often in this way, until one evening Jens said, "Good harvest this year. There would be a few extra dollars."

Her knitting needles clicking steadily, Kari answered, "The school at Yankton, the Lutheran Academy, wouldn't be such a very great cost." And so the girls went there, far away from farmers needing a passel of sons. Dagny was encouraged to become a teacher and Serianna a nurse. Though both led their classes in mathematics, science, and English, no one at Yankton Lutheran Academy said they were smarter than girls should be.

Winter wore itself out with blizzards; springtime softened snow into slush; and summer toasted grass into straw that crunched underfoot. On a Friday afternoon, working in the loft, Anders heard the scrape of footsteps in the barn below.

"You go with him then. Keep him out of trouble."

As he listened to earnest talk between his big brother Johan and their father, Anders forked hay from the loft, stabbing the pitchfork into the hay and tossing the feed down to the cows. He kept the pace of his work and the sound of it as regular as his breathing. Anders had learned to glean the grown-ups' secrets by seeming indifferent and staying invisible. *Far* and Johan often spoke to each other in Norwegian, as they were doing now. Still, Anders could translate into English most of what they said.

"Rabble-rousers, up to no good, that's what they are," grumbled Johan.

Far's voice held steady. "That I know. But if Rolf goes alone, he will come home drunk for sure, and with a broken nose, almost as certain."

Johan left the barn with an angry grunt, but both Anders and his father knew that this oldest brother would do what was required of him, as he always did.

Most Friday nights Rolf piled into his pal's Model T along with a bunch of party friends and took off, sometimes for the whole weekend. Johan rarely let Rolf borrow his shiny black Overland sedan. But this Saturday morning, as soon as Johan finished the barn chores and washed up, he rolled Rolf out of bed.

"What is this big celebration picnic party you are so wild about going to? I guess I might as well come along."

"Hey, why not? We can take turns driving the Overland to Sturgis." Rolf liked the idea of arriving behind the wheel of Johan's big four-door sedan. Anders, in the next bed, pulled the pillow over his head.

Downstairs in the kitchen, Johan and Rolf piled their plates high with eggs, sausage, cheese, and hot biscuits. Kari smiled to see her big boys so eager for a day driving around the countryside together. She packed a basket of sliced meat and bread, of apples and brown sugar cake. *"God tur!"* she called. "Have a good drive!" She waved and watched them drive away.

Two hours down the road, a commotion in the back seat made Rolf turn his head. "Good God! The kid's along!" Johan geared down, hit his brakes and brought the sedan to a halt in the dusty road as Anders struggled out from under the red wool touring blanket, coughing from the smoke and grit. Johan looked hard and long at his little brother, who waited in silence for the verdict.

"We're too far along to go back now. You don't have any idea what you're getting yourself into. You stick right by me every minute, all day and all night." Anders tried not to grin his delight, and he gave a quick nod. He would promise anything to be able to go along on his brothers' adventure.

They drove west and south, hour after hour, frequently seeing signs on bridges and fence posts: K>I>G>Y, the arrows on the signs urging them onward to the town of Sturgis, close to the Black Hills. As they passed through small towns, Johan and Rolf picked up handbills with bold black printing, "Open to everyone. Come and bring your wife and the kiddies with you. Feed stands on the grounds. Be there and hear the great principles of this great Order explained." Anders, trying to stay out of his brothers' way, watched from the car as Johan crumpled up the flyer in disgust and stuffed it into his pocket. Rolf seemed excited though and tried to change Johan's dark mood.

"What does it hurt to listen to these men? They make some good points. They say the Catholics are running over the Protestants. That's us Lutherans, I think—Protestants—ain't we? Why should the Pope be able to run our country? Washington, Jefferson, they were like us, white and Protestant. Why should runty Irish Catholics run everything? That constitution was signed by Washington and them, men like us!"

Johan shook his head and gave a quick laugh. "Washington and Jefferson were about as much like us as a king is like a cat. You ought to know by now that the rich stay rich and the rest, eating mackerel or *lutefisk*, we're just working men trying to get by."

As Johan drove the Overland onto the grounds of the cele-bration, Anders looked around at the thousands of men, women, and children gathered for a combination of partying and speech making. Rolf wandered off looking for friends while Johan and Anders grazed like the rest of this hungry crowd at the free food booths around the grounds. Men approached them from time to time, trying to talk them into joining the Klan. "For twenty dollars," one said, "you become a Knight of the Ku Klux Klan. We believe in exactly what you do already: we're pro-American, pro-Gentile, pro-White, and pro-Protestant. We're for native-born and against the foreign-born coming into our country." Johan kept on walking.

"What's that mean," said Anders. "What's that 'native-born' mean?"

"Means born here in America."

"Like me and you?"

"Yeah, like me and you."

"But—not like *mor* or *far*."

"No, not like them. Our parents are what the Klan calls 'foreign-born.'"

When darkness fell on the South Dakota prairie, Johan and Anders watched in silence as three enormous crosses, perhaps thirty feet high, burned against the blackness of the summer sky. Blasts of dynamite shook the ground under their feet as the crowd cheered, pushing forward with a wild mix of patriotic zeal and animal spirits. Higher on the hillside, three giant Ks, dug out of the dirt and filled with sawdust and oil, flamed into the night. Hundreds of cars surrounding the celebration turned their circle of headlights into the ferment of the crowd and onto the twitching, spell-binding speakers.

Anders stood hypnotized until Johan grasped him by the shoulder and led him back to the Overland sedan. They found Rolf sprawled into a drooling, drunken sleep in the back seat.

"I guess you're up front with me, going home." Anders slid over onto the passenger side, and Johan tucked himself behind the wheel. They drove slowly away from the yellow of the flames and the din of shouts and explosions.

Anders looked back at a sign like the ones that had led them to this place, written on barns, bridges, and fences. "What do those letters mean—K>I>G>Y?"

"What do the letters mean to them?" Johan asked. "Or what do they mean to me?"

"Both—to them and to you."

Johan looked straight ahead into the blackness. "To them K>I>G>Y means, 'Klansman, I Greet You.'"

They drove on in silence for perhaps five minutes. Then Johan let go of the steering wheel with his right hand and clamped it hard on Anders' shoulder. "But to me 'KIGY' means, 'Kid, I Got You!' So that's the one you remember."

He left his hand on his young brother's shoulder for some time, and even when he took it away and placed it back on the wheel, it seemed to Anders that his brother's hand was still on his shoulder and would always be there, steering him through the night.

14

Benny the Mule and Baseball

The call of the 6:00 whistle from town floated on the curve of the prairie sky out into the wheat fields, where the strong hands of young Anders held Benny's reins. The mule Benny suspended for a moment the foot he had meant to place forward in the stubble. For perhaps three seconds he stood, frozen in position, one front hoof raised. Then, twitching his ears, he drew the foot back and placed it down in the dirt, precisely into his own hoofprint.

"Come on, you stupid old mule," said Anders. "We can get one more load, at least." But he said it more as a matter of form than out of hope that Benny would obey his command. Every afternoon when the Brem town whistle blew, Benny stopped still, refusing to do a lick of work after that.

"You'd think you belong to some goldarn labor union," laughed Anders, as he pulled the reins to the side and pointed Benny and the wagon toward the barn. In truth, Anders felt the heat of the afternoon sun on his neck and the sweat of the day trickling down his back. This obstinate mule gave him a good reason to head back to the farmhouse. Everyone in the county knew that once the town whistle blew, Benny the mule wouldn't move another step until he was turned toward his feed box.

In the barn, Anders quickly filled the box with hay and oats and dashed into the house. His mother was ready with plates and food on the heavy wooden kitchen table. This was supper, mostly leftovers from the midday dinner meal. But Kari often added bread and a cake, baked with care in the oven of the cookstove. In the early afternoon, she added bits of fuel to the fire in the stove until her hand, placed in the oven, told her the temperature was right. Her cakes never fell; her bread never burned. She had learned her craft from the housewives of Nordfjord, famous for their baked goods.

The three boys, Johan, Rolf, and Anders, washed up quickly and sat down with their parents. Together with *mor* and *far,* they said grace in Norwegian. *"I Jesu Navn gaar vi til bords; at spise, drikke paa dit ord."* Anders understood this first line clearly enough: "In Jesus' name we go to the table to eat and drink on the word." The middle part of the prayer he mumbled, head down, and then joined in again: *"I Jesu Navn, Amen."* The boys each took whatever food was closest and passed the platters around. Butter melted on the still-warm bread, and glasses of milk, cream floating to the top, washed down the cake.

"Coffee, then?" said their mother.

"No, *mor,* thanks," they answered in chorus. Kari tried to use English with them now. It was true, as the teachers said, that they should all strive to become Americans. But it warmed her heart that they still called her *"mor"* instead of the "ma" used by many of the children on neighboring farms. Sounded like the bleating of sheep, she thought, this "ma!"

"Then I suppose you may leave the table," she said, and smiled at Jens as their boys dashed away.

"Baseball," he said.

"*Ja*, baseball," she answered.

Though neither of them understood this baseball, which seemed to infect their boys with a kind of madness, they did understand the wild enthusiasm that must come out in some way in young ones. In Norway, it was ski touring in the winter and hiking in the summer. Here in America, it was a strange game that made their boys hurry to finish chores so they could get to the real purpose of their lives, baseball.

Two summers before, Jens allowed a field near the barn to be leveled, and after Benny the mule had dragged the width of a heavy plank around and around, dozens of times, the land was smooth enough for the boys to lay out the bases. The bases were flat rocks, plentiful on this stony farm. The boys built up the pitcher's mound with dirt until it looked to them the same as the mound at school; the same as pictures they had seen in the newspaper of the pitcher's mound in Yankee Stadium where Babe Ruth played.

By the time Johan, Rolf, and Anders gathered the bats by home plate, other boys from neighboring farms arrived on horseback, except for Raymond, whose parents had money. He drove up in a Model T Ford, parking it at a distance, well out of harm's way.

They didn't have enough players for two teams, so they played a work-up game, with each player taking a turn at bat. The boys on the bases and in the outfield moved to another position after each out, but Raymond, the pitcher, and Anders, the catcher, kept their positions. Though the playing field itself was level, there was a hierarchy among the players, and it was recognized without argument that Raymond and Anders held particular talent for their positions and should not have to move in rotation like the others. When it was Anders' turn at bat, the right outfielder moved behind home plate to catch. When Raymond picked up the bat, whoever was at center field moved forward to pitch.

"Batta, batta, batta," the boys yelled at the guy up front swinging. If a runner slid into home safe, a raucous cheer went up. If Anders tagged the runner out, the boys screamed their delight. In their manly shouting, the boys cut short their names, so that "Raymond" became "Ray" and "Anders" became "Andy."

"They seem to be good-natured about it all," said Jens to Kari in the old language as they looked from the porch at the noisy bunch.

"Yes, not like that terrible boxing some do, trying to kill each other and calling it sport."

Jens lit a cigarette, carefully blowing the smoke away from Kari. "But what is it about baseball that makes them want to play it so very much?"

Kari looked up from her knitting. "It is American. They want that. To be really American."

"Ja, I suppose that is it. And maybe something more." He looked at her. "It has an ending, this game of baseball. At the end, they have won or they have lost. It is definite. Not like farming, day after day, digging in the dirt, planting, hoping for rain, harvesting each fall at the whim of nature, and then planting all over again in the spring. Perhaps they like the score at the end, so that they can have one clear moment of joy or sorrow."

Kari considered what he said and considered as well that this man, this husband of hers who liked so well to read books, should not have been a farmer. Yet, here they were, Norwegians both of them, with American children, living a farm life that had no clear beginning or ending to it.

They sat there in the cool of the porch, well into the summer evening, as Jens worked with a knife and awl, trimming and knotting frayed harnesses, and Kari knitted wool stockings and sweaters for the coming winter, the two of them watching this mysterious but oddly pleasing American game called baseball.

—

More than once, her boys had tried to explain the game to her. "Baseball—not bassball—'bass' is the fish we catch in Willow Lake. 'Base' means something else—completely different."

Kari straightened her back and lifted her head, queen-mother of this family. "I know the meaning of 'base.' It has to do with the choir. The lowest of the men's voices. But what has that to do with a ball, is what I would like to know."

Rolf snatched a piece of paper from the bureau and scribbled on it. "Look, *mor,* these words sound alike, but they don't mean the same thing." He pointed at the three words. "This word, 'base,' means a place you come from or go to. This word, 'bass,' can mean two things: the fish, or, if you say it another way, it means the man singer."

Kari wrinkled her nose in disgust. "What a language this is, English. In Norwegian, we say the word just as it is written. Couldn't be easier. But with English, there is no sense to it." She settled herself into the rocker and clicked her knitting needles, guiding the yarn into the shape of stockings. Her eyes, though, remained focused on Rolf. "But you still have not told me what this 'base' has to do with a ball."

"Look, *mor.* It's really about Anders. He plays baseball now whenever he can. And he's real good at it. In Brem he plays against men's teams, even them big traveling teams comin' on through, like that Kansas Negro League team. I think you should see a real game in town. Anders would like that. I'll sit right beside you and explain the game as it goes along."

Kari's mouth softened into a smile at the name of her youngest son. Well then, if he wanted her there, she would go to see this American game, however foolishly it was named.

The hot South Dakota sun dried the town infield into dust on the afternoon of the game. Kari and Rolf worked their way through the tethered horses and wagons and a few Model T Fords to the bleachers. "Here, *mor,* sit on this side with your back to the sun. Anders plays here, behind home base. You remember, 'base' means a place. This is Anders' base—his place to play. He's called the catcher." Kari nodded. This was beginning to make sense. If you play with a ball, you need to catch it.

Anders ran out on the field, tossing her a grin as soon as he spotted her in the stands. Kari's heart jumped just a little, as it always did at a look or touch from her youngest son. She nodded her head slightly and pressed her lips together in acknowledgement. It was perhaps not right that she should love this son so much; and besides that, she would not have wanted Anders to think better of himself than he ought.

Anyway, maybe he was not so special, because many young men were now coming out onto this field dressed in gray just like Anders. They spread out into a sort of pattern, three of them standing on other places—bases—and some standing farther out. They began throwing the small white ball around, but rather than catching it in the normal way, they used fat leather gloves. Was that to make things easier? It hardly seemed fair. And Anders didn't stand up straight like the other players. He crouched down behind his base as if afraid of the ball. Kari looked around to see if others were noticing her son's cowardly behavior, but the people were now shouting out names: "Go gettum' Ray! Atta boy, Stan!"—and even seemed happy about

Anders' strange posture: "Way to scoop 'em up, Andy!" She cringed a bit at this American way of cutting names in half or changing them about.

A young man in black pants and black shirt came to Anders' base, swinging a big stick carelessly about, very near Anders' head. Then he stood sideways to the base while Anders crouched behind it. Another man, very fat and rather old, stood behind Anders and shouted, "Play ball!"

Now Rolf leaned near her. "The man in the middle has the ball," he said. "The man at the plate..." He reconsidered, thinking the word "plate" would mean "dish" and confuse her. He tried again.

"The guy out in front of Anders, with the bat—the stick—in his hands will try to hit the ball. If he misses three times, he is out. But if he hits it, he can go." Rolf felt he'd made a good start. The first batter whacked a ball high into center field, and the fielder caught it.

Rolf quickly amended his earlier explanation, "But, if the man hits the ball and someone catches it, that guy is also out." Kari nodded. The next batter stepped to the plate. He smacked a line drive, stopped after its first bounce by the left fielder, who hurled the ball to the first baseman. The batter slid in ahead of the ball, safe at first. Rolf took a deep breath. "But, if the ball bounces before it is caught, and the runner gets to first base before the ball, he is not out." Kari attempted a nod, but stopped, and gazed mystified at the field.

She saw the rest of the game as a blur. Throwing, catching, running—it must be good for these young men to stretch and exercise their bodies with such vigor. In some strange way, it exercised the crowd, too, as the spectators jumped to their feet and shouted, sometimes angry, other times wild with joy. Finally, Anders threw a ball to the base farthest away, the player there caught it, and the crowd cheered. Anders threw his glove in the air and turned to her. The smile on his face told her that the game had turned out well.

"What happened?" she said to Rolf.

"Well, *mor,* it's like this. The guy on the other team was trying to steal second, and Anders threw him out."

Kari straightened her skirt as she stood to leave. "Well," she said, "I would hope so. If the boy was stealing, he deserved to be thrown out."

15

SEASONS

Summertime meant swinging a bat to Anders. In autumn, once harvest was over, Saturdays meant slinging a Winchester 12 gauge over his shoulder as he tromped through the dry straw of the mown wheat fields. Local farmers supplied him with shells, making it clear that for two shells they expected a pheasant delivered to the farm door. Usually Anders could bring down a bird with one shot and reserve the second shell to bag a pheasant for his mother's table. School, farm chores, and church filled the other six days of his week during chilly October and November.

December brought real winter, howling its way down from the north. A blinding, heartless blizzard raged across the flat South Dakota prairie. The snow did not fall in large, lazy, wet flakes as it does in some parts of the country. Fierce wind drove these tiny, frozen, piercing particles across the fields, so the snow didn't float down, it swirled sideways, piling against the fences and roadways in impossible drifts. And still the blizzard howled, hour after hour.

By 1925 the outlying farms had telephone service—a party line, good for making and receiving calls, and for listening in to the local gossip. On that night, the night of the blizzard, a man's pleading voice sounded from the earpiece of Kari's telephone. His young wife was in labor. The doctor couldn't make it out from town because of the blizzard. Would Kari come to help?

Fourteen-year-old Anders, raised to farm chores, hitched his trusted horse to the sleigh. This horse meant safety for those going out in the blizzard; even in a blinding storm, the little stallion could find its way home. Around the horse's head Anders fixed a mask, sliced from an inner tube, with slits cut out for the eyes. He wrapped another rubber tube with eye cutouts around his own face. In this way, both horse and driver could stand to breathe the frigid air, slightly warmed behind the rubber masks.

Following fence posts and the instinct of the horse, Anders brought his mother safely to their neighbor's farm in time to help the frightened young woman birth her first baby. It was not so different from helping a ewe to lamb. Kari had looked into the eyes of a ewe coming into labor and imagined she saw the same look of fear.

Kari remembered the birth of her own babies—five that lived and one that did not. She had felt that fear at the beginning pains of birthing a child—the sense of moving down a dark tunnel, no room to turn around, no chance to turn back, no way to see the ending of it. She remembered the comfort of a woman's eyes meeting hers, taking in the fear and sending back a promise. So before attending to the needs of this girl's struggling body, Kari grasped both of her hands and looked steadily into her eyes, saying without words: I will be here with you, I will not desert you, I will not leave you to struggle alone.

She turned to the husband. "Without a doctor, it is up to us and God. So this you must do, young man." Kari took the farm lad by the back of his shoulders and positioned him at his wife's outstretched leg. She placed his callused hands on the knee, with his wife's foot against his chest. Kari grasped the other leg herself. At each contraction, she called out to the young mother, "Push!" And riding the wave passing through her body, the girl shoved her feet and legs against the two of them and mightily moved the baby down the canal toward light and life.

The top of the baby's head pushed at the reddened skin around the circle of its mother's opening. Soft, wet hair covered the emerging crown. Kari whirled the dark hair with her finger. "Your baby has lovely hair—almost here now—rest just a bit— and now, push!" The top of the little head eased through, and then the miniature nose and chin, and then the small shoulders, and then quickly, swimming out like a slippery fish, the tiny body.

"So—you have a boy baby. Wait—there are two."

The mother lifted her head to see. "Two?"

"Yes—two babies! The second is just now coming to join its brother."

The second baby came more easily, but the delivery was not joyful. The babies seemed too small to live. Kari and the father held the tiny twin boys close to the face of the exhausted mother. She kissed each one, turned away, and quietly wept. Kari wrapped the babies in flannel and put them each in a shoe box—they were as tiny as that. She put the shoe boxes in the oven of the kitchen wood stove and resting her left hand in the oven with the twins, she fed twigs into the fire with her right, keeping the babies warm. The young husband gathered more twigs from dry, dead branches, and all through the night, and through the next day, and on through the next night, Kari sat at the stove, one hand in the oven, the other tending the miniscule fire. In this way, she coaxed the babies into life, oven-baked them into being, like little gingerbread men.

On the second day, Anders rode on horseback to get the country pastor, who baptized the fragile infants. Kari stayed all week until the storm subsided; and when the doctor finally came, he pronounced the twins healthy and strong. The young husband drew money out of a tin in the kitchen to pay the doctor, shook his hand, and sent him off. Then he turned to Kari, took her by the hand, and led her back to the bedroom. They looked down at the twins, each baby on a breast of their mother. With soft, solemn eyes, she looked up at Kari as her husband spoke for them both. "We know very well who should be paid for the lives of our sons."

On May Day, when the snow and ice were gone and spring had truly arrived, the young husband came to Kari's door with an armful of early-blooming yellow forsythia.

For many years after that, on the first day of May, the young couple brought flowers, filling the hands of their spirited young boys with daffodils and sending them running on ahead to her. Each time, the parents gazed into her eyes, saying without words, we will never forget, we will always be grateful, we thank you for our sons.

———

Wheat, rising tender and green from the ground after the spring snowmelt, recognizes no boundaries. Knee-high by June, the wheat ripens pale yellow, and its infant wheat heads waggle in the breeze. Then the wheat breathes in the hot summer air and absorbs sixteen hours of sunlight, growing tall and heavy through July and August. Acre by acre, mile by mile, the wheat fields own the South Dakota earth, caring not at all who claims to own it. Drought respects no section lines; hail stops for no mapped boundaries. Yet, people settled in South Dakota in the early 1900s believed they knew who owned each acre thereabouts, and if you had asked, local Scandinavian farmers would have told you this:

That Norwegian families owned all the land, six miles by six miles, surrounding the Nilsen farm. To the east of the Norwegian territory was New Sweden with farms homesteaded in the 1880s by Swedes fleeing famine in the Old Country. To the west was a settlement of Polish newcomers, unkempt and Catholic, and beyond them, the Indians, uncivilized and heathen. To the south were tidy German farms, filled with well-behaved, somber children who called their stern fathers "Papa." All of these, except the Indians, held deeds proving ownership of the land—documents certified by the United States of America.

And yet, over all the farmland, wheat bent and rose to the push and pull of the wind, grew as the rain and sun willed it to grow, and ripened by its own internal calendar, indifferent to the prayers and curses of the farmers, whether mumbled in Norwegian, muttered in Polish, or shouted in German. The wheat listened not even to pleas offered in English, the powerful American language. The wheat listened only to the wind, and the wind blew wherever it wished to blow.

Each year, the wheat gave itself generously to the South Dakota farmers. Each year they plowed and planted this same fine crop in the same good farmland. This land in America was new and fertile, not like the rocky worn-out, uneven soil of the Old Country. There a farmer struggled each summer to grow enough grass in his fields to winter-feed his goats and sheep; some winters, in fact, barely keeping them alive. But here! The land of South Dakota was strong and virile, like a young man wanting to work, waiting only for the chance to produce. And so the farmers worked it, the land, year after year.

Yet, there were times in the countryside and town, times when the land, the air, and all creatures on the land and in the air conspired against the farmers. These dark times became stories told by fathers to sons and daughters; by mothers to daughters and sons. The stories became legends, told by those sons and daughters to their children. "Be aware; be cautious," warn the stories. "Evil comes like a thief in the night. Be ready to endure."

A cloud might hold rain or snow or sleet. It could pass over in silence, carrying away whatever it held. Lightning could streak down from a cloud, striking a house with an explosion of thunder and flame. Each approaching cloud was a mystery that the eyes of farmers strained to penetrate, their faces aimed skyward.

On a day in early July, the South Dakota heat rose up from the dusty fields and descended from the empty sky. Between the bare earth and the blank heavens walked Elmer Ocre, leather boots kicking up the luckless land. He wished for rain; he prayed for rain; he raged against the Creator who denied rain to the Dakota fields until the crops dried up, withered and died. Elmer lifted his face toward the sun. His beard, bristly and red as copper wire, shimmered in the midday light.

"Mighty God," he shouted into the cloudless sky, "what are you doing to us? Just what is it you think you're doing? Are you trying to kill us?"

Then he saw the tiny black cloud moving toward him. It grew larger, then smaller. It changed shape as it came closer. The sound of it hummed and then buzzed as the swarm of bees aimed for the only bright thing on the dusty prairie, Elmer's red beard. Elmer flailed against them and ran at first as they stung his face and hands again and again. He fell down as if dead a few feet from his house. Those who found him beat away the insects, but hundreds of bees still crawled through the brush of his copper beard, so his rescuers cut and shaved it away as best they could and rushed him to the hospital.

No one thought he would live, but he did, and after slow weeks of recovery, Elmer returned to his fields, plowed them again, planted another crop, and looked to the sky for rain. But the few clouds that drifted by that summer refused to release rain. Then the scorching winds let loose another swarm, this time one that attacked not with stingers but with hungry jaws.

Kari snatched the first creature she saw from her lilac bush. A grasshopper—that was the English word for this insect. "Hop" means "jump." A bug that jumps over grass. What a silly name for this small dragon attacking her lilacs. Kari looked down at the yellow roses, and her eyes caught the downward flutter of a perfect rose leaf. The leaf jerked back, ragged and torn. Kari fell to her knees and pulled aside a small branch of the bush. Another bug. The insect chirped at her, wiggling its hind legs. She pulled the grasshopper off the half-eaten rose stem, threw it to the ground, and smashed it with a rock.

"Forgive me," she whispered. "I love all of God's creatures. But you will not destroy my flowers. What do I have in this land without my flowers?"

Jens shouted to her from the fields, something she could not understand. She stood and watched him running toward her. He shouted again, and pointed to the sky. A dark cloud moved behind him, across the wheat field. "Locusts!" Jens cried out the word from the Bible story about the plagues in Egypt. And then Kari saw the cloud descend onto the field of wheat.

All that day Jens and the boys strode through the fields, using rakes, hoes, and scythes against the grasshoppers, killing them by the tens, the hundreds, the thousands. But a thousand dead was nothing. A million more came, eating and eating, flattening the field with their voracious appetites.

Johan pulled the bill of his checkered cap down tight over his forehead and turned up his collar. He swung his hoe at the grasshoppers, chopping at piles of them as they attacked the corn. A cornstalk fell, the leaves heavy with insects and the stem chewed away. Another fell, and then another, no matter how fast he hoed. Finally, the futility of it ground into his brain, as the blowing dust ground into his skin. He bent his head into the flying insects and fought his way toward the faint outline of the farmhouse.

"*Nei*," said his mother as he pushed open the door, and he looked where she was looking, at the dozens of grasshoppers clinging and crawling on his shirt. Still, he stumbled into the kitchen and slammed the door on the hordes of grasshoppers behind him. Together, mother and son brushed the loathsome insects off him and crunched them underfoot until the floor itself disappeared under the black, broken bodies and silver wings.

Seizing the carpet beater, Kari walked out to her flower garden. With each step, her boots crunched against the grasshoppers. Now they covered her lilac and rose bushes. Kari gripped the carpet beater and knocked the grasshoppers from the shrubs and stomped them under her boots. Whack! Crunch! With a desperate rhythm, she hit each bush, watched the grasshoppers fall, and stepped on them with her heavy work boots.

Still, the grasshoppers flew and crawled onto the plants faster than she could beat them off. Crying with anger, she threw down the beater and grabbed a shovel. Pushing aside the denuded branches of the lilac, she probed for a tiny offshoot, hidden away and protected from the marauding grasshoppers. Kari forced the shovel deep under the lilac sprout and lifted it up from the ground. She brushed off grasshoppers as she stuffed the little plant and the dirt clinging to its roots into her apron pocket.

She moved to the yellow rose bush and bent down its branches. The thorns tore at her hands and she saw that they were bleeding, but her foot drove the blade of the shovel under a little rose volunteer next to the big rose bush. "So, you didn't find this one yet!" She spit the words out at the grasshoppers. Kari held the rose shoot gently, covering the tender leaves, and then she thrust it deep into her pocket beside the lilac sprout.

As the sun set, red and orange, the grasshoppers, seeming to obey some primal signal, rose to the air, and the plague moved on to some other farmer's field. Jens and the boys came back into the kitchen where Kari stood by the sink. Jens trudged to her side.

"The wheat is a total loss; I'm sure of that. We'll plow it under tomorrow and plant again. With decent rain, we could still have a crop."

Kari nodded to him, and for a moment, rested her head on his hard shoulder. He moved away to the bedroom, removed his boots and overalls, dropped onto the bed and was instantly asleep.

Still at the sink, Kari raised the pump handle and pushed down hard. The cold water splashed into the iron bucket and covered the roots of the rose and lilac shoots. The perfect teeth of the shiny dark green rose leaves brushed harmlessly against the heart-shaped, soft leaves of the lilac sprig. Her fingers caressed the leaves of both and she smiled. "What would I have in this land without you?"

———

A new place. House and barn, horses and cows, feed and seed for next year's wheat. Arnie felt about as happy and secure as a man could be on this goldarn South Dakota back-breakin' prairie. On Friday evening, Arnie Strand closed the heavy barn door on the animals and dragged the last boxes into his solid farmhouse. Shoes off, he padded into the first bedroom and tucked quilts around his three little girls. Slipping into the next room, Arnie fell into bed beside his exhausted wife.

Just past midnight, Johan Nilsen and the neighbor boy Walter drove home on the dirt road out of Brem, through wisps of fog that attached themselves to hedgerow stubble along the edges of the fields.

"Arnie'll have to get those fences fixed if he wants to keep his cows to home." Johan held the wheel steady as the Overland bounced over rocks and potholes near Arnie Strand's fields.

Walter punched Johan's shoulder. "Give him a little time, would ya? He just moved in."

"Hey, cut it out, I'm driving. If I go in the ditch, you'll go—" He stopped in mid-sentence. "What the—" Johan stepped on the gas and the car lurched up the road, getting closer to the Strand farm buildings. "Cripes! The barn's on fire!" Johan spun gravel and dirt under the wheels, careening up the drive to the house. "Wake'm up! Get 'em out. The house could go next." Walter ran from the car to the house, and Johan spun the car around to go for help.

Volunteer firemen came and so did every neighbor for miles around, but the flames burned hot and wild, licking away at the barn, too fierce to be stopped by hoses or buckets of water. A blast of heat seared skin and scorched hair on men who tried to save the horses and cows. The bellowing and whinnying of the animals drove some to cursing and others to tears. When it was over, the barn was ashes, the animals dead, seed for spring planting burned up—all gone in the hellish fire. The farmhouse was spared, and Arnie, his wife, and children were saved.

But saved for what? His wife and girls let themselves be pulled away, back into the shelter of their home. Arnie refused to move. He stood silent and looked at the still-smoldering cinders. Arnie's Uncle Frederick stood beside him, saying nothing, for what could you say? Wiped out. The two men stood side by side for perhaps an hour, faces warmed by the heat of the blackened heap. Then Arnie turned, and they walked to the house, Frederick's hand on his nephew's shoulder.

The next thing happened as naturally as a worthy cloud forms tiny droplets, gathering together moisture to provide the earth with rain in due season. The local farmers and their wives and their children were given to understand, as they slept a few hours that evil night, that they could put back together the farm and livelihood of this family. In the morning, it began. Strong hands used rakes and pitchforks to clear away the charred rubble. Anyone who could swing a hammer worked on building the barn. A gang of kids picked up scraps of wood and nails at the end of each day. At noon on workdays, women put together a big feed for the whole community: roast beef, potatoes, gravy, carrots and peas, hot rolls, and great sheets of frosted cake.

Every farm family donated an animal or two: a team of horses, some chickens, enough cows so that the Strands could get through the winter by selling milk and butter to the creamery. In the spring, neighbors came again with seed to plant, seven tractors tilling the rich black soil. By fall, when the harvest came in, the Strands were back on their feet again.

Nobody thought much about it. That's just what you did.

Part Two

WORK DID IT

16

BERIT AND GUSTAV

"Good day, Mrs. Rose," said Dagmar Lundeen, as the two women turned over bolts of cloth in the dry goods store. "Good day to you, Mrs. Lundeen." The voice of Mrs. Rose echoed around the room, reverberating from the heavy beams to the scarred wood floor.

"I had been thinking of you as I watched my daughter Berit scrubbing the floor yesterday." Mrs. Lundeen's Swedish-accented words, as musical and nimble as sixteenth notes, fell softly onto the bolts of cotton and disappeared.

"What is that you say? Your watch fell on the floor? I am sorry but I only hear half your words." Men sitting beside the potbellied stove turned to look.

"Mrs. Rose, I will talk plain then. My daughter Berit is strong and works hard. She can cook and clean and milk. She would be able to help you, if you needed a hired girl this fall, now that our harvest is over." Mrs. Lundeen had rarely spoken so many English words together in one breath.

A grand smile wrapped its way around the thin face of Mrs. Rose, the corners of her lips reaching almost to her cheekbones.

Her ebony eyes laughed themselves closed, as she shouted out something in a foreign tongue.

"Now I do not understand you," whispered Mrs. Lundeen.

"Pardon my Yiddish," Mrs. Rose cried out. "I said, 'From your lips to God's ears.' I have been praying for a nice, strong girl to help with the cooking and cleaning. Your Berit is an answer to my prayers!"

At sixteen, Berit Lundeen could cook up a noontime dinner for ten farmhands, milk a barn full of cows, and stitch closed the holes of a dozen socks, all in a twelve-hour day. Still, it seemed wasteful to her parents to keep their strong, healthy daughter at home, when she could be fetching a solid dollar a week as a hired girl for another household.

And so it was that Berit walked, carrying a satchel containing her nightgown and an extra housedress, to the neighboring farm of Benjamin and Becca Rose. Without children of their own, they often took in foster children and hired other youngsters to help about the place. Just now, though, their only foster child was a young boy, taken in more from charity than his ability to work on the farm.

On her first workday, Berit rose at 5:00 to wash clothes, hanging them out by sunrise. By 7:30, Berit had breakfast on the table for the boy, a hired man, and Mr. Rose. By 8:00, Mrs. Rose came to the breakfast table, still dressed in her nightgown and wrapped in a robe. Mr. Rose, rather than scolding her for getting up so late, greeted her with a kiss on the cheek and a gentle squeeze on her arm as he murmured little words of endearment in her ear.

Then he turned to Berit. "So this is the fine young helper we have now. What a breakfast! A prince could ask for no better!" Benjamin Rose, who had marched with General Sherman in the Civil War, spun around smartly and strode out the door.

Mrs. Rose raised her coffee cup. "So, Berit, sit a minute with me and talk to an old lady." Her tone, kind yet commanding, turned the request into an order. From this beginning came their daily pattern: three hours of early morning work for Berit, followed by a little talk over coffee with Mrs. Rose. Nothing in Berit's life seemed too private for them to discuss. Mrs. Rose asked about her brothers, her parents, their house and animals. She asked about Berit's health, her appetite, and her monthly cycle. She gave advice about Berit's future—what she should read, what work she might do, how she could earn money, and what sort of man she should marry.

"You see my Benjie," she said. "He worships me almost to idolatry. And how does it affect me? I live for him and I would die for him. So it should be with you and the man you marry."

Berit thought of the farm boys her age, and she could see no possibility of such a marriage among those Swedish boys.

"Or then," Mrs. Rose saw the skeptical expression on Berit's face, "there is also another kind of marriage many have found quite satisfactory. Marry a man with property and be his partner in life, providing for yourself and any children, God willing, you may have. Money and security, there is no great sin in that and quite a comfort in your old age."

Thinking again of the men on neighboring farms, that seemed to Berit a more reasonable goal.

Days revolved for Berit around the chores of the farmhouse and barnyard. On clear mornings, she did the wash, keeping Mrs. Rose's good dresses and nightgowns separate from the men's work clothes that she carried in baskets to the clothesline. On some winter days, clothes froze stiff before they dried in the feeble sunlight. When snow fell, the clothes hung in the enclosed mudroom on wooden pegs pounded into the wall.

As Berit observed Mrs. Rose through the year, she saw that this small woman was an important part of the prosperity of the farm. She packaged eggs neatly into crates and sent them off to the grocer. She rented out extra furniture to newcomers, selling the chairs and beds to them later, if they could afford to buy, or collecting a user fee each month. Bent over a leather-bound ledger, Mrs. Rose dipped her pen into black ink and wrote figures in careful penmanship. She sat Berit down beside her one day and explained the system.

"The money coming in goes in this column," she said. "And the bills are paid and recorded in this column. Any profit goes to buy more land, or it goes in the bank. Or perhaps for some little bauble for the queen." She said this last with a laugh as she flashed the ring on her hand, a gold ring, delicately formed around a dazzling blue stone.

"Every woman needs something of her own." Now she was solemn, looking directly into Berit's eyes. "Every woman needs something she can run with, or sell, if the evil eye is on her family, to save her people."

So the wisdom of Mrs. Rose and the respectful admiration of Mr. Rose strengthened Berit, for she was unused to this kind of attention from her own family, who believed that parents should not waste time teaching girls and that praise of any kind led to wicked pride. As the year passed, it seemed to Berit that there was a sort of magic in these people. It came, perhaps, from the candlesticks on the table or the violin on the sideboard. It was a magic that, if she observed it carefully, she might blend with her Swedish strength and stubbornness and use someday to lift herself up.

Gustav Gustavson stood straight-backed and wore thick-soled shoes, making all he could of his height of five feet and four inches. His head seemed large for the size of his body, perhaps expanded by a thousand bits of flinty wisdom he had collected in his first eighteen years.

From his mother, Olga, he learned tenacity. When her husband abandoned their hardscrabble Dakota farm, fleeing bad winters, failed crops, and Olga's shrewish yammering, she pressed on. It was not in her to quit. Left with little, Olga used what she had. She forced the dirt floor of her sod shanty to lie smooth and dustless. She twisted prairie grass into knots and burned it for heat. She harnessed the oxen and horses and plowed the fields. She raised her boy to work. With him, she dug a well and built a simple wooden farmhouse. As neighbors said with respect, she made a go of things. And when her little girl died, Olga buried the tiny body herself in the hostile earth.

From country school, Gustav learned English and ciphering numbers. Olga relied on him more and more, at first for labor and then for dealing with clever merchants. By the time Gustav left school after fourth grade, he could do sums in his head as Olga bought sugar, pins, and coffee in town.

From the fierce Dakota winters, Gustav learned to be watchful and wary. In January of 1888, a fierce blizzard struck. That morning, seduced by a beautiful sunrise, some farmers had hitched up their wagons and headed for town. Other farmers tended to chores in the fields, encouraged by the glimmer of winter sunshine. At 10:00, Gustav trudged to the well to draw water for the animals, his feet crunching a pathway through eight inches of snow that had fallen the night before. As he walked, a dark blue patch of sky in the north turned hazy and pushed its way south.

The snowstorm hit without warning, and within minutes swirling, icy particles erased any sight of roads, houses, or barns. Gustav fell to his knees and with his bare hands felt for the packed snow of his footprints leading back to the barn. From there he could hear his mother calling to him, over and over, from the house, and he followed her voice home. Tying a clothesline to the kitchen door, he made his way back to the barn to feed the stock before pulling himself along the icy rope into the shelter of the house. A boy on the next farm grabbed a cow's tail and was towed to the safety of his barn. Other farmers, staggering in from the fields, froze to death a few blind yards from their buildings.

From the land itself, Gustav learned that the earth, when worked, can feed a family. He learned that rich loam provides better than rocky dirt. And in the last years of the 1800s, he learned that there was still acreage available for homesteading.

He homesteaded land up north for the time required to clear the title, and then he sold the acreage for cash. With money in the bank, Gustav courted seventeen-year-old Berit Lundeen, the neighbor girl who worked for Mrs. Rose. As Gustav presented Berit with his proposal, he made the match seem sensible, almost inevitable. He asked her first if she could milk a cow and second if she would marry him, and she said yes to both. She did not do this blindly or without forethought. She compared this short, serious man to the big, joking lads from other farms in the area. She observed that Gustav did not drink or gamble. She took into account that, while he chewed tobacco, he was accurate in his aim at the nearest spittoon and that he wiped his mouth clean with his shirtsleeve. She noticed his sharp pencil as he figured costs at the feed store and interest at the bank. Taken together, these were enough.

Not enough though for Berit to be content living in the same house as her mother-in-law, Olga, that sharp-tongued, skinny little woman with hard hands and eyes. Olga fully expected her son Gustav to remain in the wood-frame farmhouse they had built together, whether or not he was foolish enough to buy the grief that marriage to this girl Berit was sure to bring. So they started, the three of them, living together.

Each morning of her first year as Gustav's wife, Berit's back stiffened against the sting of her mother-in-law's criticism. Olga sputtered against the bitterness of the breakfast coffee, fussed over the extravagance of throwing sugar into it, ranted about the waste of lye soap in washing up the coffee cups.

"Hot water, that's all that's needed. Boil water on the cook-stove and dip the cups into it. Save the good lye soap for scrubbing real dirt out of the work clothes." Olga grimaced as she ran her tongue over the edge of the cup. "The taste of soap never goes away." She wrinkled her nose. "I can smell it." And she spit into her saucer.

Berit thought of the words of Mrs. Rose, "Marry a man with property and be his partner in life. Provide for yourself and your children." Mrs. Rose mentioned nothing about a complaining old mother-in-law. Still, from the beginning Gustav and Berit had the partnership Mrs. Rose described, each seeing value in the other's business sense. When they heard of a reasonably priced farm seven miles away next to the town of Brem, complete with a barn and a small house, Gustav convinced his mother to loan them money to buy it.

"A miracle!" Berit held her lips tight against a smile as Gustav told her that Olga had agreed.

In the month before they moved, Olga gave not a jot on the subject of Berit's coffee making and housekeeping, chattering on and on about her daughter-in-law's wastrel ways. Yet she said nothing against the new farm, and when moving day came, Olga bid them both a cordial goodbye. "I suppose we will still see enough of each other," she said with a nod.

One month later, Olga sold her farm and with that money bought a little plot of land in Brem, half a block from Gustav and Berit's farm. She had a cottage built on the lot, and there she lived out her days just a stroll away from her beloved son.

She watched him with silent pride for the final eighteen years of her life, seeing in Gustav's grit a fragment of her own grinding determination. He dug and removed glacier-deposited rocks, sized from pebbles to boulders, from fields meant to be plowed. He sawed the old barn in half, pulled the two sections apart, and erected a hay loft and horse barn between. He added fences, a hog house, a machine shed, a chicken coop, and a tile-covered silo. When a storm blew the silo down, Gustav built it again.

He added acreage to his holdings. Like a little bulldog, he attacked his business adversaries with single-minded focus, viewing his target with clear eyes, challenging the landowner with unwavering persistence, hanging tenaciously onto the deal, and finally, strutting away with his prize.

Gustav observed the moneyed men in town, and he learned to use the sharp tools of business success: be watchful, be shrewd; borrow only to buy property—and never begin or close a business deal on Friday, the unluckiest day of the week.

17

PUSHING AHEAD AND PULLING APART

B erit's firstborn came forth without a cry. The baby boy's face was wrinkled and solemn and his little body sturdy as a soldier, so they named him Wilhelm, thinking the name had a military sound to it. Two years later, a second baby boy pushed his way into the world with a willful yell. They named him Henry.

From the beginning, Gustav took the boys in hand, allowing no pampering from Berit or Olga. By age two, Wilhelm toddled about the barn. His playmates were the barn animals that sniffed and nudged him about. His toys were miniature tools: a hammer, a rake, and a shovel. His father taught him the importance of sharpening and cleaning farm implements. Wilhelm learned his numbers by memorizing the cost of a wagon tongue or axle when some precious wagon part broke and had to be replaced.

As soon as Gustav observed curious little Henry squeezing a few drops from the teats of a cow, he began twice-a-day training sessions, teaching the boy how to milk a dairy cow. Before their feet could reach the planking of the wagon, both Wilhelm and Henry learned to drive the horses that pulled the hay stacker.

Little Wilhelm grew keenly alert with his eyes and ears and in his sense of responsibility. One day, the scurry of a mouse in a dark corner of the kitchen caught the boy's ear. He reached across the wooden table and grabbed the kerosene lantern, wrapping his fingers around its glass chimney. In the upward, turning motion, half a second into it, he felt the hot glass blistering the skin of his fingers and the palm of his hand. He did not drop the precious lamp but, his eyes wide with the pain of it, turned back to the table and gently settled the lamp onto its pine surface. He was six years old.

Berit's two daughters were also born in the small brick and plaster house that came with the farm on the edge of Brem. It was through the windows of the old house that the little sisters, Mildred and Evelyn, watched as their Pa directed big brother Wilhelm and the other builders. The girls watched as the foundation, walls, and roof grew; watched as the stones and boards climbed up and over; watched the creation of their new farmhouse.

The sturdy structure might have been seen as an immense box but for the fanciful turret on the left-front corner of the house. The exterior wall of the turret began with rocks harvested from the fields. Atop this foundation, sturdy beams held solid lumber in place. The inside of the turret remained unfinished for some time, less important than the façade. Gustav had not thought what use he would make of the room, but only that a tower attached to his house would make it from the outside seem defensible, even invulnerable—indeed, give it the look of a Swedish castle.

On moving day, their first day in the new house, the little girls claimed the turret room as their play space. They slipped under a crude opening into the round room and declared it their own. Through the long, narrow windows they could peek out, without being seen by grown-ups approaching the house. The curved interior walls became the inside of a cave or of a battleship, of a tepee or a witch's cauldron. The little ones furnished the space with blankets and pillows filched from bedrooms. They peopled it with dolls and imaginary friends. Enemy tribes or armies might try to reach them, but these sturdy walls, built by Wilhelm, Pa, and his workmen, would keep Mildred and Evelyn safe from harm.

Farm money financed this house—cash from sales of milk, of wheat, of corn, of beef, of chicken and eggs. With his fourth-grade education, Gustav Gustavson could not have spelled "diversified," but he knew as if by instinct that a farmer shouldn't bet on one crop. In any given year, the price of wheat might drop through the basement or a surplus of corn might make that crop worthless. Blight could blacken flax; hoof and mouth would decimate cattle. No, spread your money around, and even in the worst year, some of it will come back to you, multiplied.

If the schooling of a child of his went beyond basic reading, writing, and figuring, Gustav considered it a waste of time. He paid no attention to the good report cards that his children brought home. Only at Berit's insistence did he permit his sons and daughters schooling past the primary level.

Wilhelm spoke only Swedish when he started school. He carried home English phrases to his little brother Henry as secret passwords, so that when Henry came to school two years later, he could answer back the English-speaking toughs. If some sadistic boy persisted in tormenting Henry, Wilhelm stepped between them, and soon enough the bully ran away bawling. His reputation grew with his size and strength, so that when Wilhelm walked Mildred and Evelyn to their first day at the elementary school, the scruffy boys standing at the doorway moved aside.

In the September of his third year of high school, with near-perfect marks in all of his classes, Wilhelm refused to go back to school. Gustav Gustavson, after careful deliberation, had taken out a mortgage to add a quarter section of land to the farm. Wilhelm understood as a boy at his father's knee that interest was something to have coming in, not something to be paying out; and that debt could beat a farmer into bankruptcy. So in his sixteenth year, as his younger brother and sisters walked off to school, Wilhelm stayed home, working on the farm to lift the weight of debt off the back of his father. In December of the next year, Gustav paid off the loan, tossed the payment schedule into the fire of the kitchen stove, looked Wilhelm in the eye and gave him a nod of approval.

Two more children, Herbert and Russell, were born to Berit in the new farmhouse, so six in all, four boys and two girls. The girls Gustav left to Berit, but the boys were his assets to be trained for farming. Gustav brooked no nonsense from his sons about work. From the age of ten he had been able to subtract money going out from money coming in, checking profit and loss—and he did not, by God, intend ever to take a loss on his farm. He acquired adjoining land, bought milk cows, and improved the herd through careful breeding. He planted corn, wheat, barley, and oats. When one crop failed, another survived. He cut a deal with owners of the local dairy to sell them starter milk for churning great vats of butter.

It was work that did it—Gustav's work, his hired men's work, and his sons' work.

His first-born son Wilhelm strode about the farm as steady and faithful as the strong draft horses. Up at dawn, he milked cows, fed the pigs, cleaned the stalls—whatever job needed his strong hands and arms, he threw himself into it. Each afternoon, he paused for a few moments as his younger brothers and sisters came onto the farm from school and ran over to tell him their stories of the classroom and the school yard.

"Good," he told them. "Study hard—and play some, too!" Then, rumpling a blond head and patting a small shoulder, he sent them off to their mother's kitchen and bent his back to the lifting and hauling of farm work.

Henry, Gustav's second son, was unfortunately a reader. Spent every spare minute bent over a book. In his father's opinion, he should have been finished with schooling, ready for farm work. But the teachers yakked on about his good mind, convincing his mother that Henry must stay with his studies.

Still, after school he could work.

On Friday Berit blocked Henry's path as he dropped his schoolbooks on the kitchen table. "Pa and the men are haying out beyond the pasture. Take this foodbox out to them on your way to getting the cows in. It's getting late."

She stacked pork sandwiches and frosted cake into a crate and placed the box onto Henry's outstretched arms. Henry stumbled across the pasture with his load, setting it down twice and shaking out his arms before picking the box up again and trudging on. When he came to the hay wagon, he called out, "Pa, Ma has eats here for you."

Gustav Gustavson motioned for his men to put down their hayforks and sit in the shade of the wagon. As they reached for the sandwiches, Henry sat down by Mickey Sullivan, the youngest of the men. Mickey opened his sandwich and looked sadly at the slice of pork.

"Well, then, me lad," he said to Henry. "You'll be wantin' a bit more meat in your sandwich, I'm thinkin'." He carefully lifted the slice of pork from his sandwich to Henry's bread, so that now Henry's sandwich had meat both in the middle and on top of it.

"Why?" asked Henry. He had never seen a hired man give away food before.

"Well, you see, there are two things here you would want to consider: the first would be, this is Friday; and second would be, I'm Catholic. The priest says only fish on Friday, and that's what my Ma will be fixing us tonight. And if I come in, my breath smellin' of meat—well, I might as well be smellin' of whiskey, for all there'd be hell to pay!" Mickey grinned and bit down into his buttered bread.

Farmer Gustavson rose to his feet and moved toward the wagon. Knowing this signal, the men stuffed the cake and frosting into their mouths and jumped up. Henry picked up the box and turned back toward the house.

"Henry, you'll be up here." Henry heard his father's voice, unyielding as a hand clutching his shoulder. He turned, dropped the box, and looked up. Gustav reached down, grabbed Henry's hand, and lifted him in one motion onto the hay wagon.

Henry knew the routine. The hired men tossed forkful after forkful of hay onto the wagon, and Henry spread it around evenly across the wagon load. The October sun warmed the hay and lifted the scent of it to Henry's nose. Again and again, the men threw mounds of hay onto the wagon, and Henry used his fork to lay it out smoothly, until another flurry of hay landed around him. He saw his father watching him. He distributed the piles over the wagon load. Too much hay on one side or the other and the load could slide off, wasting hours of work.

Then Henry's head began to ache. He felt a bit dizzy. "Pa," he said. "I feel sick." His father didn't answer. Henry forked around the next heaps of hay. He leaned against his pitchfork. "Pa, I really do feel sick."

"You might as well go on home," said his father. "You never did like to work anyway." Henry dropped to the ground, and tried to smile as Mickey patted his shoulder and gave him a wink. He trudged back to the cow pasture, wrapped his fingers around the collar of the lead cow, and pulled her toward the barn, as the other cows followed. "Come on, Maggie, time for milking." Henry clutched at the cow's neck as much to hold himself up as to lead her to her stall.

From the barn, he shuffled wearily into the kitchen and sat down on a chair. "What is it?" asked his mother, looking suspiciously at his red and perspiring face.

"I guess I'm sick. Pa doesn't think so, but I feel awful bad."

His mother touched his forehead, wiped his face with a cold, wet rag, and led him off to bed. She muttered quiet oaths against her husband, who was a good provider; no one in Brem could say he wasn't. But for a man to see his sons only as farm workers and nothing else! She covered Henry with just a cotton sheet, for he was burning with fever. "Sleep," she said, praying his young body would fight off this deadly flu, because there was no medicine for it, only rest.

For weeks the farm women had dreaded the influenza, a sickness that had already killed many on the East Coast. In this year, 1918, the Great War blew like an evil wind across Europe and America, leveling healthy young men, first with bullets and then with a pestilence the boys carried with them from their barracks, into the troop ships, down to the trenches, and back to the hospitals in America. By the third week in September, its sickness and death darkened the farmlands of the Midwest. Some called it the Spanish Flu; others whispered of a German plot. In Brem and in the South Dakota countryside, houses of the sick were quarantined. Brem's school closed, not to open for six weeks.

Within days, Gustav himself was in bed, grumbling about the work he had left undone. The flu struck Wilhelm next. A quarantine sign went up on the door.

Neighbors came in to do the barn chores. For the first time in anyone's memory, all work by the Gustavson family stopped, except that some in Brem did credit as work Berit's nursing of her husband and children. She bathed their feverish bodies, changed the sweat-soaked sheets, brought them water and broth, and sat night and day by one bed or another.

"Ma," said Henry after his fever broke and he was able to sit up in bed, "why didn't you get sick?"

"No time," she said and pushed a spoonful of soup into his mouth.

Brem's doctor stood at bedsides, helpless against this capricious killer. Patients died or survived randomly, whether or not they were treated. All faith in medicine gone, mothers tried folk remedies: herbal teas, garlic, onion baths, or brown sugar burned on hot coals to fumigate the house. And yet babies, old men, young girls, and able farmers fell into their beds with influenza. Some lived through it and some died, with no sense to it at all, whispered weeping women to each other.

Finally the influenza epidemic in America blew itself out, like a tornado drifting back into the sky. It left in its destructive path six hundred thousand dead in the U.S. alone—and millions upon millions worldwide.

———

Berit heated the beef chunks, cabbage, onions, and carrots to a rolling boil, building a hearty soup to protect her family against the early October frost. *"Sjukdom, håll dig borta,"* she muttered, wishing away the last effects of the deadly influenza.

"Say it in English, Ma."

"So, Henry, *är svenska inte bra nog nu?*" Berit directed the words and her formidable gaze at her son, but he did not lower his eyes. She repeated her question in English. "You think Swedish is not good enough now?"

"It's just—it's the war, Ma. People don't like any foreign tongue, and Swedish sounds a lot like German to these English and Irish. Grandma can't seem to talk English at all, after living fifty years in America. You've seen the yellow paint on the Schmidts' fence. We're American now. We have to sound American."

Berit wiped her hands on her apron and looked hard at her son. In *det gamla landet,* the old country of Sweden, a son would not correct his mother so, shaming her in her own kitchen and criticizing his old grandmother. Yet at thirteen, Henry knew American ways and spoke English perfectly, so here in South Dakota he acted like a wise parent, and she felt like a foolish child. She turned back to the stove.

"Another thing, Ma. We could start calling Wilhelm just 'Will,' making it shorter. The Irish say 'Mike' for Michael and the English call Robert 'Bob.'"

Berit stirred the soup and said carefully, "And what would be the purpose of that?"

"'Wilhelm'—you know—that's the name of that old German ruler. People might think our Wilhelm was named after him."

Berit dropped Henry's soup bowl on the table. Startled at the clunk of the bowl and the splash of the soup, he studied her face, but now she did not look at him.

"Ma, I need to tell you these things. You don't notice, but it's important to change. Last Sunday there was an American flag up by the altar. That's a way of saying Lutherans are loyal Americans, even if some came from Germany."

"And do I look like a German spy to you?"

"It's not about me, Ma. It's about other people. It's about the government. We need to be careful."

———

The knives in the butcher shop gleamed. Polished and honed to a razor's edge, they hung in descending order of size on thin leather thongs, convenient to the sturdy hands of butcher Heinrich Schmidt. Pork, beef, lamb, and poultry—whatever meat a Brem housewife wanted, Heinrich Schmidt cut and wrapped in tidy paper packages and marked them "pork chops," "beef brains," or "stewing hen." At times, his spelling faltered or his hand moved of its own volition to write *"wurst"* instead of "sausage." On those occasions, Heinrich unwrapped the meat, wrapped it afresh, and wrote the proper American word on the package.

Gustav Gustavson walked with short, quick steps along Brem's only business street, grateful for his restored energy and health. He stopped briefly at the post office to try to read the poster there. Pictured on the poster was a man wearing a little white chin beard and dressed in striped pants. This old man pointed to a ship in dock, but he seemed to speak to a muscular young man pictured in work clothes. Some words were short, so Gustav could read them. "This is where I need you, Lad!" But other words on the poster were unfamiliar. Gustav could sound them out, using his primary school phonics, but the meanings escaped him. "Slimy German submarine," said one line. "Devilish cunning of the hellish Hun," said another. "German" was a word he understood, and "devil" and "hell"—the pastor spoke of them often enough at his Swedish Lutheran Church— but what was "slimy" or "cunning" and what did "Hun" mean? He walked on to the butcher shop.

"Ah, Heinrich," he called ahead, and as Heinrich stepped out into the sunshine, Gustav added, "Fine day!" The two men looked at the yellow October sun in an indigo sky, and then at each other.

"In some ways, *ja*." Heinrich wiped his hands on his white apron and looked down at the traces of blood.

"What, downhearted on a day like this?"

At that moment, John Collier strode by, and before either man could greet him, John spit tobacco on the sidewalk, just at Heinrich's feet, and without a word, walked on.

"What is this?" Gustav was offended by such carelessness. There were spittoons around the town for those who chewed tobacco, after all.

"This is about the war, you know," said Heinrich. "You may not want to be seen talking with me."

"War? In Europe, you mean? We all left there to get away from one war after another. You left Germany and I, Sweden. What has that to do with us now?"

"It has to do with us now. America is in it, too. And John Collier's son is fighting over there." Heinrich turned to the front of his shop and gestured to the yellow paint splashed over the door and window. "This I found Monday morning. Yellow, you know, meaning coward or traitor. Last week it was on the fence of our house."

Gustav frowned, and then forced a smile on his face. "Well, my friend, this is nonsense and will be quickly gone. Let me buy you a cigar. A good one—a ten-cent cigar!"

Heinrich lifted his eyes from the yellow paint. "Too much for me, though I thank you for your kindness. A five-cent cigar, I will smoke with you." And so Gustav went next door into the mercantile and quickly emerged with two nickel cigars. The men smoked them in silence and with a nod parted, Gustav walking back to his farmhouse on the edge of town and Heinrich stepping back into his butcher shop.

In the dim light, he saw the row of knives arranged from smallest to largest, seven of them in all. He lifted two off the rack, one in his left hand and one in his right, feeling the heft of them. He dropped the smaller knife on the chopping block and felt the sharp edge of the larger knife by running his index finger along the blade. A fine line of blood formed on the tip of his finger.

Carrying the knife, Heinrich the butcher stepped out the back door of his shop and into the alleyway. He stood for a moment between a red delivery wagon and three white milk pails. He climbed into the back of the wagon and lay down, his torso flat against the wooden wagon bed. He looked again at the endless blue sky, and with a practiced hand, he cut his own throat.

In this way, Heinrich missed the celebration three weeks later, when Kaiser Wilhelm abdicated, and the Great War came to an end. Those left behind found it hard to say which was most deadly—the ghastly war itself, the poisonous vine of influenza that wrapped itself around it, or the lingering stench of mistrust, one neighbor for another. Venomous gossip now grew from the shade of a man's skin, the rites of a woman's religion, or the brogue detected in a child's first words.

18

Evelyn

L ittle Evelyn Gustavson wiggled her toes deep under three quilts piled on the iron-post bed, finding a warm spot near Mildred's feet. Mildred moaned, snuffled, and turned away, never breaking the rhythm of deep sleep. The chime of the clock in the downstairs hallway struck 2:00. Evelyn flattened her back against the mattress and stared into the blackness. Time inched toward morning, the seconds measured by the sound of an icicle dripping outside her window. 3:00. Did she sleep at all? As the clock chimed 6:00, she heard her father's clattering boots and her big brother Wilhelm's quiet footsteps down the stairs, then a creak and click as he closed the door. She slipped from under the quilts, gathered her clothes, and crept down to the kitchen to dress in the warmth of the blazing cookstove.

Her mother, Berit, standing near the stove, lifted a pot of coffee off the iron surface and splashed its black liquid into a cup. She added milk and cream to the coffee, so that the cup held a third each of coffee, milk, and cream. Then she scooped a tablespoon of sugar into the mix and handed it to Evelyn.

"Ma, you know about the play tonight?"

"What?'

"I'm in the play tonight at the school."

Her mother turned to the stovetop griddle covered with browning chunks of potatoes and sizzling eggs. Evelyn felt for the plates high in the cupboard and set six places at the table. The family sat down at the table in twos, Wilhelm and Pa in from the barn, Henry and Mildred ready for school. Evelyn sat across from Ma's empty plate, which would be used only after the family left. As Evelyn and Mildred cleared the dishes, little Herbert toddled in. Evelyn swept him up into the highchair and kissed him on the nose. "I'm going to be a Dutch girl tonight," she whispered into his ear. Ma spread a thick rusk of bread with butter, cinnamon, and sugar and set it along with a cup of milk on the tray of the highchair.

By 7:00 that evening, the seats in the gymnasium were filled with older school students, parents, and other townspeople, all gathered to see the Brem grade school operetta, *Dutch Windmills*. Heavy cloth curtains separated the stage from the chairs set in rows for the audience. Evelyn grasped the edges of the curtains where they met in the middle of the stage. She parted the curtains slightly, creating a slit between them, and she pressed one eye to the sliver of light. She scanned the audience, row by row. Near the front were Henry and Mildred, talking to their schoolmates. In back, leaning on the frame of the entrance door, stood her oldest brother, Will. Evelyn searched the faces of the audience again. They might still come. They might just be late. She felt a hand on her shoulder. Miss Fosburg gave her a serious look. "We're about to start, Evelyn. And remember to frown a bit on your first line. Your character Katarina isn't sure she wants to dance with the boy Jacco."

The music started and curtains flew apart to reveal a Dutch village. The boys skipped in, dressed in ballooning black pants, white shirts with black buttons, and ribbon ties. Black caps covered their patchy farm boy haircuts. Evelyn and the other girls wore long, bright blue dresses draped from waist to hem with white pleated aprons. Matching white hats, folded and pressed in the pointy Dutch fashion, topped the head of each girl.

Evelyn stepped forward and tried to frown as she said her first lines, but she couldn't stop smiling as Knut, the only boy worth liking in the whole school, bowed to her and took her hand to dance. Boys and girls stomped around the schoolhouse stage in wooden shoes that knocked and rattled with every step. They had learned to stiffen their elbows and rotate their arms in graceful imitation of windmills caught in an onshore breeze. As they danced, they sang about the clackety-clack sounds of windmills in Holland:

Dancing, dancing in our little wooden shoes.
Dancing two by two in white and blue.

And Knut—Evelyn secretly called him "Knut the cute"—had chosen her. He had to, of course, because he was Jacco the Dutch boy who danced with Katarina the Dutch girl in this play. Still, it seemed to her that Knut didn't mind a bit holding her hand as they stomped their wooden shoes.

Afterward, big brother Will lifted Evelyn into the wagon behind Mildred. He slipped a small bag of hard candy into her hand. "For your first big play," he smiled. "I suppose you will be on stage in Minneapolis next." He climbed onto the driver's seat beside Henry and snapped the reins over the backs of the horses.

The four of them rode in the wagon back to the Gustavson farmhouse on the edge of Brem. The house was already dark, and they moved up the stairs in silence and slipped into their bedrooms. Evelyn undressed in the darkness and crept into bed, where she found a warm place for her toes against her sister's feet.

———

Berit stared in stolid resistance at the dishes piled high in the iron sink. *What do these have to do with me?* The question wandered though her mind with no reply. Sunlight sifted through the flaxen weave of the muslin curtain. Pushing it back, she looked out the window at the straw-patch chicken yard and the weathered red barn beyond. White chickens scratched at dry South Dakota dirt, pecking at a bug or a dust devil with equal zeal.

"*Galna kyckling*—crazy chicken," she said, and grasped the handle of the chicken-feed bucket with one hand as she pushed open the screen door with the other.

The chickens scurried around her ankles and clawed at the grain as it hit the dusty ground. "*Ägg och middagsmat*—eggs and dinner, that's all you are!" she said to the hens, but she said it with affection. Along with Gustav and her children, the hens were her best companions on the farm, and money from their eggs belonged to her. She flung the grain across the barnyard, making the chickens flutter and run after it.

"Yes! Work for it," she shouted. "Else you don't deserve it!" Then she lowered her voice to an apologetic whisper. "*Var så goda*—come and enjoy—and make me good eggs to sell, eggs with bright orange yolks." The chicken's feathers gathered grime and birdshit from the swirling dust.

Something of beauty was what she craved. Her soul knew it, if her practical brain did not. Berit carried the empty feed bucket back to the porch. She stood by the stove and watched as her husband put his arm into his coat sleeve.

"Well," said Berit, "if you are walking to the feed store anyway, you might as well stop by the train station for a newspaper."

"The Webster paper is right here on the table."

"I was thinking of the Minneapolis paper," she said, as if the thought had just entered her head.

"I suppose it would be good to get the commodity prices. We could see what ridiculous price those lazy bankers are giving a poor farmer for wheat this week." To Gustav, all financiers, whether in the stock market or at the racetrack, were bankers and therefore leeches, sucking the blood of farmers. And to Gustav, all farmers were poor, even those who, like him, lived in substantial houses on large landholdings.

"Well, then." Berit tossed her words over her shoulder. "You would want to buy a *Minneapolis Star* for that." She said it as though buying the paper was first his idea.

Gustav walked into town with purpose. Anyone watching would know that this little man had no time to waste. His short legs clipped off the steps like pruning shears, snip, snip. And each small stride brought him closer to wherever he wanted to go—first to the feed store, then the mercantile, and finally to the train station where he picked up the *Minneapolis Star*. He opened the paper to the financial page and let his eye move down a column of farm prices to those that concerned him. Corn, wheat, barley, flax, hogs. He shook his head in disgust at the prices and muttered a mild swear word in Swedish. The farmers standing nearby grumbled sympathetically about the cost of working the land for such meager return. Some used even stronger oaths in English, there being no women around.

Gustav folded the paper and clamped it under his arm. Perhaps later he would scan the obituaries for familiar names.

He marched in quick-step back to his farmhouse on the edge of town, circled to the back of the house, and stepped inside the kitchen door. The newspaper landed with his hat on the table as he passed by on his way to change into his work overalls.

Berit waited until he tromped his way to the barn. Then she touched the edge of the paper, unfolded it gently, and smoothed out the wrinkles. She looked past the political headlines and lingered over the clothing store ads. Not that any sane person would buy a tailor-made dress at those prices, but a woman could look.

She turned then to the back pages where little entries told of items people wanted to sell—wagons, tables, and butter churns; animals, too, and farm birds—chickens and turkeys. A word stopped her, "Peacock." From her Swedish childhood into her mind flew a bright bird, the fan of its tail a miracle of color, as if the paint box of a Gypsy artist had spilled over.

She pictured herself as a girl of Småland in *det gamla landet,* the old country, Sweden. In the big manor house on the hill above her parents' poor cottage, lived the local aristocracy, surrounded by acres of lush farmland and added acres of forests and lakes. In the pond nearest the great house floated water lilies, white and pink and purple, like little clouds reflecting the setting sun. Around the pond strutted peacocks, each turning and spreading the brilliant fan of his tail in display, screaming for the attention of the peahens. "Cocky males," thought Berit. "And yet, so very beautiful." Each peacock tail feather fluttered a dark fringe around a centered blue and purple eye, winking and beckoning the passing females.

Berit looked out on the dark soil and weathered fences of the farm. Brown in summer, white in winter, and mud in between, those were the colors of Dakota. Truth to tell, these were the colors she knew best. How splendid it would be to have a peacock in the midst of the barnyard, walking through those silly chickens, lording it over them all, waving his magic tail for her. Berit stood up and stepped over to the cupboard. She scraped the bottom of the tin box where she kept her egg money. Enough, she nodded as she counted. Berit wrote an address from the newspaper on an envelope, scribbled a message, stuffed it inside with folded dollars, and sealed the envelope. She strode to the mailbox with the letter and deposited it in the box. Then she fixed her eyes on the drab farmyard and smiled for the first time in weeks.

It took careful planning and considerable pushing of the men in her life, but by the 4th of July she had what her soul needed: a wide, shining pond, dug for her by her sons. In the pond floated water lilies, thriving in the prairie sunshine. A noble peacock and his lady, the peahen, paraded through their little kingdom. On Independence Day morning, Berit told the family to leave her be—to take the wagon to Webster for the celebration and patriotic speeches, too long and hard to understand. In the quiet after they left, her eyes rested on the pink and white lilies and the hopelessly proud, useless, and beautiful peacock, and her stern mouth softened in wonder at her own inexplicable extravagance.

19

HARVEST

As it did every afternoon, unless a blizzard stopped it dead on the frozen track, the Great Northern train rumbled past the Gustavson farm at 2:00. This day in early September the train slowed to a crawl along the fields as it approached Brem where it would stop to unload passengers, supplies, newspapers, and mail. The Gustavson farm looked inviting to Billy, a non-paying passenger, riding not in a train car, but on top of it. Clinging to the ironwork, hiding from the railroad guards that his fellow free-riders called "bulls," Billy rode the miles from one Midwestern farm town to the next, looking for work when he could find it or a handout when he couldn't.

This farm near the town might just do for a while. Billy climbed down the side of his slow-moving train car and jumped clear, landing with a few running steps before stopping to look around the acreage. The wheat seemed ripe for harvest. The farmhouse gleamed white with fresh paint. Roses bloomed near the kitchen door. A man on the move for a day's work and daily bread learned to observe such things.

As Billy approached the screen door, he removed his cap, spit on his hands, and wiped the grime from his face. He hunched forward slightly, cleared his throat of the train's coal smoke, and knocked on the door. A young girl's face appeared. She was perhaps fifteen. "Ma," she called, looking at him.

Behind the girl loomed a woman of impressive size. In one motion she swept her daughter behind her and filled the doorway with the bulk of her body. "What is it you want," she said, not unkindly but in a voice that warned they'd have no nonsense around this farm.

"Ma'am," said Billy. "I'm looking for work in the fields, if you'd be needing a strong worker. And I been travelin' all day and haven't had a chance to eat."

There was a pause. Billy waited, his eyes locked on hers. If he looked down or spoke now, it would be easier for her to turn him away.

"You can't come in here," she said finally, "but you can sit on the porch, over there in the shade. I'll fix you a plate."

"Thank you, ma'am." Billy stepped out of the harsh sunlight and into the pleasant dimness of the shade. He sat down on a wicker chair. Yellow roses climbed a trellis over the kitchen door. Chickens ran about in a pen across the yard. Billy sat up straight and squinted into the glare reflecting off the hinges of a red barn door. What was it, this strutting bird—a kind of turkey? The bird turned and bobbed its shiny blue head. It faced Billy directly and lifted and spread its tail into a dazzling design of shimmering color. "It's a damn peacock," muttered Billy.

Then the girl pushed open the screen door with her hip, her pale hair shining as she stepped into the sunlight. She carried a tray over to Billy and set it down beside him. "There," she said. On the tray was a plate heaped high with potatoes, gravy, and slices of beef. Tiny beads of water clung to the sides of a tall glass brimming with milk. Next to the glass Billy saw thick bread with butter and a square of yellow cake.

He looked at the girl. "I thank you," he said. "Tell your mother, I thank her."

The girl nodded. "It's what we feed the threshing crew at noon. They started in today. Ma says if you want work, you can get on out there in the far field, once you've eaten."

Billy's mouth, filled with meat and potatoes, could not speak an answer, but he nodded his head.

"Evelyn!" The mother's voice rattled the doorframe. When the girl turned and walked back to the house, Billy closed his eyes and smiled as he felt a little river of gravy run down his chin.

By Friday night, Billy's back ached with the strain of bending over and lifting the heavy bundles of grain. Billy and the other crop workers leaned the bundles against each other, forming grain tepees, so that rain spilling out of a rogue cloud would run off the grain and sink harmlessly into the dry earth. Ten hours of that work, six days in a row, could do a man in, especially when the man's usual occupation was riding the rails. Still, there was breakfast every morning and dinner every noon—good food and lots of it—and there was a bunkhouse to sleep in, and pay at the end of the week, the cash slapped into your hand by the little Swede who owned the farm, Gus Gustavson himself. Not so bad in these hard times.

———

Her older sister, Mildred, pitied the horses pulling the binder, but Evelyn did not. It seemed to her that Buster and Prince, the two larger workhorses, sensed the urgency of harvest time and sniffed excitement in the sweat and spit of the men who harnessed the horses and hitched them to the binder. The lead horse, Buster, walked on his own with great dignity to the proper work rig after his morning feeding and drinking. And strength? Not on any of the neighboring farms had Evelyn seen a horse as large and mighty as Buster.

Buster often pulled loads alone in a single harness, but at harvest time, four horses were hitched to the binder. The men trusted Buster to be the "grain horse," walking along the standing grain and guiding the other horses in a straight line. The men trusted him, yes, but in one way, Buster bore watching. His uncommon horse sense and harvest experience had taught him to edge away from the line of grain, so that the binder would cut a narrow swath, thus gathering up an easy load for Buster and the three other horses to pull.

The work horses varied in color from white, gray, and buckskin to shades of red. Their intelligence, according to Henry, ranged from "good sense to hammerhead." Still, he'd slap Buster on his hindquarter and mutter a blessing: "Patient and faithful you've been for all these many years."

Evelyn watched the two McCormack binders at work. Each had a platform with a sickle in front and a reel above, composed of six or eight revolving slats. These tipped the cut grain onto the platform canvas, which carried the cut straw to another set that elevated it to the bundling mechanism. The bundles of grain were dumped onto a carrier, which dropped them, six or eight bundles at a time, for shocking in groups of a dozen or so. Men, some of them local farm boys and others roving hobos, followed the horse-drawn binder and balanced the bundles against each other in triangular shocks.

Less than a week later the threshing crew grabbed pitchforks in their callused hands and tossed the sun-dried shocks into the hayracks that hauled the bundles of grain to the threshing machine. The thresher gulped down the workers' offering of shocks and separated the wheat from the straw. It blew the wheat down a funnel onto a lumber wagon, which carried it to the Brem grain elevator next to the railroad tracks. Left behind, straw became bedding for the farm animals.

Midmorning, Mildred and Evelyn ran water, coffee, sandwiches, and cake out to the men, who flopped themselves down in exhaustion as the girls arrived. With ferocious appetites the men devoured food—two, three, and even four sandwiches, great gulps of water, and cups of coffee with cake. This all happened within fifteen minutes. Then the men jumped back to their work, and the girls gathered up the few leftovers. It would have been humiliating to the Gustavson family if there had been no leftover sandwiches or cake, as if they had been too lazy or too poor to provide enough food for these sunburned, sweating workers.

For noontime dinner, the men scrubbed hands and faces at the pump, grateful for the shock of the cold well water. They stumbled into the kitchen and sank into the pine chairs around the long plank table, already piled high with platters of roast beef, boiled peas and carrots, and mashed potatoes. Tureens of gravy followed the potatoes around the table, and the workers gobbled slices of white and brown bread, fresh from the oven. All this, with Mildred's molasses and sugar cookies, big as saucers, fueled the men for the afternoon's work. Final gulps of milk and water, and they were out the door into the harsh September sun and relentless heat.

———

"Well, she's not afraid of work." Mildred announced this as a sort of absolution.

In spite of her raucous laugh at the threshers' crude jokes, Gretta, the new hired girl, redeemed herself in Mildred's eyes every mealtime when the exhausted hungry men sank into the chairs around the kitchen table. Gretta strode with Prussian efficiency from the stove to the table, filling plates with pork chops, potatoes, and gravy as fast as the workers could devour the meal. Without this food, the threshers could not toil; without their work, the crop would not be harvested; without the harvest, the farm, and with it the family, would be lost. Work was sacred; work meant life.

The men labored from before sunup until after sundown during the harvest, no matter the heat and dust. As darkness fell, Mildred's brothers staggered from the fields into the barn to milk the cows. Mildred saw a thin red line across the top of Wilhelm's upper lip. Sweating blood, he was, in all that heat. Will and any man past thirty years fell into bed after a day in the fields, immediately unconscious until the next morning. Somehow the younger men—cousin Steph at seventeen, the handsome neighbor Isaac, twenty-one, and Billy, the new-hire who had jumped off the train, maybe twenty-five—somehow each young worker revived himself, pouring a bucket of water over his head or changing his shirt, so that he could drink a beer or two and lose or win at poker in the bunkhouse.

Mildred watched the young men after work sometimes—watched Isaac tonight strip to the waist and douse his sweaty body with icy water from the well. Watched him walk back to the bunkhouse for the poker game. Then feeling Evelyn's curious eyes on her, Mildred busied herself with the pots and pans.

Just before midnight on Friday, Mildred wiped the final supper dish. She rubbed a stubborn crumb from the rim of the glass bowl. "It's a darn poor towel that won't take at least half the dirt," she muttered. As she placed the bowl on an open shelf and hung the towel by the cookstove, Mildred heard footsteps and glanced out the window. Light from the kitchen caught the brim of a cotton cap, the kind of cap that Isaac wore to keep the worst of the sun off his fair skin. Isaac's cap—she was sure of it. The cap and the slender man, his face in the shadows, moved up the outside stairway to the second story of the farmhouse. Mildred heard the rap of knuckles on a door upstairs. And a door opening. The door of the hired girl. Gretta's door. Opening and then closing.

At 5:00 on Saturday morning, the women began boiling coffee, frying eggs and bacon, and tossing hunks of bread on the griddle to catch the final juices. Gretta was there, humming a Bavarian tune as she bustled about the kitchen. Mildred turned the eggs, throwing her wrist into it, spreading the yolks over the whites and spattering bits of grease on Gretta's arm. *"Gott im Himmel!"* Gretta jerked her arm away. "What's got into you this morning?"

Mildred slid the eggs with the bacon onto a platter. "I think Isaac wants these," she said. "You'd better see to it." She said it with authority, her head in the air. Mildred spoke to Gretta in a new way. She spoke as a daughter of the household speaks to a servant.

Just as Isaac plunged his fork into the eggs, Billy, the new hired man, swung the kitchen door wide. With perfect accuracy he pitched a cap at Isaac. The cap settled on Isaac's blond head, the bill of it off to one side. "There," said Billy, "I grabbed the wrong one last night. Don't look like that. I don't have no lice."

"I'm not counting on that!" laughed Isaac. He tossed the cap to Mildred.

"Wash that for me?" His smile made her look away. "Use boiling water," he said.

Mildred lifted her eyes then and smiled back. "For sure I will," she said.

After Saturday's workday of sweat and dust, Billy walked back to the bunkhouse with his pay for the week, and he thought about sending some money home. Not all of it, but a few dollars for his ma. He peeled off two bills, smoothed them flat, and slipped them into an envelope. With a pencil, he carefully printed an address on the envelope. He tore off the corner of a feed catalog and wrote, "Ma—don't spend this all in one place—ha ha—your son Billy." He slid the note in beside the money and stuck the envelope under the blanket of his bunk. Billy carefully folded the rest of his pay into a snug, square packet and pushed the money into his pants pocket. He stepped out into the glare of the late afternoon sun and strode across the field, the fingers of his right hand rubbing against his week's pay.

—

"Well, it's about that time, ya know," said Hilmer.

"Pretty close, now," added Arvid.

"Are you ready for it, then?" asked Sten. The worried brothers looked into each other's eyes and then down at their heavy work boots.

"Ja, vel, I think we can handle what comes," said Hilmer with conviction.

"I can tell you what comes from Minneapolis for the whole harvest season is the one called Jack." Arvid cracked his knuckles and rippled the hot air with the thick, gnarled fingers of each hand.

"And I hope to tell you, I will keep an eye on Jack!" Sten's broad forehead gathered up in a scowl.

Every harvest season took strong arms and backs as the men handled eight or ten bundle sacks. This punishing work Hilmer, Arvid, and Sten could do, sweating gallons of salty water.

But Jack was the worry. On Saturday nights harvest workers hunkered down for a poker game that could last till Monday morning. The three brothers gathered their wits every threshing season, honing their poker skills to win serious money from all but their closest neighbors. As Sten often said, "Playing cards beats milking cows to heck and gone for earning pocket money, and the wife's got no cause to know about it neither."

Yes, but Jack. His slick, shiny hair parted just to the left of center on top of his angular head. His dark eyes darted everywhere and wouldn't meet your own as an honest man's would. His black eyebrows hung bushy beneath his pale forehead, the skin of his whole face unnaturally white. He was no rough laborer, you could bet the farm on that. Minneapolis card shark was more like it. And his knife flashed quick enough to make a man stand an arm length away.

So it was that in the early evening of the sixth day of harvest, a blazing hot Saturday, the farm workers downed an enormous supper, bringing life back to their tired bodies for a night of poker. They crowded into the bunkhouse, the local farmers, honest and innocent, mostly, and the Dakota and Minnesota drifters, whose good-natured smiles encouraged trust, confidence, and a festive spirit.

"Hiya, Sten, you young buck! At your age I was chasin' girls, not losin' money to old guys like me!"

"Figure on takin' you right down to your socks, Arvid. Willy here yet? He's got a pocket a money with my name on it."

"We're not holdin' up the game for him. Deal them cards!"

Cigar and cigarette smoke clouded the room. Badly aimed snoose spit splattered bare wood walls. Home brew loosened tongues and wallets, and betting turned heavy. Sten stood to one side, watching as Minneapolis Jack cleaned the pockets of the entire threshing crew.

Arvid's stocky body blocked Jack as he gathered his winnings and turned toward the door. "I think," said Sten, "that now you and I will play cards. But this time it will be a real honest game." Sten drew out a revolver and placed it on the table near his right hand. In two hours, the pile of money moved dollar by dollar from Jack's side of the table to where it rested in a heap in front of Sten.

"Now," said Arvid with the rest of the farmers standing behind him, eyeing their redeemed cash hopefully. "Now, get outta Dakota and don't come back."

Jack backed out of the bunkroom in a helpless rage. That night he, who was used to Minneapolis hotel rooms, slept in a haystack. The next morning, Jack jumped onto the train as it passed by Brem on its way to Andover. Pistol in hand, he moved through the cars, robbing passengers of their cash. But bad luck followed Jack. By chance, Andover's Sheriff Fossum was waiting at the train station when the train rolled in. For a few moments, Jack seemed in charge as he faced the surprised sheriff, his gun pointed at the lawman's badge. Then someone on the platform dropped a steel bar, and the clang drew Jack's eyes for an instant. The sheriff pulled out his gun and got off six shots. Minneapolis Jack fell dead at Fossum's feet.

Back on farms near Brem, wives fed their husbands well that Sunday morning, and praised them a little, too, for hanging onto the threshing money this time. Each farmer brushed it off, and said, yes, of course, did she think so little of him that she believed he would lose it all on cards and moonshine? Then, in every farmhouse, a man thanked his lucky stars for a good neighbor and clever poker player named Sten.

Breakfast Monday morning on the Gustavson farm crackled with workers' talk about the poker game and Jack. "By God, I knew the man was a card shark, but I didn't think he'd be robbin' trains!"

"You think he was in with the Barker Gang?"

"They work all of 'em together, not like Jack. He was always a loner."

Mildred and Gretta passed the eggs, bacon, and fried potatoes around, fast and efficient as ever. Gretta turned to Mildred and pointed to the empty place at the table.

"Billy's late this morning," she said. Mildred nodded, but both girls knew that no man was ever late for breakfast during threshing season. More likely he had tired of the work—maybe of Gretta, too—and was riding the rails again.

The threshing crew moved as a team out into the field. Last week had meshed the local farm boys and the rail-riding hobos into a practiced squad of men, each one knowing his job. The crew worked the far end of the acreage until midmorning, breaking briefly for the water and sandwiches Mildred, Evelyn, and Gretta carried to the field. Then the men sweated in the hot sun until noon when the drivers shut down the machinery for dinner.

They ambled along past the haystacks, slowed by glare and heat. The sun's fierce light caught a dark edge of something against the yellow hay. One of the hired men stopped and looked hard. "That looks like the heel of a boot," he said.

"Maybe a rock," said another. Still, they walked over, curious about the mention of a boot, when good shoes were hard to come by.

"Two boots," said the first man. And then they stopped, silent for a moment.

"Drunk, you think?" A man could freeze to death if he fell down drunk in winter, but more than one of them had spent a night sleeping off a summertime bender in the hay.

Two men pushed some of the hay away above the boots and uncovered the man's legs. They pulled on them, others pushing off more hay. Then they turned the man over.

"Billy," someone said.

"Shot," said another.

A town meeting was held that evening. Sheriff Hartley asked questions: Money in his pockets? None. Suspicious characters around? Someone mentioned Jack and the card game. Others looked around the room and muttered that two of the hired hands seemed mighty uneasy, but what could you prove with that?

On Tuesday morning, the work crew again tramped across the field to the waiting wheat. Though it was Gretta's job as hired girl, Mildred went with her to take the blanket off Billy's bunk for washing and airing. Together they found the envelope and opened it.

"He was sending money to his mother," said Gretta. "We must send it on. I must write her a letter." Her eyes brimmed with tears. "He was a good man."

"Yes, I believe he was." Mildred wrapped her arms around Gretta, and in the cool darkness of the deserted bunkhouse, she let her cry.

20

ANDERS IN BREM

In the summer of 1927, Anders Nilsen helped a neighbor dig a well. It was understood that no one had money to pay a youngster for help; but maybe something could be found.

"Kid, would you have a use for some parts off them cars in the lower field?" None of the farmers knew how to do any but the most basic car repairs, so if a Model T ground to a halt, most times it would be hauled off to a side field, and the farmer would buy some other wreck of a car that was at least running.

But farm boys grew up with cars, knew them inside out, loved to get the smell of oil and gas on their hands. "Sure, I'd tinker around with some car parts, if you're sure that's all right."

"Got no use for that pile a junk myself."

Anders took this and that and put the parts together in a car frame that lacked a body around it. The engine and frame were so light that the vehicle slipped and slid and spun around on the gravel farm road, Anders grinning behind the wheel. The thing was to save up money for a car body. And he did; he finally saved enough to surround his engine and frame with a windshield, doors, fenders, and two bumpers. Cost him fifteen dollars total.

All summer long, Anders squirreled around the country roads with his pals in the mismatched wreck of a car. September brought the heat and sweat of harvest as he worked alongside Johan and Rolf, who had both dropped out of school to farm. His sisters were gone—Serianna working as a nurse in the Moorhead hospital, and Dagny studying in her final year at Yankton Lutheran Academy. In October, Anders chugged and rattled his car to Brem and the town high school. Baseball lived there, basketball, too—and high school girls.

He arrived a month after the start of town school. Farm boys worked the harvest first, while town kids were learning the basics of mathematics and grammar. As Anders stepped into geometry class on the first Monday in October, he felt his new classmates' eyes crawl over his baggy clothes and bowl-shaped haircut. Two girls giggled. His face went red. An older boy, big as a gorilla and almost as hairy, growled something to a pal across the room. "McIntyre! That's all!" commanded the teacher, and the boy slumped back into his chair.

Anders left school late Friday afternoon, as soon as he could escape from his tutoring session with the geometry teacher. After a week of rain, Brem's dirt streets were pockmarked with mud puddles. Waiting down the way was McIntyre with his brothers, stamped with the same face and only slightly smaller. Heart thudding against his ribs, Anders brazened his way toward the gang. He circled around an enormous puddle and stopped just beyond it, planting his feet in the softened dirt.

"Gettin' your shoes kinda dirty, aintcha, farm boy?" McIntyre tossed his cigarette into the road.

"Well, out on the farm we're used to that. Guess you town boys keep yours polished all the time." Anders forced a grin across his face, calculating his slim odds against the three brutish brothers. He decided to try to talk his way by them.

Then McIntyre yelled, "Let's see how you pig farmers look covered in mud," and the three hulking bodies, in a flying wedge, came at him, arms aimed at his midsection.

Instinctively, Anders jumped sideways. The three flew by him and into the dirty puddle. The jarring impact as they hit rocks beneath the mud and felt the shock of cold, dark water splashing into their mouths and eyes left all the brothers sputtering. "How'd you do that?" one yowled.

Anders strode briskly up the road and called back over his shoulder, "Our longhorn bull taught me to get out of the way real quick. Old Big Red, he had a nasty temper, too."

As the school year progressed, basketball turned that scrappy, muddy beginning for Anders and the McIntyre brothers into wary respect and exacting teamwork. In this small high school, Coach Fallon welcomed any able-bodied male who wanted to be part of the basketball team, including the disorderly McIntyre brothers and the new kid from the country named Andy.

Coach drilled the boys, running them back and forth across the gym. He ran them harder if he smelled cigarettes on their breath or if he'd heard about a Saturday night brawl. He deliberately turned their anger against himself and against any team that challenged them. He made them loyal to each other and ready to fight any outsider for the team. These boys who sweated out basketball season began to hang around together after school and at the town dances held Saturday nights at the grange hall.

Sheriff Hartley was a small man with only one good eye, but he was Brem's cop, and he'd usually be at the town dances to keep the peace. One night four strangers walked into the grange hall with a local, Pete Peterson, who could himself be trouble. The five of them pushed around the dance floor, loud and drunk, and Hartley, small though he was and blind in one eye, asked them to leave.

"No dirt-town sheriff is gonna tell me what to do," hooted one of them as he stumbled toward Hartley and took a swing at him. The boys from the basketball team were standing right there, and Sheriff Hartley turned to the boys and pointed to one after another: "I deputize you; I deputize you; I deputize you." He said it five times, fast, dodging away from the drunk.

Now the four strangers and Peterson tried to run for it. They made a dash for their Model A Ford and ducked inside. Just as fast, the basketball team and the sheriff jumped on the running boards and hung on, Hartley up in front near the driver. The sheriff reached inside, grabbed the driver's hand on the key and wrenched it to the "off" position. The driver yanked the key back to "on," and the car jerked forward. Sheriff Hartley tried to steer it into a barn, but the driver pulled the wheel away from him. The Ford bounced down a three-foot dirt bank and into some trees where it crashed to a halt, scattering basketball players on both sides.

The driver, still drunk and by now mad as heck, shoved his way out and popped the sheriff in his one good eye. Hartley grabbed the guy with one hand and reached in his pocket with the other for his "sap," a little leather pouch filled with shot. One rap on the back of the drunk's head did it; he was out cold. Seeing that seemed to take the starch out of the rest of them.

Sheriff Hartley and the basketball team hauled the bunch to jail and locked them up. Peterson, the only one of them that knew folks in town, yelled threats out between the bars, "I'm gonna get you, Magnuson!" The boys laughed, feeling lucky that he was too drunk to recognize anybody: there was no Magnuson on the team.

The next day the boys found out just how lucky they were. The South Dakota state troopers searched the car, top to bottom, even ripping up the floorboards. Turned out the strangers were bootleggers, running whiskey across the border from Canada. They had stashed that bright, shiny new Model A with gallons of whiskey and a fair number of loaded guns.

———

On weekday evenings, brothers Wilhelm and Henry Gustavson harnessed up the two delivery horses, Lady, with black and white markings, and Fly, the red chestnut. Fair-haired Will conducted his duties with military order and precision, checking the leather on the harnesses for tearing or roughness, and moving the horses with a firm hand, as a sergeant positions recruits. Henry, his dark skin and black wavy hair looking more Latin than Nordic, refined the appearance of the cart, shining the gold trim on the black wheels and polishing the silvery sides of the supply can. Finally, he attached two leather straps, each holding four bright bells, one strap on the harness of dappled Lady and one on the harness of cinnamon Fly.

"All set, Will!" Henry jumped in the cart.

The bells jingled their dissonant duet along the streets of Brem. As each housewife heard the clip-clop of the horses' hooves and the jangle of the bells, she ran to the street with her bucket. Using the wagon's dipper cup to measure, she ladled milk from the wagon's supply can. Often a mother sent her son or daughter to the milk wagon. Henry watched for the third house on Main Street and jumped off the wagon to help pretty Lucille fill her bucket. He tried telling her his joke about a bucket with a hole in it, but Lucille had heard it before and scampered back into the house with her milk.

On Second Street sat a boarding house occupied by country boys who moved into town for high school. From the boarding house porch sprang a lad wearing a baseball cap on his blond head. He dipped out a bucket full of milk and then began dipping a second bucket full. He grinned up at Henry and Will. "Bunch of hungry guys in there for Mrs. Reidling to feed."

As their wagon rolled on, Will broke his usual silence. "He acts like he knows us."

"New guy in town," said Henry. "In from the country school. Plays basketball, baseball. And I think he has his eye on Evelyn."

At the mention of his sister, Will snapped the reins over Fly's gleaming chestnut back. "I guess she has the good sense to stay away from a country kid like that."

"Yeah, sure," said Henry, trying to keep the smile out of his voice.

———

"*Alting må mot styrken vike,*" said cousin Knut with a wink.

"And what does that mean, exactly." As the youngest in his family, Anders was a bit shaky on the nuances of Norwegian proverbs. He could navigate ordinary conversational Norwegian, and, in fact, for confirmation memorized Luther's catechism in Norwegian, as God willed and as the pastor commanded, but these old Norwegian sayings mystified him.

"*Alting må mot styrken vike,*" repeated Knut. "All things must, against strength, give in."

"And how does that apply to the town dance?"

"Obvious, Andy. Evelyn Gustavson ignores you. Her mother probably hates you. But if you persist, you will wear them down like water dripping on a stone."

"Just how am I supposed to do that?"

"Do something for Mrs. Gustavson first. Make her grateful. Make yourself look harmless. Then, when her mother isn't around, do something a bit dangerous in front of Evelyn. Girls are drawn to dangerous men like moths to a flame."

"Another one of your bits of wisdom, this time in English."

"I can educate you in any language about women, *stakkars liten!*"

"Poor little guy, is it? I can take you in wrestling, basketball, baseball—you choose!"

"*Ja,* you could do that. But it is not me you want to take—to the dance or anywhere. And it is not for me—but for Evelyn—to choose. So you'd better listen to me, your cousin, who may not be a man of sports but has more experience than you in the ways of winning the hearts of women."

Anders looked around at the sky and the shed and the house, anywhere but at Knut, who had indeed pointed out his dilemma: how to convince the lively, lovely sixteen-year-old Evelyn to come with him to the town dance, when she didn't seem to notice him at all, and when her mother, Mrs. Gustavson, the fierce, unfriendly Swedish farm woman, seemed downright hostile to him.

He considered his cousin's advice—to do something to make Mrs. Gustavson grateful to him. Something that would make him seem harmless. Then to do something dangerous in front of Evelyn. Well, one thing at a time. First aim for the mother's gratitude.

In the afternoon, Anders drove to town and parked his patched-together Model T near the feed store. As he approached the store, he heard arguing inside, a loud confrontation between a woman and the storeowner.

"Mrs. Gustavson, please, you can see that the store is full of customers, and my helper is home sick. You wouldn't want him here, would you? Tomorrow is the earliest I can deliver that chicken feed. I'm sure your chicks can scratch around till then."

"And you, Mr. Murphy, can cancel any future orders if you cannot do a simple delivery to the edge of town. You know that Mr. Gustavson and I spend plenty of good money here, and if you can't—"

Anders felt that fate had placed him in the store at that precise moment, and he spoke with quiet confidence. "Excuse me, Mrs. Gustavson, Mr. Murphy. Maybe I could help. My car is parked just outside. I'd be glad to take Mrs. Gustavson and her feed over to her farm."

Mr. Murphy sighed with relief, while Berit Gustavson nodded unsmiling that she was willing, though not pleased, for this arrangement. Anders, strong from farm work and athletic from baseball and basketball training, could have easily hauled all three bags of feed to his Model T in one armload, but his cousin's words echoed in his head: make her mother grateful; make yourself look harmless. So he made three trips out to his car, bending in apparent strain under the load of each bag. He muttered apologetically to Mrs. Gustavson about back trouble and related a fictional family story about his being a sickly child. Berit Gustavson's frown twisted into a scornful smile as she compared her own sons, burly and vigorous, with this Norwegian weakling.

As he unloaded the bags at the Gustavson farm on the other side of town, Anders stumbled, and then made a clumsy excuse about his hand-me-down shoes being a size too big. Berit snorted a bit at that, but thanked him properly for his help. She clipped a few yellow roses from the bush near her front door and told him brusquely that perhaps his landlady, Mrs. Reidling, would like them.

Anders looked sheepishly down at his shoes and tugged at his hair, a gesture he had not made since he was six years old on his first day of school. "Well, thank you, Mrs. Gustavson," he said. "I'm just happy to help anytime." He could see in her eyes that she saw him as a weak, pathetic, insignificant boy—and that made him very glad indeed.

He shuffled back to the Model T, hands in his pockets, and started up the car. He was careful to chug along the dirt road slowly and carefully, driving like an old man rather than a seventeen-year-old. As soon as he turned the first corner, rolling down the little hill into town, he saw a gaggle of girls, school books in arms, dallying along toward home. And in the midst of them, her short, wavy blond hair shining in the sunlight, he saw Evelyn.

"Do something dangerous. Girls are drawn to dangerous men like moths to a flame." Knut's words rang in his ears, and before he could consider what to do, he found himself flinging the car door open and standing, one foot on the running board, one foot on the steering wheel, right hand clutching the roof of the car, left hand waving wildly as he honked the car horn with the toe of his shoe. The girls stopped, and all in one motion turned, first to look in the direction of his car and then to look at Evelyn. They nudged her and pointed at him, laughing uproariously.

Anders came treacherously close to Mrs. Larson's lilac bush as his car picked up speed. He eased himself back into the car and brought it under control. He turned right, out of sight of the girls and considered what had just happened. He had made a complete fool of himself, that was clear. Yet, why had the girls pointed to Evelyn, when she always seemed indifferent to him? This was the first time he had publicly displayed his affection for her, if you could call this tomfoolery a display of affection. His fair cheeks burned red above the blond stubble on his chin. In spite of his embarrassment, hope now burned in his heart:

hope that Evelyn liked him, perhaps even felt attracted to him; perhaps had confessed this attraction to her girlfriends.

At the next road, Anders turned his car left, back into town, where he stopped at the tavern to buy two cold bottles of low-alcohol near-beer, the closest thing to a real drink a man could buy since prohibition started. He drove to Knut's house, popped open the bottles, and handed one to his cousin.

"What is this then?" asked Knut.

Anders raised his bottle in salute. "It's as you said, cousin, *'Alting må mot styrken vike!* '"

21

STICK TOGETHER

Just a slip of a girl. Curly blond hair capped her perfectly round head and framed her animated, rosy-cheeked face. An inch or two over five feet tall, she would barely come up to his chin, if he could ever get that close to her. Only a look now and then, just a glance from her was all she tossed his way in the school hallway. And he was grateful for that.

"She plays basketball, you know," said Knut.

"Who plays basketball?" asked Anders.

"Evelyn, of course."

"Listen, Knut, you almost got me killed with your last advice. 'Dangerous,' you said. 'Do something dangerous, girls like that.' So I almost ran my car into a bush in front of all her girlfriends, and now she thinks I'm nuts."

"That's good, Andy. Just like I told you. Girls don't like average. Girls don't like normal. They like a guy who's a little bit crazy. They can't quite figure him out, so they keep thinking about him."

Anders shook his head. He paused. "What was that about basketball? She's pretty little for basketball."

"She's a guard—and very fast. You'd better watch a game. Girls like guys who show up for the girls' sports."

"Funny thing, Knut. You have all this advice, but no girl-friend yourself. How's that?"

"I'm waiting, watching for the right one. Then I'll make my move. Come on—let's go watch the girls dribble that ball."

As Anders pushed open the gym door, the crowd of girls cheered. "See, they like you here already," laughed Knut. But the girls perched on the bleachers were screaming encouragement to the Brem girls' team, just beginning their game with Holmquist. Anders spotted Evelyn at one end of the court, her short yellow gym dress barely covering her matching bloomers. The hem of the dress flipped up and down as she bounced on her tiptoes, like an athletic ballerina, right at the black line painted about ten feet in from the edge of the court.

"What's she doing?"

"Girls' rules," said Knut, once again the expert. "She's a guard. She can't leave her part of the floor. She has to hand off the ball to the passing centers, and they pass it on to the forwards."

"That's insane." Anders could hardly believe this.

"Girls, you know—can't run like us or they won't be able to have babies or something." Anders thought of the farm women he'd seen, his own mother, in fact, who lifted heavy milk cans, dragged huge bags of feed, and ran all over the farm, day after day—each one with her own passel of children.

Anders looked back at the basketball floor, marked off in three sections. He knew every girl on the Brem team: Sigrid, almost six feet tall, standing mid-court; Lillian and Gladys right beside her; Hazel on the near end of the court, next to Evelyn;

Ruby and Hattie on the opposite end. Matched up against them, one on one, were the players from Holmquist.

The referee took the basketball to the center and held it between Sigrid and a tall Holmquist girl. He tossed it high in the air and blew his whistle. The two girls jumped, desperately reaching for the ball. Sigrid tipped it off to Gladys. Gladys bounced it twice and leaned over the black line dividing the center court from the forward court. The Holmquist girls, guarding the Brem forwards, tried to knock the ball out of her hands, but Hattie grabbed it, bounced it twice, and shot the ball expertly into the basket. Anders and Knut cheered, their masculine voices booming to the far corners of the gym.

Did Evelyn look in his direction? It seemed so to Anders, and he lifted his hand to wave, but she had already turned back to the game. Another tip off, this time going to the Holmquist team. Their passing center handed the ball to the Holmquist forward, a tall girl with massive shoulders. As the shot went up, Evelyn jumped and reached, the tips of her fingers nudging the ball enough so that it missed the basket. Hazel grabbed the ball, and another cheer went up from the crowd. The big Holmquist girl shoved Evelyn, and the referee called a foul.

"She'll get a free throw," said Anders, bursting with pride for this girl who seemed to have no interest in him.

"Girls' rules," said Knut. "A Brem forward gets the shot." And, indeed, the referee threw the ball to the far end of the court. Hattie took the shot, holding the ball with both hands, flexing her knees, lowering the ball between her legs, and shooting at the basket. She missed.

"Evelyn would have made that shot," moaned Anders.

"Tell her that," said Knut cheerfully. "Girls like guys who notice what they're good at."

"Sure, Knut, if you say so." Anders picked up his jacket and hung it over his arm. "Well, I guess I might hang around."

"You do that, Andy," said Knut walking toward the door and then turning back. "And remember, '*Alting må mot stryrken vike.*' If you never give up, all things must give in—even little blond basketball players."

After the game, Anders leaned against the brick railing outside the gym doors. The two doors banged open and a group of girls pushed through. Anders pushed his cap back and called out, "Good game!"

Sigrid smiled at him. "Thanks for cheering us on, Andy. I saw you there."

Anders tried again. "Evelyn—good defense!"

It seemed to him that Evelyn looked his way for a moment, but she kept walking with her friends.

"Never give up," Anders mumbled to himself, watching curls bounce on the back of her head.

On Friday, Anders found a small, square envelope on his home room desk. He slipped the card out and read, "You are invited to the birthday party of Evelyn Gustavson in her home at 7:00 tonight." He stared at the letters of the words, every vowel perfectly round and every consonant slanted evenly to the right. "You are invited..."

The party was one of card games and punch and, finally, dancing to the Victrola. Anders didn't attempt the Charleston or any of the other fast dances. He stood against the living room wall and watched the short skirts of the girls flash above their knees. The cheeks and lips of the girls seemed unusually red, and he thought perhaps they used a bit of paint here and there, which made them seem to him quite wild, something he had not suspected of his well-behaved classmates; something which attracted and intrigued him. On the next slow dance, he nudged

Knut aside and asked Evelyn to dance. She looked up and smiled at him, while Knut nodded and stepped away.

"You were good on the court." Anders stepped in a square, one, two, three, four, as his sister Serianna had taught him.

"You're a good guard, too. But you should take more shots at the basket."

"You go to the boys' games?"

"All of them."

Anders felt himself being guided into the rhythm of the tune—one, two, three, one, two, three. It was beginning to feel natural.

When the party was over, Mrs. Gustavson stood at the door. Each high school boy and girl thanked her for the cake and punch. When it was Anders' turn, before he could say a word, Mrs. Gustavson stepped toward him.

"Anders Nilsen—a Norwegian name?"

"Yes, from Norway's west country."

"When I left Sweden, we still controlled that Norwegian land, but things change." She frowned in disapproval. "But I do thank you, just the same, for your help with my feed sacks last week."

"Of course, Mrs. Gustavson, I was glad to help."

"I could have managed myself, you understand."

"Of course, Mrs. Gustavson," he said, feeling himself wither under her gaze.

Still, his heart sang to the dance tunes as he walked back to the boarding house.

A week later, on Saturday night, Anders spotted Evelyn and her sister Mildred looking into the window of the drug store. He ambled over to them and asked, "Like to have a banana split? My treat." He had meant to ask only Evelyn, but Mildred answered first, "Sure, if you're buying!" He dug into his pocket and felt two quarters slide against each other. At fifteen cents a sundae, that would do it. But he could forget about seeing movies for awhile. They stepped inside the shop and sat on stools at the soda counter.

"What'll it be?" Anders smiled at the two girls as if to say, money is no problem. Evelyn's eyes narrowed, and he felt he saw in them a reflection of her mother's disapproving look. Still, both girls seemed delighted when the treats arrived, a banana split for Mildred and a tin roof for Evelyn. Chocolate sauce and peanuts covered the tin roof sundae, and Anders watched Evelyn dig her spoon deep into the ice cream, lift it high, and slip the dripping spoon into her mouth with pleasure. He felt his cheeks turn red, and he had to look away, grateful that she could not read his mind. He stirred two straws in his nickel soda, explaining that his big boarding house dinner left no room for a sundae.

On Wednesdays after school, Abeline, the generous, good-hearted German woman who owned Brem's only restaurant, opened an upstairs hall for high school parties. By running café food up the stairs at irregular intervals, she kept a close watch over the local youngsters. Card games, sausage and mustard—that kept the kids busy and out of mischief. And yet—Anders glanced across the table and caught Evelyn watching him. Evelyn handed Anders whist cards and her fingers brushed his.

So it began. First Anders' school friends, then teachers, and finally others around town began to notice the two of them together. Her brothers observed and suspected. Her mother was the last to know.

On Saturday evenings, Brem came alive with country and town folks walking the wooden sidewalks and driving up and down the several streets that made up the town. Evelyn and

Mildred closed the door behind them as they left their farm-house on the edge of Brem. From the kitchen they could hear their mother calling after them, "You girls stick together now!"

"Right, Ma!" they shouted back in unison, "we'll stick together!"

And together they did stay—until they reached the corner of the first block. There they paused as a Model T Ford pulled up, and Evelyn jumped into the patched-together car driven by this boy called Andy. Mildred strolled off with a girlfriend for a few hours, as Brem settled into the warm springtime night. Later Mildred waited on the same corner until the Ford rolled to a halt and Evelyn bounced out. The sisters walked back to the farmhouse and into their mother's question: "Did you girls stick together?"

"Yes, Ma, we stuck together."

When she finally heard the gossip that Evelyn and Anders were often seen about town together, Berit Gustavson confront-ed her daughter. Why not a nice Swedish boy? Plenty of them in Brem and the countryside to choose from. Then, seeing the stiffening of her daughter's back and the flash in her eye, Berit relented but set down rules, the chief of which was that Evelyn must be home, inside her house, by 10:00.

And Anders tried to get her home on time, but the hours went by so fast when they were together that often they were late, closer to midnight than the curfew. Berit flew down the bedroom stairs when she heard the car rattle into the drive. "Let me get my hands on that Norwegian!" she raged as Evelyn blocked the doorway with her body and outstretched arms, like the feisty little basketball player she was, and Anders drove quickly away.

By the beginning of summer, with some confidence, Anders began to call Evelyn his girl.

Berit Gustavson fumed as she watched her daughter slip from her grasp into the arms of this Norwegian boy. He seemed to have changed in a year's time from a bumbling bumpkin into a handsome, charming fellow who drew her daughter to him like iron filings to a magnet.

Yet, there was something about him. There was something about the two of them together that captured Berit's attention. In them, she saw the magic between a man and a woman that Mrs. Rose told her about. "My Benjie worships me—and I would die for him," Mrs. Rose had said. Berit's own sensible and businesslike marriage to Gus Gustavson had produced bushels of top-grade wheat and six healthy, hardworking children. But watching Anders and Evelyn, she observed a certain joy that, while she didn't understand it, made Berit glad for her daughter.

Anders sensed he had been accepted by Evelyn's father when Gustav led him one evening around to the barn, offered him a chaw of tobacco, and lectured him about the fine blood lines in the farm's new breeding bull. Anders knew Evelyn's mother had warmed to him when she introduced him to her visiting cousin. "He's Norwegian," said Berit. "But he's just as good as any Swede."

And so, the following spring, when the junior class at the high school began planning the prom for the seniors, Berit gave Evelyn permission to host the party in the Gustavson home. Evelyn and her friends in the junior class opened up the parlor, the dining room, and the living room to make a space big enough for a dinner and dance in honor of the seniors. The dark wood paneling gleamed in the early evening sunlight, streaming through the parlor windows. In the big bay window of the dining room, red geraniums and petunias cascaded almost to the floor. Even the giant fern by the player piano had been dusted and polished with flax oil.

After sunset, the junior girls lit candles around the room and in the center of the table. They carried in platters of thinly sliced beef and bowls holding mounds of white, fluffy potatoes. Then they sat daintily beside the boys to flirt and perhaps to eat something. Their mothers moved quietly about the kitchen, preparing still more food to satisfy the seemingly endless appetites of the junior and senior boys.

"So what will you do now that you've gone so far as to graduate from high school?" Gus Gustavson's question after the party was the one that Anders and all the other seniors heard from their own parents and from every adult.

"Well, farming I guess. Dad's been sick for this last month and my brothers could use the help."

Gustav gave a quick nod. Any farmer could use help in these days of dust and drought. But a decent rain would do a farmer far more good than another worker tromping around the parched fields.

⎯⎯⎯

The next year, after her own high school graduation, Evelyn went away to Alexander Normal School and earned a teaching certificate at age nineteen. She was hired to teach Polish kids in a one-room country schoolhouse twenty miles west of Brem. Her students ranged from a sweet, baby-faced kindergartener to a lanky six-foot farm boy with a stubbly beard. She lived in her students' homes, boarding with a new family each month. Some housewives fed her well. Others dished up her plate grudgingly, wanting in those hard times to keep the food for their own children. For two years, Evelyn saved every cent of her paltry pay.

Each evening, she wrote a letter to Anders. In the summer she came back to Brem and lived on the home place.

Anders worked beside his father and brothers and scrambled for odd jobs on other farms and in town. No profit in farming in this drought, but even meager crops had to be harvested, and farmers would pay something for extra help. Housewives eked out a few nickels from their budget to have wood chopped and egg crates hauled. Every bit of change he earned from these chores went into the blue canning jar stowed under his bed, but it wasn't enough. Finally, in June he sold his calf.

Many evenings in early summer, Evelyn and Anders walked together to the Brem train station and gazed at the poster of a majestic woman, her bare feet touching the top of the world, her hands stretched high over her head. They whispered to each other that they would save enough money and that they could convince her parents. They would overcome every obstacle and go to the 1933 Chicago World's Fair.

"Ma, it's educational. I can learn about scientific discoveries and teach my students about them in the fall." Evelyn heard in her own voice a begging quality that was never effective in influencing her mother.

Berit turned her back and walked away in silence. In a firmer tone, Evelyn spoke to the tightly wound bun at the nape of her mother's reddened neck. "Herbert could come with us. He'd be with us all the time. I'd watch out for him, and he'd watch out for me. We'd stick together." Having her fourteen-year-old brother along might be the only way to get her mother's consent.

Berit stopped, nodded, and continued into the kitchen. "I had been married for two years and had a baby when I was her age," she muttered. The word "baby" made the farm woman hesitate again. Herbert traveling along with Anders and Evelyn might protect her, if she wanted protection, and at least it would slow tongue-wagging in town. Berit stomped to the sink and scrubbed at the pots and pans. Being a practical woman, she did not waste time worrying over something she could not control.

———

Anders, Evelyn, and Herbert arrived in Chicago by train on a Wednesday. On Thursday they walked to the shore of Lake Michigan, under a sign announcing "Century of Progress Rainbow City" and into the dazzling displays of the fairgrounds. Herbert ran ahead of them along the edge of a man-made lagoon. Multicolored buildings held fabulous designer cars: Nashes, Cadillacs, Lincolns, and Pierce-Arrows. Exhibits created scenes from Chicago's hundred-year history. In one show, sixty midgets pranced about, while at the fair's nightclubs, Judy Garland and the Andrews Sisters pulled in the crowds.

"I've gotta see Sally Rand. Now don't give me that shocked look. Every guy in Brem'll be asking me about that!"

"Fine, Andy," said Evelyn, "but don't ask me to go with you to see a stripper. Or Herbert either." So it was agreed that the three would look at different exhibits until 5:00 and then meet in front of the Old Morocco club.

Just inside an open archway, a baby caught her eye. A baby in a clear glass bottle, a wide-mouth canning jar. A baby, afloat in pale liquid like brine in a pickle vat. The baby's body was perfectly preserved. Its tiny fingers formed two fists, clinging to nothing as it floated serenely in the jar, suspended in limbo, while farmers, city folks, foreigners, and locals filed by, peeking through the glass of this baby's peculiar coffin. She was a girl. Except for that difference, the baby seemed identical to Evelyn's baby brother, just after his birth, when the nurse brought Russell out of their mother's bedroom to show to his father and to his brothers and sisters. The tiny feet, the curved legs and rounded belly, the little arms reaching out randomly, the head topped with tufts of blond hair, the wise old face, the brow creased with indecision. The infant girl in the jar held for eternity the look that newborn Russell had discarded a few days into life.

Only after five full minutes of gazing at the baby did Evelyn realize she was standing at the wrong end of the line. A tall man of perhaps forty, dressed in a blue suit, addressed her in an annoyed tone. "Miss," he said. "You are blocking the exit of this exhibit." She turned and met his glare. "I'm so sorry," she said with a farm girl's blush at a social blunder. He took a step backward for a fuller look at the blond curls framing her Swedish blue eyes.

"Quite all right, miss. Are you enjoying the fair?"

But Evelyn moved quickly to the entrance of the exhibit. "The Beginnings of Life," said the bold letters overhead. The first enormous placard was an artist's rendition of a single human egg within the uterus, and a thousand squiggly sperm inside a scrotum. Standing in front of the second drawing, Evelyn's eyes widened as she viewed the army of sperm attacking the egg, and one victorious combatant breaching the ovum wall.

Now the artist's work was complete, and a series of liquid-filled glass jars stretched ahead: in the first, an undifferentiated clump of cells. In the next, a tadpole. Then a creature with a head of sorts, and arms and webbed fingers. The fourth jar encased what was clearly a baby, as yet hairless and undersized; followed by a larger container holding an infant with hair, fingernails, and eyelashes, awaiting birth. Evelyn reached the final cylinder, the one she had first seen, with the newborn girl-child floating in the lucent tomb of a glass jar. Evelyn bit her lip, awed by the wonder of the miracle displayed and filled with an immense sorrow for these infant lives unlived.

Dazzled by the sunlight as she stepped outside the building, Evelyn squinted at the buildings around her. The midway glittered just down the walkway. On each side of her stood massive art deco structures, their sharp angles and bright colors demanding her attention. It was too much to take in. Her eyes swept over the huge buildings and fixed on a sign: "Live babies in incubators." She entered that exhibit and moved along with the line of people waiting to see this miracle of science. Tiny babies, kept alive in warmed glass enclosures lay naked to be viewed by the crowds. "How wonderful," said a woman. "Unnatural," murmured another. Evelyn felt in her stomach both a need and a fear. Her hands rose from her sides as if to touch the encased infants, but she clasped her fingers together against her chest. "What if..."

In her mind she heard echoes of the secret conversations she and her high school girlfriends whispered, bedroom doors firmly closed against listening parents. "What if? What would you do?" The questions hung suspended amid the tight circle of girls as they pictured the dark streets of Minneapolis where a desperate woman might find a doctor willing to perform an abortion. But how would you find such a doctor? And would it be a doctor or a fake with dirty instruments who might leave a woman damaged, diseased, or worse? "A girl would have to leave and say she was visiting an aunt. Give it up for adoption." That was Sigrid's advice. But word would get around in a town like Brem. And the other choice, a shotgun wedding—how could you know if a man really loved you if he was forced to marry you?

At 5:00 when Evelyn found Anders and Herbert, they were already trading stories, Herbert gesturing with arms and hands to illustrate the twists and turns of the wild midway rides, and Anders raising his eyebrows and lowering his voice as he described the long slender legs and the feathery fan of Sally Rand. Evelyn ignored them both, and with a toss of her head led them away from the fancy Old Morocco club to a stand-up eatery with ample portions and cheap prices.

After four days of the fair, Anders, Evelyn, and Herbert boarded the train back to Brem, their heads spinning with displays of science, industry, art, and amusement. When the train steward pushed a handcart down the aisle, Herbert hailed him. "Ham sandwich," he said, and turned to Evelyn for money.

"I gave you an allowance at the beginning of the trip, Herbie," she said.

"Just fifty cents for a sandwich."

"If your money's gone, that's nothing to do with me." She pushed her purse firmly into her lap.

"Come on, Evie." Anders' pockets were empty, too. He tried to take her hand. She pulled it away from him and fixed her eyes on the train window and the yellow wheat field slipping by. The steward and his handcart moved on.

What was he to make of her? Anders looked at the tidy wavelets of her hair. The shine of them held a glint of wiry copper, a gleam of polished brass. He could do little to shape her. It seemed that she swayed him more than he influenced her. Though he could often make her laugh and could coax her into his arms, she lectured him frequently against gambling, alcohol, and wasting money. As he puzzled over this, Evelyn turned, and with a soft look, took his hand again. He held her small hand gently, and in that moment the lightness of it outweighed tenfold the loss of his wandering bachelor ways.

22

Loss and Change

Anders drove slowly down the road from Brem to his family's weary farm. What exactly had changed in the last years, he could not say, except that everything on the farm seemed old. The barn and house looked in need of paint. The animals and the very soil of the farm appeared to be worn out. His mother grew tired in the summer heat and sat with her hands in her lap. She seemed weaker still during harvest. It was something everyone in the family observed but no one spoke of.

Through the winter months, Kari resisted any mention of her health. She believed January darkness caused her lack of energy and that the springtime sun would soon invigorate her heart and lungs. To that end, she sat early one morning in the sunniest part of the kitchen, her face toward the light.

Kari squinted against the glare of a sunbeam that peeked through the small eastern window of her kitchen. Such a small streak of light to be so bright. The light entered her body through her eyes and struck the base of her skull. The sudden pain made her grit her teeth, and in spite of that effort, a little cry escaped her throat, like the whimper of an injured lamb. She clutched the edge of the table. Perhaps this was something momentary that would pass. The room felt hot and airless, though the morning sun was just above the horizon. She turned her head away from the sunshine and felt a tightness grip her like a stiff leather harness around her neck and back. She rested her head against the cool pine table. Sleep, that was it, she needed to sleep.

Anders bounded down the stairway from his bedroom, strode across the hallway, and pushed open the door into the kitchen, his voice arriving before his spare frame, "Sorry, *mor*, I slept too long..." He froze at the doorway. "*Mor*..." he said and crossed the room to where she sat, slumped against the table. He touched her shoulder, and she fell to the side. He caught her in his arms and lifted her limp body onto the long table. She was damp with fever. He bent over and put his ear next to her mouth to hear the shallow whispers of her breath. He slipped his arms under her body and rolled her next to his chest. He carried her up the steep staircase to her bed, placed her gently there, and raced down to the telephone. Women's voices on the party line chattered to each other in a gossipy mixture of Norwegian and English. "*Nei, nei, du seier ikkje det! Seier du det?* No, no, you don't say! Do you say that?"

He held his voice calm and said, "This is an emergency!" And then bluntly, "Get off the phone, this is an emergency," as one silly woman wanted to know what kind of emergency. He rang the operator and asked for the doctor. "My mother is very sick," he said. "I can't wake her." He put down the phone and ran to his father in the field.

———

The doctor stepped back from Kari's bedside and gathered up his stethoscope. He led Jens, Anders, and Johan out into the hallway and closed the door. "I've seen a few of these cases. Not many, thank God. I won't lie to you, this is very serious. She is in a comatose state. I believe it is encephalitis. We don't know the cause, might be something in the air. We have no cure. But some recover after a time of quiet and rest."

The room was kept dark, quiet, and cool. Daughter Serianna came home from the nursing hospital and sat by her mother's bedside, cooling her forehead with damp cloths, replacing them every few minutes as the fever pressed itself into the cotton fabric.

Jens, Johan, and Anders went back to the fields, walking every few hours up to the house to stand helpless beside Kari's bed. She seemed absent from her body. It seemed so to them. It seemed so to her.

Kari felt no pain now, nor did she feel hot or cold. In this timeless space, she could see light, but it no longer threatened her. She felt neither happy nor sad, only secure, as though held in her mother's arms. She saw a robed figure walking toward her and watched him stop at the foot of her bed. It was Jesus, his face as she had seen it in the Bergen cathedral windows, luminescent, lit from behind as through stained glass, his face the color of flax, his eyes blue, and his hair flowing like wheat lifted in the wind. She would gladly go to him and be his forever.

Whispers came to her from another place. *"Kjære Kari, kom hit."* Jens' soft plea reached her. She recognized the voice of her husband, very near to her, calling her "beloved," speaking her name, asking her to return. She watched with sadness as the face of Jesus faded. She opened her eyes and saw instead Jens' face, his eyes filling with tears. In all their years together, she had never seen even a mist in his eyes.

"I have seen Jesus," she said. He looked at her, speechless for a moment.

"Then I thank him for sending you back." He drew her hand to his lips and held it there as he blinked away the dampness in his eyes.

"Open the curtains," she said.

"It's night—almost midnight."

"Open the curtains."

Jens pulled back the white muslin fabric and sat behind Kari on her bed, so that she had a clear view of the night sky. The moon hung low, a thin slice of melon, a citrine arc. Light spilled from it into the darkened field. Pinpoints of stars made a scattering of light in the sky. The stillness drew them in. Jens helped Kari as she struggled to the window and pressed her forehead against the cool glass, shaping her hands around her face to shut out the room's reflection. It held them motionless: the slim orange moon locked in the black sky, the moonlight stretched across the bare land. Silent. Still. Then a bright meteor streaked down in a precise diagonal, right to left, over the suspended moon. Kari tried to grasp the meaning of this sign, but she could only say, "Beautiful, you are so beautiful."

———

Farmers on the South Dakota prairie heard the 1929 stock market crash as a muffled and distant thunder. Financiers could shuffle numbers, but hard work and decent weather still produced fat crops and cattle. Then the weather turned hot, rainless, and windy. The good prairie soil burned to dust and drifted against fence posts. Windstorms blew the dust into houses and over the prairie in airborne layers until powdery dirt darkened the sun. On the worst days, farm wives lit lamps midday against the gritty blackness. Starving cattle were slaughtered. Anders cured Russian thistles for hay to feed the few remaining horses and cows.

The Depression and scorching sun seared the dirt and dried up their last dollars. The telephone company cut off service. Electric lights faded as batteries wore out and could not be replaced. Mortgage payments became impossible to meet. The Nilsen family let the home quarter go, along with the big farmhouse, and moved back into their old house.

In less than a month, Jens fell sick with a terrible pain in his jaw. Cancer, the doctors said and blasted him with an x-ray treatment, which sapped his strength. He looked tired, slumped deep in the big leather chair, and very old. Kari stood beside him, straight and sound, feeling ashamed of her own restored health. His sea-green eyes regarded her from under shaggy blond and gray eyebrows, the wiry brush of his eyebrows massed over his bare lids, as if his elderly eyelashes, lonely for company, had fluttered up and perched on the ridge of his brow.

He reached up and pulled her down in his lap. She relaxed there and felt his chest against her bosom, the lift and fall of his breathing pushing gently against her. Her forehead lay against his chin, and she felt the stubble of his unshaven beard.

Jens tightened his arms around her, "Kari, I would like the pastor to come over with communion." He spoke in English, the language of business between them, not in the Norwegian they used in their intimate, private times.

She did not move, but whispered into his warm neck, *"Nei, slett ikkje no."*

"Do not say no," he said. "It is time, and it is what I ask of you. I saw them again last night, the children—angels, they could be—standing by my bedside. They do not speak, but they make me to understand that I am not to be afraid of what is coming."

The couple rested then in silence, pressed against each other, breathing together, each drawing comfort from the body of the other.

She sent Anders to request that the pastor come, not wanting to speak this message on the prairie telephone party line. Now Jens lay in bed, too weak for the parlor chair. He insisted that a bowl of soapy water be brought to his bedside with a razor. As Kari sat on the edge of the bed, holding a small mirror, he shaved away a week's growth of beard. Then he relaxed back on his pillow, weary from the effort. Still, as the parlor door opened and closed and he heard the subdued voice of the pastor, Jens reached for Kari's arm, and with her help, straightened himself, and sat on the edge of the bed.

As Anders followed their pastor into the bedroom, Kari stepped to one side. The pastor, dressed all in black, moved with dignity and a certain formal grace, as he approached Jens' bedside and sat down beside him. "Så, Jens," he said. "Det var då trist—men må Gud Fader sjå i nåde til deg." Anders translated in his mind: "So, Jens, this is sad, but may God the Father give grace to you." Jens smiled a little, nodded, and met the pastor's kindly gaze.

The pastor opened his black case containing a small container of wine and a little silver box of wafers. He gave a glass communion cup to each of them, and looking from one to the other, said in Norwegian the words of communion—that Jesus, on the night he was betrayed, took the bread and broke it, took the wine and poured it and said to his disciples, this is my body, this is my blood, do this in remembrance of me. He passed each a wafer and poured a little wine into each communion cup. Jens lifted the wafer into his mouth and the cup of wine to his lips and took this sign of immortal life into his dying body.

Then the pastor prayed for the blessing of God over all the family, that angels might guard and protect Jens, surrounding him with comfort and love. At the word "angels," Anders glanced at his mother, and she at him.

Jens eased back into his bed and slept, while Kari served coffee and sweet rolls to the pastor in the parlor. He thanked Kari for her hospitality, for making the effort to serve him with her fine baking, even at such a time. Then he turned and spoke to Anders as a man who must now be strong. "Please call me again if your father has need of scripture; but I think now he is at peace."

For the next three nights, Kari slept curled next to Jens, his body unmoving except for soft breathing. His breath came less frequently, and sometimes a minute, perhaps two, would pass without a breath, and then he would gasp and begin the quiet sighing again. On the third night, she awoke to a profound silence. She lay still and listened, her hand resting on Jens' side. She rose from the bed and called for her sons, who were sleeping in the next room. She lit the lamp, and as Johan and Anders stepped in, she looked at them for a moment, unable to speak, and nodded toward the chair at the bedside.

Johan remained standing, his body pressed against the doorframe. Anders sat down in the chair beside his father, though he knew at once that his father's body was empty of life. Some say that the spirit hovers over the body for a time, even days perhaps, but Anders felt nothing of that. The soul of his father had left his crumpled body and was nowhere near. Kari's youngest boy, now very nearly a man, stood and moved to his mother and wrapped her tightly in his arms.

23

ANOTHER KID IN MINNEAPOLIS

Dagny's schoolteacher pay of sixty-five dollars a month now provided the family's only cash income. For the five months after Jens was laid to rest in the church graveyard, thirty dollars of her paycheck went to his doctors for the x-ray treatment and to the undertaker for his burial.

Quiet, bright, and unflinchingly realistic, Dagny saw a bleak future on the farm for her young brother. She borrowed against her own life-insurance policy to pay tuition for Anders to go to Dunwoody Institute, a technical school in Minneapolis. And so one morning Andy the Kid, as his brothers and teammates called him, stepped onto the train and into the world of the big city. He would soon learn that he was not the only "Kid" in town.

Minneapolis in the 1930s was wide-open and wicked, and Anders, used to the dirt and muck of farm life, breathed in the smell and grit of the city. Bodies jostled against him on the crowded sidewalks of Hennipan Avenue. Faces passed inches away from his own; faces of Norwegians and Swedes as on the prairie, but also of Italians, Jews, Indians, and Greeks. Every face was a stranger.

To pay room and board, Anders washed dishes in a Greek restaurant. On his second night there, two enraged cooks, arguing over a woman, threatened each other with knives. One grabbed a chisel from the counter and threw it across the room. The chisel missed the other cook, whistled past Anders' head, hit the wall, and dropped into his sink full of dishes. The furious restaurant owner screamed a command in Greek and instantly brought the kitchen to order.

Each weekday, Anders went to technical school, fixing in his brain the twists and knots of electrical circuitry, gas engines and steam boilers. Before and after school hours, he wised up to the corrupt politics and grimy street crimes of the city. One morning after breakfast in the neighborhood café, a man in a suit asked him to carry a small briefcase for a few blocks to a cigar shop down the way. The gentleman promised a nice tip for the help. They walked more or less side by side, and when they arrived at the cigar shop, Anders stretched out both his wide country grin and his free hand as he put the case on the sidewalk.

"Oh, no," said the man politely. "If you wouldn't mind, just place it inside and I'll pay you there."

"Sure," smiled Anders as he opened the shop door, walked in with the case, and again put it down. He accepted the tip, then waited politely while his new acquaintance chatted with another well-dressed man, handed over the case to him, and walked out.

Anders cheerfully fingered the silver dollar in his pocket as the second man carried the briefcase to a back room.

"Hey, kid," said the cashier quietly. "Hey, kid, I wouldn't do that again." The old man at the cash register looked with concern at this rube from the country. "That was probably dope you was carrying. If the cops had come, that guy woulda been gone—and you'da gone to jail."

Cops were not, as a general rule, a hindrance to illegal trade during this era in Minneapolis. As entwined as holly and ivy, police departments and underworld gangs created safe twin nests in Minneapolis and Saint Paul for men and women dabbling in vice or lashing out in brutal crime. John Dillinger, Baby Face Nelson, and Ma Barker's gang launched kidnappings, bank robberies, and killings from Twin Cities apartments and hotels. Lesser crooks controlled bootlegging and prostitution.

Occasionally underworld types, looking like a bunch of over-age, undereducated fraternity boys, hung out together at the Greek restaurant where Anders worked. Their faces became as familiar as those of the cooks, waiters, and other regular patrons. The restaurant's customers played slot machines before dining on pheasant year around, whether or not it was legal hunting season. Anders had turned down good money to drive a truck filled with pheasants, covered over with wheat, from Clark, South Dakota, to the Minneapolis city limits. There city truck drivers, knowing they had paid-protection from Minneapolis police, took over driving the trucks to supply restaurants with all the plump pheasants their customers could eat.

One afternoon, to Anders' surprise, a policeman walked into the Greek restaurant. He ordered a near-beer, took one drink, placed the glass back on the counter, and left. "OK" said the boss. "We gotta get these slots down in the basement." Within half-an-hour, the slot machines were locked in the basement cooler. That evening, police raided the restaurant, looked around the main dining room, declared it legal, and left.

"Move 'em back up," yelled the boss, confident that a cop would tip him off to any future raids.

Behind the kitchen doors, Anders and the cooks marveled at the nerve of Walter Liggett, a mouthy reporter for *Plain Talk* magazine. Prohibition had dammed up the supply of liquor that Minnesota thirst demanded, and brewers eagerly bootlegged their way to success. Although businessmen of many ethnic backgrounds supplied drinkers of every clan and tribe, Liggett targeted bootleggers Bennie and Abe Gleeman, along with liquor-consuming Scandinavians, in this bit of verse:

"Ten thousand Jews are making booze
In endless repetition
To fill the needs of a million Swedes
Who wanted prohibition"

Walter Liggett didn't stop with nickel and dime bootleggers. He attacked both gangsters and the state's crooked politicians who allowed the corruption to thrive. In *Plain Talk* magazine he wrote that Minnesota "is dripping wet; that speak-easies, blind pigs, beer flats, and brothels flourish in abundance...gambling joints operate without fear of molestation...police and other officers protect the bootlegger, the gambler and the prostitute."

When he became editor of *The Mid-west American,* Walter Liggett's exposés brought him first threats and then beatings. Still he railed in print against corrupt politicians and gangsters. Finally, on December 9, 1935, two gunmen shot Liggett down as he carried groceries into his apartment house. Mrs. Liggett identified one of the murderers as Isadore Blumenfeld, more commonly known as "Kid Cann," a Romanian immigrant and a powerful Minneapolis liquor and gambling mobster. Though the attack happened during daylight hours on a busy city street, only one other witness stepped forward to testify, a naive out-of-towner named Wesley Andersch.

Kid Cann was arrested. The dishwashers and cooks where Anders worked speculated as to how this slick, swaggering crime lord, who frequented the Greek restaurant, would jump free of this charge. The trial date was set, and the city of Minneapolis waited. A day after the trial was to have been held, Kid Cann strode into the restaurant for a plate of spanakopita. Waiters hovered attentively, and then the owner called from across the room, "Hey, Kid, how'd your trial turn out?" Kid Cann waved his hand in dismissal. "This was nothing," he said. "Naturally, the jury acquitted me. None of the witnesses even showed up."

Quickly the story behind the story spread through the kitchen. The judge had changed the time of the trial to midnight of the night before the originally scheduled date. Witnesses were not notified; so, indeed, none showed up. Acquittal, Minneapolis style.

The grime of Minneapolis street life chipped and smudged Anders' farm-boy innocence. Now he trusted no man whose face did not reflect honest emotions: the barber, for example, who laughed through clenched teeth; or the corner cop who smiled as he cursed the local drunk and kicked him awake.

In the frigid winter of 1936, drifts of unsullied snow covered the frailties and softened the violence of Minneapolis streets. Neighborhoods of substantial two-story homes held honest citizens eager for the FBI political housecleaning soon to come. Anders would not stay around to see this change. Head filled with the workings of steam engines, gas-powered machinery, and electric circuits, eyes wide with seeing city ways, Anders crunched his way across the icy platform, stepped onto the Great Northern passenger car, and headed west.

He jumps from the truck, waves his thanks to the driver, and strides up the snow-covered road to the old farmhouse. She sees that he does not look to the east, does not look in the direction of their big, fine farmhouse, their home for two decades, sold for a pittance. He looks neither right nor left but straight at the old parlor window. Kari stays hidden behind the lacy curtain. She needs to hold this moment, her first view of her son back from the city. His steps stretch longer than before, and his arms seem loosely connected to his shoulders, so that they move easily in an even, balanced rhythm at his sides. As he comes closer to the house, she can see the beginnings of a beard, reddish brown around his chin and over his upper lip. She sees that with each step his legs provide a bounce upward as well as forward, as though propelling him from boat to shore, from rocky cliff to mountain meadow. She thinks of Vikings and sees a wild, bright spirit in him that neither the dull farm nor the harsh city has dimmed. She sees with pride and regret that in these months away from her, the boy has become fully a man.

In the weeks that follow, Kari feels it in her bones. She hears it as a dirge in the creaking of her rocker and the chiming of the clock. As surely as she fled poverty in Norway, her children must scatter to survive. Her girls are gone already: Serianna, a hospital nurse in Rochester; Dagny, a teacher in Marsh county day school. Out of their meager paychecks comes tax money for the farm.

Her sons have changed from baseball-playing boys into men, so different from each other that it seems impossible she carried each in her womb. Rolf, her middle son, comes and goes, careless as a sparrow. When he is home, he works cheerfully enough for some days, but soon grumbles about his lot, muttering about the unfairness of it all. Then he is gone again for weeks at a time, not saying where he is going or what he is doing. She no longer asks. Anders, her youngest, child of her old age, views everything as opportunity, even this time of drought and dust. Just over the horizon is his new chance. Just around a twist in the road is the next possibility. "Look at it this way: things couldn't get worse. They gotta get better!" And then his boyish grin to melt her heart.

Only Johan stays his course, steady as the sun and moon, rising at the same early hour each day, working long and hard, eating with thanks what is placed before him, respecting his elders and caring for the young. Some would say he lacks imagination. Kari sees in him a rare faithfulness, and she thanks God for this, her firstborn.

As the parlor clock strikes one, Kari stops the rocking of her chair, stops the clicking of her knitting needles, and watches the dark silhouettes of her two beloved sons, ten years apart in age, at the end of the hallway. As the sunlight shifts and gleams through the hall window, she sees by their faces that they speak serious words. The two men look into each other's eyes for a moment and then shake hands. She knows without hearing that an agreement has been reached: young Anders will give up his share of the farm and with it the responsibility for his mother's care.

With a nod of his head, big brother Johan accepts the endless work and obligation of this arrangement, setting his cockeyed optimist of a little brother free, penniless though he is, to go wherever the wind blows him—perhaps landing for a time with Aunt Inga and Uncle Mathias in Montana. At the instant of their handshake, Kari thinks, children do this, as they must. As I did. She rocks again, back and forth with the sorrow of inevitable loss and clicks her knitting needles in a cheerless, steady rhythm.

This country, this prairie, seems no longer her home. She yearns for the crushing roar of a Nordfjord waterfall and the blush of a midsummer night sky. A fiddle tune jingles in her head, but she can't remember the words. How can I sing the songs of Norway in a foreign land?

She gazes at a shriveled cluster of *revebjelle* nodding under a few flakes of new snow just outside her window—fox bells in the Norwegian word. Americans call them foxgloves, and she can imagine the tiny hands of little foxes slipping into the cone-shaped purple blossoms. In Norway they grow in the shade at the edge of the forest, dark and beautiful reminders of death. Grandmothers there tell stories of trolls making a poisonous brew of the leaves of these flowers to give to small children who stray from home. She feels pulled to these blossoms, nevertheless, drawn to their promise of final security, of eternal safety, of comfort and peace. She releases the knitting needles into her lap and rests her hands on the unfinished knitting of a winter sweater. *"Om Gud vil,"* she whispers. As God wills.

She can no longer remember the name of the pointed mountain that stands just above her father's farm in Nordfjord. And she has forgotten the word for soft snow melting into the edge of a river; Norwegians have a precise word for that. She is mystified by the loss of these words, flown out of her head like chickadees scattering under the shadow of a circling hawk.

Having neither the exact Norwegian words nor the right English words, Kari turns her thoughts into pictures as Anders prepares to leave her and the South Dakota farm. She sees her own leave-taking as a girl from her mother and father on the farm in Norway. She sees the mountains covered with snow in winter. She sees the sheep and goats in the summer pasture, when the warmth of the sun makes the flowers blossom in the meadows and brings forth the fragrance of earth and grass, of lamb's wool and goat's milk.

The scene blurs and her mind-picture refocuses on Anders as a little boy, chasing pheasant chicks through the wheat. She watches him running for her skirts as the pheasant mother flaps its wings and screeches. Her arms reach down, and she lifts him, feeling his baby smooth skin, soft as duckling feathers, against her face. Then a new picture comes to her, and she sees a young man and feels the strength of his arm wrapped around her shoulder after his high school baseball game—sees her own cheeks glowing red with pride and unexpected joy at this unseemly public display. "We won, *mor!*" she hears his excited voice. "We knocked their socks off!" She pictures him running then, from her to a pretty girl with wavy blond hair and a short red skirt. He lifts this girl up and hugs her, and it seems she hugs him back for a moment and then pushes him away, both of them laughing. All this Kari sees in pictures without words, as she rocks and knits on the wintry day Anders is to leave the farm for Montana.

It might seem that Anders feels only excitement about leaving. But Kari knows her son and hears in his voice a slight tremor, subtle as an eyeblink, that tells her of his fear and grief at leaving this farm and his brother and mother—the unexpressed pain, held just beneath the heart, of leaving all behind.

She puts together an enormous package of food—meat, cheese and bread with a jar of fresh cold milk, fits it all into a blue cotton bag and places the bag in the back seat of Johan's car next to Anders' brown metal suitcase for the ride to the train station.

"Goodbye, *mor.*" Anders wraps his arms tightly around her slender frame. "I'll be back soon. Gotta go where the jobs are." His face brushes against her own. His chin is rough, and his brown plaid shirt smells of hay and scratches like tree bark against her bare shoulder. Then his hands, calloused and knotted from farm work and baseball, hold her own, and she looks into his slate-green Norwegian eyes, half hidden by shaggy brows. She might have said a few words, but the sound of his gentle voice pours over her, sweet and smooth as warm cream. So with only a kiss on the forehead, she sends him away.

Part Three

Home

24

INGA AND MATHIAS

"You come with us for awhile, nephew. *Ja* sure, you come live with us. Inga makes a buncha food, *klubb* and bread, that'll fill you up, skinny guy like you. Didn't your mother Kari take little Inga in, only sixteen years old, when she come from Norway years ago? Wouldn't we like to have Kari's son with us? Kari, Inga's *eldre* sister, that we can do for her, and glad to do it, y'know. *Velkomen*, Anders, to this house, such as it is. *Ja*, you come with us for awhile."

Uncle Mathias said it all in a breath, pointing and gesturing with his glowing pipe. Eyes shining, head nodding, he puffed the words out into the frosty air after rings of fragrant tobacco smoke. Then Inga rushed down the snowy path from the log farmhouse, apron flapping around the pillows of her bosom and thighs. "*Ja, vel,* Anders! Kari wrote you might be coming. *Kom! Kom!* Dinner's pretty near ready. *Ja, eg er so glad—*Anders *kom!*" Inga's low laughter interrupted her waterfall of lilting Norse-English words.

Mathias and Inga gazed with admiration at their nephew; traveled by train across prairie and mountain all the way from South Dakota, he had. Well, yes, here he stood, bone and muscle and spruce-green eyes from his father's side. But there was something of Kari's smile in that grin. They marched him into the warm kitchen, Inga backing in before him and Mathias flanking him from behind. Willing captive, Anders dropped his battered suitcase at the door and surrendered unconditionally to their terms: that he eat mounds of potatoes and venison, that he soak in an iron tub filled with steaming water, and that he sleep in a bed of goose feathers.

The feather bed wrapped itself around him, trapping in the heat of his body still rosy from the hot bath. Frozen beads of snow rattled against the square-paned bedroom window; and from the roof overhang, sharp icicle swords pointed toward the frozen earth. Inside, on the chinked log wall above him, a black bearskin hung head down, so that Anders looked directly into the bear's teeth and mouth. He burrowed deep into goose-down bedding. Safety. Though he was high in the rugged mountains of Montana, seven hundred miles from the South Dakota homestead, farther west than he had ever been, he was with his own people. He was home.

At first light, Anders opened his eyes and blinked at sharp teeth in the open mouth of the unlucky bear whose furry hide hung over the bed. He heard pots and pans clanging against the iron top of the wood stove downstairs. Quickly he pulled on pants and a shirt, and hustled down the cold stairway and into Inga's warm kitchen.

"*Ja so!* Early up on your first morning here! *Har du sove godt?*" Mathias' narrow nose was red from below-zero weather outside, and his mouth curled up toward it in an impish smile.

"Sure, I slept good. But a guy couldn't smell Inga's bacon frying and not come down to eat it! I wouldn't want to insult her cooking and get off to a bad start."

"No, and you better sit and eat, both you men. It's a cold day and lots to be done." Inga frowned at the two of them as she scraped fried eggs and a rasher of sizzling bacon from the wood-burning cookstove onto their plates. To a large platter in front of Anders, she added a pile of fried potatoes. Then lifting the heavy metal coffee pot from the stove by its towel-wrapped handle, she filled their cups. "Eat now!" she ordered, but a chuckle escaped from her plump throat as she watched the men devour her breakfast. "Well, that should hold you 'til *kaffi og smørbrød.*" Inga wiped her hands on her wide apron and turned to roll out the dough for her cardamom sweet buns.

Morning in this Montana farm kitchen was not so different from Anders' childhood breakfasts in South Dakota country. Aunt Inga turned out fried eggs and bacon and big bowls of cooked cracked wheat, as her sister Kari had in better times on the prairie. Uncle Mathias stumbled into the kitchen after early morning chores, cold wind pushing at his back, much as Anders' brother Johan did in Dakota every dawn after milking the cows.

Evenings, too, felt like the quiet, dark, firelit winter nights in South Dakota. Uncle Mathias sat smoking his pipe, reading and re-reading mail from Norway, or splicing a worn harness. Anders' young cousins, Betty and Norman, pressed stubby pencils against the long division and percentages of their homework. Inga knit socks and sweaters almost as fast as her sister Kari in the same traditional Norwegian patterns. She couldn't get exactly the same colored yarns as in the old country, but spinning her own wool and dyeing it herself, she could come pretty close. Like the shape of Norse words on her lips or the lilting song of the fjord fiddle in her ear, the yarn that she spun and dyed and knit preserved for Inga the touch and texture of Norway.

Sometimes a friend happened by in the late afternoon, stayed to dinner and lingered after. One evening, it was Arvid Roe who pushed his expanded waistline back from the table. "*Ja*, I had it so good in Norway. Did I ever tell you about the dances there? You can bet I danced with all the pretty ones, and they liked me well enough, too." Arvid winked at Mathias.

"So you were such a one, Arvid, a regular Valentino, maybe."

"*Ja*, you can laugh, but I'll tell you this much. I danced one night with Sonja Henie! We flew around the floor in circles, just like she spins when she's skating on the ice!"

Inga, even more than the men, laughed aloud at this outrageous tale. "Arvid, such lies you tell! You left Norway before Sonja Henie was born!"

"Well, *ja*, but what's the difference? I danced with her mother when she was already pregnant with Sonja!" Arvid looked around the room in amazement at those so persnickety about the details of a good story.

In this way the days and nights passed in the farmhouse here, like the days and nights in his boyhood home, with farming, housework, handiwork, and talk. But when Anders stepped outside the farmhouse, he saw a world bearing no resemblance to the flat, wide lands of his youth.

South Dakota prairie grass and wheat had turned to dust in the drought, but the walls of Inga's kitchen, made of thick logs stacked evenly twenty feet high to the upstairs bedrooms, spoke of a northwestern Montana backcountry anchored by deep-rooted trees. Mathias built his solid barn of logs, too, from this never-ending forest. Most of this land had been woods when he arrived from Norway. By clearing the fields, he felled all the trees he could use for his house and barn, with wood left over for burning in the long winter.

Land good enough and flat enough for farming was rare in these mountains, but native grass held the soil down, and trees and mountains blocked the wind. Fiercely cold in winter, mild in summer, encircled by rugged peaks, this part of Montana was as near to being Norway as Inga and Mathias could find in America. No fjords, that was true, but you could walk out your door any day of the year, look up at the mountains, and believe you were back in the old country. Perhaps it was the mountains, isolating these immigrants, that kept them more Norwegian in language and culture than their cousins in Dakota.

In winter, Montana snow drifted deep, reminding Inga of the Myklebust glacier near her family farm in Norway. Indeed, Montana had its own glaciers. Inga wrote letters to Norway about that, telling her folks about a wondrous place of mountains and glaciers just to the north and east of them, now a park for the entire nation. Those in Norway sent letters, too, filled with precious gossip of the rocky little Norwegian farm community of Byrkjelo: news of difficult births and unlikely marriages. Who would have thought the Halvorsen's fair-haired Sofie would have set eyes on that lumpy Olaf Hauge? Well, the Hauge farm was a big one, of course, and maybe that was what Sofie saw when she looked at him. Inga clapped her hand against her cheek, shook her head, and laughed.

But, when the solemn postmaster pressed a dreaded black-edged letter into Mathias' unwilling hand, he pushed it deep into his pocket. This *dødsbodskapen,* this death message, was bordered with an inch of darkness, as black as the feather of the raven, God's grim messenger to mortals. Such a letter from Norway was always of a death in the family, but before the death letter reached the small town of Axeton, Montana, traveling by ship and train, the dear one's cold body would have settled well into the grave.

Mathias carried the unopened letter from the post office in town back to the log farmhouse. There he and Inga sat silently by the cookstove, looked at the envelope, and thought of their loved ones in mountain-rimmed Byrkjelo, seeing them gathered at *middag* table and picturing their faces, candlelit in the white wooden church. Which one was dead? A tired grandmother, ready to go to Jesus' arms? Or a child, snatched away?

Inga carefully slipped a kitchen knife just above the black border to slice the paper cleanly. She unfolded the smooth paper. Her eyes stopped at the cross at the top of the page, followed the length of the cross down to the formal, printed Norwegian words, and finally rested on the name of the deceased. Well, there it was. An old uncle, a dear one, too, but it was his time. The children, for now, were spared, thank God.

25

MONTANA ICE AND SNOW

When Anders was a child, the flocks of native Dakota prairie chickens dwindled to near extinction, their hiding places in the tall prairie grass plowed under. Hoping to replace these native birds, farmers ordered eggs of ring-necked Chinese pheasants and set them under brood chickens. The hens seemed confused as their odd-looking chicks emerged and hustled for feed around the yard. Farmers released mature birds into the fields and found that the Asian pheasants prospered in the ditches and weeds along the fence lines, multiplying into thousands. Not much of a trick to hunt them, really. Tromp through a field, listen for the whir of wings as a pheasant flies skyward, get off a steady shot, and bring home dinner.

Anders had learned the skills of hunting in those wide fields and open skies. By the age of fifteen, he held a friendly understanding with his neighbors. Farmers trusted his young hand and clear eye, and they agreed to the deal he offered: for supplying him with two shotgun shells, Anders would bring a farmer back a pheasant. Most times, he could bring a bird down with one shell and have the extra one for shooting his own game.

He told Uncle Mathias about his arrangement with the South
Dakota farmers, but his uncle was not impressed.

"So, young fella, you tink you're some kinda hunter, shooting birds in Dakota. *Vel,* here's a different place altogether,
don't you know? This here's Montana!" Mathias divided the
word into three parts, "Mawn Tawn Ah!" the middle syllable
stretched wide. "And so you used a shotgun for them pheasants?
Ja, vel you wouldn't much stop a bear or elk or even a deer with
that kinda popgun. So then, take ahold a this rifle. It's ready for
ya, loaded and ev'ryting."

Mathias positioned the Winchester 30-30 rifle in Anders'
hands and against his shoulder. "Now, vat you do, you see a deer,
follow him along, squeeze slow on the trigger."

Then Mathias laughed and wagged his head side to side.
"You'll never hit the first one you shoot at, you know. Like the
resta them new hunters, you'll get buck fever and freeze up. But,
Jeese, y'know, after that I guess you'll be as sharp as your Uncle
Erik, who's half wild animal himself!"

Mathias slapped his young nephew on the shoulder and
hurried off to the morning chores. Standing on the porch of the
log farmhouse, Anders peered through the rifle sights at the
scaly bark of a spruce. How hard could it be to shoot a target
as big as a deer? Every fall, birds scattered wildly against the
blazing South Dakota sky, and he picked them down like apples
from a tree. He could certainly bring a deer home for the table.
If he could find one.

Anders pulled the flaps of his cap down over his ears and
stepped onto the new snow. Easier to track an animal in the
snow. He walked beyond the barn and across a field. And there,
not thirty feet away, coming out of a grove of hemlock, was
his deer. Anders slowly lifted his rifle and held the deer in his
rifle sights. The deer was still. Easy shot. Anders squeezed the

trigger, felt the kick and heard the gun's sharp report. The deer lifted his head and looked back at the sound. Again Anders shot. Bang! The deer wandered carelessly back into the brush.

Mathias listened with sympathy to the embarrassment in his nephew's voice as he told his story. "I don't know, Uncle Matt, I sure thought I held the rifle steady. Maybe you're right about buck fever. I just couldn't hit him."

"Vel, you was pretty cocky, pretty sure of yourself." Mathias was grinning now and leaned forward to tell a secret. "I did to you what was done to me, and it might seem mean, but if it humbled you a little, you'll be a better hunter for it. You had blanks in that rifle. I loaded them myself. But tomorrow your Uncle Erik takes you on a real hunting day, and you'll learn more from that soldier and mountain man than from a farmer like me."

Early the next morning Uncle Erik, veteran of the Spanish-American War and the Great War, trapper and hunter, led Anders through rugged, forested mountain country. Three inches of fresh snow sifted onto the trees and brush, and the crisp frost of it fell to the forest floor as the two men pushed their way into the wilderness. "*Styggkaldt*," muttered Erik. Ugly cold.

As they walked, Erik schooled Anders in the cryptic messages of this wild land, of its weather, birds, trees, and animals. You can read the snow, Erik said, once you know its language. Crisp tracks on a still day. The squirrel makes a sloppy hop print in snow, leaving drag marks with its tail. Rabbits are over-hoppers, reaching their back feet over their front feet. Mink. Weasel. Black bear. Grizzly bear. Study their marks and you can decipher who has passed by. Or who has tangled in desperate battle.

Or who has robbed what another has gathered up, said Erik. The noisy nutcracker, with its long beak and special pouch under its tongue, carries pine seeds each fall to secret caches on the south sides of slopes. The bird marks the hidden stores with twigs and pebbles, but by winter the nutcracker's little brain forgets some of them. A hungry bear prowling by could find a stash of pine seeds and devour them all with a quick paw-swipe. Only rime-frosted claw marks and scattered seeds in the snow would tell of the robbery.

Though the seeds would be but a mouthful for the bear, every meal is important as winter sets in, especially to a female bear. Bears mate in the spring. If the mother bear is strong and well-fed, the male bear's seed plants itself inside her in November and grows as the mother hibernates. If the female bear doesn't find enough to eat over the summer and fall, the male seed passes out of her. A hard autumn followed by an early winter, when food is scarce in the wild, means less plentiful game for hunters the year after.

In a quiet undertone to the snowy silence, Uncle Erik whispered that elk mate in October under the spell of an odd perfume. The male elk pees in a mud puddle, lets the mixture go rank, and then rolls in it. The smell that covers him somehow attracts the female. Sad to say, all this rolling and coupling, added to the crash of head-on banging with those big antlers, shortens the life of the king. After a few years of fathering calves, he usually dies young, felled by harsh weather or disease. Still, every spring, elk calves are born, and as though unrelated to their stinky, rutting sires, the newborns are completely odorless. Or so Erik said. Picturing the elk roiling around in the foul mud, Anders laughed out loud, his breath forcing noisy explosions of white mist into the silence of the falling snowflakes. Erik frowned and muttered, "You wanna announce us to da deer?"

Anders stumbled, kicked against a small rock, and watched as it skittered down the ravine in front of them. He winced at the noise. Except for Erik's quiet nature lesson, the two hunters had moved in near silence, their footfalls softened by the covering of snow.

Erik scowled. "You stay right here. Don't even move. I'll go down the draw and scare any deer up to you, if they ain't all gone by now." Erik held his Krag-Jorgensen Carbine close to his side. This was the rifle used by Teddy Roosevelt's cavalry as they rushed San Juan Hill. The 30-40 Krag shot five rounds—smooth and reliable she was, and a highly accurate and effective deer gun, too. But today Erik kept the rifle close and quiet. Today, with some skill and more luck, should be young Anders' day.

So—this was it. Anders had real shells in his rifle, shells he loaded himself. He planted his feet and lifted his rifle. Far below in the ravine, he could hear Erik beating his rifle butt against a tree. Then a rustling in the brush, and a deer pushed through across the clearing. Anders held steady and shot. The deer kept moving. Another pull on the trigger, recoil and bang! The deer still pushed ahead. On the third shot, the deer jumped sideways and into the woods.

From the other side of the clearing, out of the ravine, Erik jumped up sputtering. "Three shots and no deer! I never seen such pathetic shooting!" Anders dove hopelessly into the thick woods, and Erik, cursing like a soldier, plunged in after him. Only three long strides and they stopped. A splash of red stained the snow at their feet. Just beyond, the deer lay dead, fallen on a mat of yellow larch needles, its brown head resting against the tree's bright cinnamon bark.

Anders felt sickened by the beauty and the stillness of the animal. Erik examined the carcass expertly. "One shell grazed the throat. The second across the back. The last one through the heart. Not so bad, after all."

The two men cut up the meat and divided the load in half to pack it back the five miles to the farm. Erik, army veteran in his mid-fifties, set a brisk pace up and down the steep and treacherous terrain. Soon he'll stop, thought twenty-four-year-old Anders. He'll stop and we'll rest. But Erik carried the heavy load straight and steady, saying nothing, mile after mile until at last the farmhouse was in sight. Then he turned to Anders. "Not so bad, nephew," he said. "Not so bad, after all."

The next Saturday, Mathias' and Inga's daughter Betty begged to come along.

"You can't keep up," Anders teased her as he had his own sisters, "and if I bag a deer, you'll be in the way." Betty, a spunky, chunky girl, short, but spit-in-your-eye sassy, blocked his way to the door.

"You'll never shoot another deer, Andy. You can't without Uncle Erik along. I know you can't. I'll make you a bet. If you shoot a deer, I'll haul it myself, all the way back to the house!" Anders glanced out the window at the snow. It looked to be a foot deep at least.

"You're on!" he said, picking up his rifle.

Anders got a deer that day, and after he dressed it out, he told Betty to start pulling. She was game to try. She pulled the deer a ways, slipped, fell down, got up, pulled again, slipped and fell. Anders laughed and walked alongside, told her he was darned if he was going to help, and she didn't complain. Finally he reached down and got a firm grip on the carcass, and together they hauled the deer home.

All that winter, Anders supplied Inga with venison for *klubb,* a steamy broth bubbling with dumplings, each one hiding a mouthful of savory meat. On Sundays she served the family crusty venison cutlets with wild berry jelly and red cabbage simmered into soft, purple mounds. From shelves filled with canning jars, she pulled preserved carrots, peas, and beets. She sent Betty down the cellar stairs to bring up apples and potatoes from wooden barrels. As the weeks went by, Anders felt a comforting tightness against his belt and used the point of his hunting knife to make another hole in the leather. Inga chuckled and nodded against her several chins.

From January to March, as he tramped through the Montana woods, Anders learned from winter. When it gets cold enough in Montana, snow and ice talk to you, teach you what you need to know. At forty degrees below zero, frigid air groans as it cracks frozen rivers, pushes against icicled waterfalls, and freezes spit midair into bits of glass. Cold says pay attention. It says respect me. It says disobey and you will be punished. Sternly it speaks, like a strict schoolmarm.

High overhead, snow gathers silently on fir branches, piling up until a final sprinkle of snowflakes weights the limb to bending. Whoosh, the snow whispers as it slides from the branch. Whoosh. Just enough warning to duck your neck into your collar. Never enough time to dodge out of the way. Whoosh, and half-a-second later, a snowy baptism blesses your head. Though your sins be scarlet, they shall be whiter than snow. Or colder than snow. Though your sins be hot, they shall be colder than snow.

In springtime Montana the streams and waterfalls, like the *elvane* and *fossane* of Norway, gush through rocky crevices and plummet to the valley floor. The weather warms in April, filling Pearly Creek with melting snow, so that it overflows into the woods wherever the banks of the creek slump low. Then temperatures dip near to freezing again and snowflakes drift down, big, wet and lazy. Thaws come and go until May, when shimmering green grass pushes up quite suddenly, aiming to match the bright new leaves of the aspen and cottonwood. Behind the chartreuse of spring-green leaves, the needles of spruce and fir look black. Jagged crests of Snowshoe Peak and Mount Snowy in the Cabinet Range loom in the distance. Purple lilacs bloom against blue sky. The people of Axeton shed winter boots and jackets, exposing their pale skin to the sunshine. A fifty-degree day feels balmy after the deadly cold of winter, and women sit midday on their front porches in sleeveless housedresses, watching their children play in the sun.

Anders hiked the springtime fields and woods to see schools of fish splash in the streams and deer, elk, mink, and bear nose through kinnikinnik and huckleberry. He fished at sunrise in Pearly Creek, learning to lift the fly on the end of a light line just above a quiet pool before letting it dip in where a trout could bite. A quick flick of the pole tip set the hook, and they all had trout for breakfast. He felt himself settling into the life of Mathias' and Inga's farm, treated more like a son than a visiting relative.

After snow patches disappeared and sunshine warmed the fields, the brush and tree-covered foothills of Montana's Cabinet Mountains still hid surprises. You couldn't stomp through undergrowth like you could over Dakota wheat stubble. Sometimes you had to push your way through tree limbs. One day in early summer Anders crawled on his hands and knees with Mathias' rifle through scrub and brambles. An animal, maybe more than one kind, had tunneled through before him. He imagined a deer hesitating around the next turn, a young buck waiting to become venison for Inga's table.

Head down through the brush, Anders crawled ahead. Then he looked up and into the black eyes of a black bear. The bear sat on its haunches, solemn as a judge. The woods fell silent, except for the bear's rasping breath. Anders crawled back slowly, away from the bear, feeling the tunneled opening behind him as he guided himself by touch rather than sight. He held the bear's eyes with his until a turn moved him out of the bear's gaze. The bear did not follow. Still, Anders slid his knees backwards over rocks and twigs for an hour, not feeling the pain of it, until he had worked his way out of the underbrush.

"Vel, you coulda shot him," Mathias said that night. "But, y'know, them fellers can yust keep comin' at you—one, two, or tre bullets in 'em. Ja, I tink you done right." Mathias nodded and took a long puff on his pipe. "Anyhoo, dat's the fun of it. You get yourself into a bit of trouble—and den you get yourself out of it!"

Inga clucked around Anders' chair, pouring his coffee and spooning more pudding into his bowl. "Vel, I vil not write min sister Kari about that one. She won't need that to keep her up at night!"

"Now settle down, tante Inga, I think maybe the bear was as scared as I was."

"Ja, and I'm Sonja Henie! Now, thank your Maker you are home safe, and have a skvett of cream for your coffee."

26

MAKING DO

Dagny bounced along in the back seat of a car driven first by cousin Velma across the dry landscape of South Dakota and then by cousin Elsie for the mind-numbing miles of eastern Montana. Velma took the wheel again and steered her way into the twisting roads of Montana's mountain country. Finally at Mathias and Inga's farm, Dagny disentangled herself from the sweaters, bags, and blankets that had become her nest in the car's back seat and waved goodbye as her cousins headed on to Tacoma to visit Velma's daughter.

"School's done?" Anders hauled his sister's suitcase into the farmhouse.

Dagny frowned and shrugged. "Report cards handed out, schoolhouse swept, scrubbed, and closed for the year."

"How's *mor*?"

"Still cooks for Johan. Eats like a bird herself. Seems healthy. Knits. Sent a sweater for you."

"And the farm?"

"Hanging on. Just. You might as well stay here if there's any work at all. The dirt's still blowing off the farms back there. The whole Gustavson family moved to Oregon. Had an auction at the farm—tractors, milk cows, horses. Old Gustav scooped up the pile of money and drove off a week later. Evelyn got a job in Spokane. You probably heard that." She paused to check Anders' reaction and saw that he nodded.

The next day, Mathias offered Anders his car. "Take the girls for a ride," he said. Dagny sat beside Anders in front, and young Betty settled in back. As they bounced along the dirt road, Dagny told him her plans.

"I've applied for correctional work in West Virginia. Alderson, a women's prison. I took a test."

"Well, you'd do good on any test. You can work from the neck up. I have to work from the neck down. I heard there might be mill jobs soon in Axeton. And they're building a water supply dam, too. There oughta be something one of these days. Meantime, I can help Uncle Mathias out, right Betty? Your pa hasn't kicked me out yet." He craned his neck to glance back at his cousin.

"Keep your eyes on the road. Pa'll kick you to the moon and back if you wreck this car of his!" Betty hung tightly to the rear seat cushion as the Model T Ford sedan rattled along the rough roadway.

Anders brought the car to a halt at the rocky ending of the dirt road. "That's as far as this bucket of bolts goes." He set a stone behind each rear wheel and grinned as he turned to the jostled passengers, Dagny and Betty. "Ready to meet the wild mountain woman?"

Betty shoved against his shoulder in reply. "She's not so much wild as just wanting to be left alone. We take her a few supplies once a month, and she makes it on her own after that, just her and the goats and the dog." The three trudged up the steep mountain trail. "You gonna be able to make this, you flat-landers? South Dakota's got no mountains, I hear."

Anders grabbed his young cousin by the scruff of her neck. "We hike through blizzards and march through dust storms. Montana's got nothing we can't handle."

Betty shook him off and ran ahead. "Race you up this trail!" And she disappeared up into the early morning mist. Dagny and Anders hiked faster then, as fast as they could; for in truth, fit as they were in their mid-twenties, this mountain air felt thin and dry, and their lungs complained at each upward step.

Two miles they hiked, up and up the tree-covered mountain. Betty waited for them, tapping her foot in mock boredom, as her cousins plodded up the last stony steps to her side. A dog barked in the distance.

"Hund is telling *tante* Tilda that we're coming."

"Hund?" gasped Dagny, trying to catch her breath. "She doesn't have a real name for her dog—just calls him 'hund'— 'dog' in Norwegian?"

"Tilda likes to keep things plain and simple. You'll see." Betty motioned them to follow behind her.

As they stepped into a clearing in the trees, Anders could see through the window of a cabin. A figure pulled a garment over her head and wriggled into it, tugging at the hem. She stepped out onto the porch and looked down at them. Anders saw in a glance that Betty was right: the place was plain and simple. A few goats bleated and jostled against a fence of willow stakes. Hund, the dog, braced himself, legs stiff, between the porch and the visitors. The house itself was more shack than proper mountain cabin. Tilda stood motionless on the porch, small and sinewy in a flour-sack dress.

"It's me, *tante* Tilda," called Betty. "Me and some cousins from South Dakota, *tante* Kari's son and daughter."

The words seemed to glide slowly through the cool mountain air from Betty to the porch, passing through Tilda's ears and into her mind. Finally she motioned them onto the porch. "Hund!" she called sharply, and the dog ran onto the porch and lay at her feet. Again she motioned her visitors, and they stepped into the cabin itself.

The darkness of the cabin's one room shivered with light and shadow from the crackling fire in the wood stove. The fire warmed the room, pushing away the morning mountain chill. Tilda nodded that they should sit down, so each looked for a chair or at least a perch. Dagny moved a pile of newspapers from a wicker chair, placed them on the floor beside her feet, and sat gently on the edge of the seat. Anders leaned against a heavy wooden table, causing kerosene to slosh against the sides of a glass lantern in the middle of the pine slab. Betty found a worn cushion with the faded image of a country church embroidered on it. She plunked herself down next to the fire.

"Yes, *tante* Tilda, *dei er dine tremenningar*—second cousins—Anders and Dagny, children of your cousin Kari, my mother Inga's sister. We've brought you some jam from Inga and some bread from her oven just this morning."

Tilda smiled brightly at this. Whether she was happy to see them or the jam and bread was difficult to say, but she nodded again to Anders and Dagny as Betty said their names. She took the bread and jam from Betty and then moved toward a door on the back wall of the cabin, out of their sight. She came back with a jar of pale liquid. *"Limonade,"* she said, looking to them for approval.

"Yes."

"Thank you."

"I like lemonade."

They all spoke at once, eager to fill the silent cabin with conversation.

As the wiry little woman moved purposefully against a plank along the wall, her back to them, Dagny thought of the stories told about Tilda: that as a girl she married a newcomer to Axeton who disappeared within twenty-four hours of their wedding; that she moved to this remote cabin on her own with a few goats and a dog. Years later she married a man as reclusive as herself, and when he died she remained in the mountain cabin, never leaving. Relatives in the valley supplied her now and then with the few items she needed.

Tilda brought a plate of bread and jam to the young people. She handed them china cups filled with lemonade. Each delicate cup was painted with a wild flower—a buttercup for Dagny, a mountain bluet for Betty, and a forget-me-not for Anders. She herself drank from a bent tin cup.

Anders held a slice of bread in one hand and lifted the cup to his lips with the other. A cool salty, sour liquid splashed against his lips. He watched as Dagny tasted the lemonade; he watched as the instant of surprise moved from her lips and tongue to her brain and eyes; and he watched as Betty experienced the same shock. Their eyes met and exchanged a message: Tilda has flavored the lemonade with salt instead of sugar. They all watched as Tilda swallowed a sip of her lemonade and looked confused. She quickly gathered up the cups and took them back to the sideboard. Grabbing a spoon and two brown crocks, she tasted a spoonful from one and then the other. Choosing the second crock, she ladled scoops of white granules into each cup of lemonade and brought them back to her visiting relatives. There, her look seemed to say, that fixed it.

So Anders, Dagny, and Betty drank the lemonade, now a noxious mixture of three strong flavors: salt, sour, and sweet. Their faces held a pleasantly neutral expression as their mouths and stomachs protested each swallow. Each developed a private strategy for downing this undrinkable stuff. Anders took his in one gulp and then filled his mouth quickly with Inga's good bread and jam. Dagny sipped hers delicately, with a small bit of bread in between each little slurp. Betty dipped her bread into the lemonade, hoping that the blackberry jam would mask the grim taste. Tilda's metal cup sat forgotten on the sideboard as she watched them intently.

Tilda gathered the cups and took them to a water-filled bucket. She lowered each cup carefully into the water and turned back to her visitors.

"Glad you come," she said. It had the sound of dismissal, so they shuffled to their feet and stood some distance away from her. Dagny moved slightly closer, but then stopped as Tilda looked at her with the wild eyes of a frightened deer. Betty took Dagny's arm and gently moved her back.

"So, *tante* Tilda, I see you are all right here. The goats are still giving you milk and cheese?"

Tilda smiled for the second time that morning. She nodded and straightened herself. "*Ja,*" she said with pride. "*Mjølk og geitost.*" They understood her smile, for they had been raised on flavorful goat's milk and strong, brown goat cheese.

"Goodbye, then, *tante* Tilda and thank you for the lemonade and bread. *Mange tak!* Many thanks!"

Tilda watched as they entered the path into the woods. They paused for a moment and looked back at the cabin. Just inside the open door, Tilda pulled her dress over her head, revealing another dress underneath.

"She keeps a clean dress ready for visitors," said Betty. "She pulls it over her work dress and then takes off that layer when we go, so she can get back to work."

"I see," said Anders. "She likes things plain and simple—like her lemonade."

They chased each other down the trail, stumbling, almost flying, until they reached the car two miles from the cabin, finally sure that Tilda would not hear them as they collapsed into the bliss of youthful laughter.

——————

"*Ja, vel*—what can you do? Horses got to run, and then when I need 'em they're near wild, off in the woods. Looks to me like today we better catch them horses for plowing."

So on a June day, Mathias and Anders chased, coaxed, and finally captured the plow horses. Waste of time, thought Anders. While his hands gentled and wiped down the horses in the barn, his mind revolved around his brother Johan's Overland sedan, his own patched-together Model T, and the engines he learned to tune up at Dunwoody Institute in Minneapolis.

"I'm taking a little trip to Spokane, Uncle Mathias. I've got an idea about something."

"*Ja,* and I know about your idea. A Swedish girl lives there, that much I know."

Anders kicked at the dirt. "All right, maybe that's part of it. But I have an idea about plowing, too. You need a tractor. Now wait just a dang minute. I know you can't afford it. But this isn't going to cost that much if it works out."

Before dawn of the following day, Inga watched Anders set out toward town. So off he goes, this last-born son of *mi eldre syster* Kari. Without any money to speak of, who knows how he travels? By boxcar maybe? In these years men do that, riding in a boxcar, if they find one open, or on top of one. Some die that way, too, or lose a leg trying to jump onto a moving train. Inga shook her head and worried about her sister's dear and foolish boy. *Ja, vel,* and aren't they all in need of angels' care, these young ones?

In Axeton, Anders walked quietly around the freight yard, listening for other footfalls on the gravel next to the tracks. The catch light of the early morning sun glanced sideways off bright metal wheel rims where black grease wore thin. He watched for "bulls," the train yard detectives who chased away boxcar transients. He looked around, too, for lifetime bums, the tough, sometimes criminal, older men who rode these trains and mixed in with boys and young men made jobless and penniless by drought and the Depression. The boxcar doors were closed, and when Anders pulled on a handle, he felt a sharp wire cut into his hand. The railroad company ordered its employees to wire the doors shut, but sometimes a sympathetic worker neglected a car or two. Well, not this morning.

Anders climbed up the side of a boxcar and lay down on his back, exactly in the middle of the top of the car, where no roving railroad cop could see him. The cold and damp soaked into his lanky body as he watched the gray morning sky turn blue. He held the cloth flour sack containing Inga's meat and egg sandwiches next to him, under his coat. He was secure in his next meal, for sure, and a certain Swedish girl named Evelyn might feed him pretty well when he got himself to Spokane. It would take some doing, this tractor for Mathias, but it could be done.

The train rattled, creaked, and moved forward. Once his boxcar rolled past the edge of town, Anders could sit up and enjoy his unobstructed view of the mountains, rivers, and trees. There was something powerful, even kingly, about being pulled along atop his private coach. He held fast to a metal tie bar as the train careened around a bend and onto a bridge high above the Kootenai River. Then, straight ahead he saw the curved entrance of a tunnel. It looked small, hardly able to accommodate the bulk of the train. Anders flattened himself against the top of the freight car and gasped one last breath as his body slipped into the black, airless tunnel. Metal clanking, wheels against rails, rattled into his ears. He counted the seconds: eighteen, nineteen, twenty. Suddenly the world turned bright, and he sat straight up and whooped into the sunshine with the joy of a survivor.

Even in 1937, with the ruinous economy slowing commerce to a crawl, Spokane rattled with cars and trucks. Anders viewed the confusion of the city as his train slowed. He envied the drivers hauling goods in a Seattle-built Kenworth. He watched as two young men unloaded freight from a Ford truck into a boxcar. The Ford's sedan front gleamed black, and the green slat-sided load box advertised, "George M. Laler & Sons." Double tires in back, no surprise. Ford beat out all the others in building trucks. Then a GMC T-96 rolled down the street. Six-cylinder, 173 horsepower gas engine, a six-wheeler that could pull another loaded four-wheel car. "Overnight Motor Freight Service," said the sign in white letters on its side.

No use crying in the bucket over what you can't have. Anders knew from South Dakota farming that you make do. And he learned at Dunwoody how to fit together whatever mechanical parts you have into something that'll work.

Once in the Spokane train yard, Anders slipped off the far side of the boxcar, jogged his way over the tracks and onto a side street. He checked into a rundown hotel near the train station where the clerk was used to trading shabby sleeping rooms for the pocket change of smoke-smudged, train-hopping men. For a nickel, the clerk pointed out a phone, and Anders called Evelyn at the house where she worked as housekeeper and secretary for a woman doctor. Evelyn couldn't talk long on the phone, but she said she'd meet him for a picnic lunch in the park near Spokane Falls.

Anders scrubbed off as best he could in the hotel bathroom and walked the distance from his hotel to the falls. Sitting on a blanket with her, eating sandwiches, fried chicken, and chocolate cake, looking, looking into her lovely blue eyes, watching her mouth curve into a smile, and yet being able only to touch her hand—the combined pleasure and pain of it made him as dizzy as going through the train tunnel.

"I'll find a job soon, Evie—and then..."

"Yes, soon," she said, "and then..."

She handed him a bag stuffed with more sandwiches. "I have to get back." She gave him a hug and a quick kiss and pulled away with a sad smile.

"Write, Andy."

"I will."

The next morning, Anders got what he needed with the money Uncle Mathias had entrusted to him. First he bought an old four-door Hupmobile Touring Car. The 1924 model cost plenty when it came out, but now, twelve years later and times tough as leather, the topless Hupmobile came cheap. These days, any man who had money to buy a new car wanted a modern hardtop sedan to protect his family from rain and snow. Still, the old touring car's windshield was intact and should keep bugs off a driver's teeth.

Checking around wrecking yards for the best prices, Anders bought a Warford transmission and a Ford truck with a Ruckstell axle. Picking out all the parts he needed, from transmissions to attaching bolts, Anders stacked them in the backseat of the Hupmobile and topped off the tank with cheap gas. He gave a firm twist to the door handle, pulled the car door open, and slid behind the wheel. He aimed the car, backseat filled with well-chosen junk, toward Mathias' and Inga's Montana farm.

The topless Hupmobile rolled on its spoke wheels into Idaho and through the town of Sandpoint. As he approached the far edge of town, Anders saw an old woman standing beside the road, so he stopped to see if she needed help. Yes, she said, she would much appreciate a ride to Bonner's Ferry where her daughter lived. In she jumped, spry and alert as a little girl. She chatted all the way, about her daughter and about wanting to make this visit, never pausing for a reply from her young driver. For the already weary Anders, Idaho road miles stretched long, and the old lady's chatter rattled on and on. Finally, in Bonner's Ferry, the woman pointed to a grassy corner on a cross street. "This is it," she said. "I want to get off here." With some relief, Anders waved goodbye to this yakety woman as he drove on in blessed silence toward Axeton.

By 11:00 the next morning Anders rolled beyond Pearly Creek, out to where the gravel road turned to packed dirt edged with a few summer mud puddles. He saw the log barn first, framed by the buck-and-rail fence. He pounded on the car horn, and the honking echoed loud and brassy against the hills. Then, as the touring car rolled to a stop, Mathias stepped out of the barn, and Inga's round face popped out of the farmhouse kitchen door.

"*Vel*, vat you got there?" Mathias shook his head as he looked at the topless car and the pile of engine and transmission parts in the back seat.

"Let the boy eat first," said Inga, wiping her eyes with relief at seeing her nephew drive up to their log farmhouse.

"But vat is it, all of this?" Mathias said, waving his hand at the stack of metal.

"Don't you worry, Mathias. I'll fix you up with all the tractor you'll ever need! Now, Inga, I'll take you up on that food."

The three of them sat down in the usual way to noontime dinner. Above the clanking of forks and cups, the radio crackled out news. First came a local incident. A confused older woman, a mental patient, the announcer said, had been missing from Sandpoint, Idaho. She was later found safe in Bonner's Ferry. It was a mystery how she got there, since she had no friends or relatives living in the area. Police were seeking information. Anders choked on his coffee and then told Inga and Mathias about his part in this story of a missing woman. At first they all sat in silence, solemnly considering what they should do.

Then Inga giggled. She laughed. She shook from her round shoulders to her plump ankles. *"Vel,"* she said. "I tink these Idaho folks can take care of their own crazy ones. I got enough trouble watching out for you two, with Anders running off to Spokane and spending good money on God-knows vat kinda machinery to run our horses out of a job!" She cleared the table, still chuckling at all the nonsense in this world.

In the days that followed, Mathias got on with his chores, casting a glance from time to time at his nephew's impossible project. Anders cut the frame of the Hupmobile in half. He hooked the Warford transmission into the Hubmobile transmission. Behind that, he attached the Ford transmission and the Ruckstell rear axle. Then he stood back to look at what his work had produced: a very short, odd-looking tractor with thirty possible combination shifts.

Even when Anders had finished assembling the tractor, Mathias had grave doubts that this freakish makeover would ever run. Plenty of real engineers, fussing around with new designs for tractors, had failed and become jokes in the countryside. When was it, 1920 maybe? When that Durant feller showed off his Iron Horse Samson tractor, supposed to take the place of horses. The farmer could operate the rig with horse reins, pulling on them to stop it and letting the reins go slack to speed it up. Almost ruined the whole General Motors Company before they got rid of that one. And now Anders got his own experiment. Still, as an act of faith in his nephew's work, Mathias attached the tiller to the back of the misbegotten machine where it stood on the new green grass.

"When I start the tractor up, those fork tines are gonna cut up the lawn," warned Anders.

"If you can get this thing to move, go to it!" Mathias stepped back a couple of paces, as if expecting an explosion. Anders started the hybrid tractor in its lowest gear, and the machine dragged the tiller relentlessly across the grass, ripping a deep brown scar in the green turf.

"Hold it right there, *sinnssvake*, crazy man!" Mathias yelled. Anders plowed on, unable to hear over the noise of the engine. But Mathias' impish smile pushed into his cheeks as he pictured all the field work that ugly tractor could do for him.

Indeed, the tough little tractor dragged Mathias' plow all summer. It turned his fields and readied them for planting. It pulled a wagon filled with tools from the barn to fences that needed mending. Beyond that, it lured many visitors to the place, neighboring farmers who came to shake their heads in wonder that a machine so graceless in form could actually run and do the work that was required of it.

These farmers brought rumors of a change in the economy. They spoke of it quietly, not wanting to raise false hopes for jobless young men. "I hear the Axeton water supply dam's underway. Some kinda federal deal."

"Guess so. I heard that myself around the post office. Could be."

One August evening at supper, Anders made a request of his uncle. "You got some business in town? Give me a lift there?"

"*Ja*, got some stuff I oughta pick up. Could go tomorrow."

In spite of dark clouds and drizzle, the two men headed into Axeton the next morning. Mathias dropped his nephew off at the far edge of town, and Anders struck out on a walk through the countryside, leather satchel in hand, to the town water supply project. A persistent rain probed his wool cap and trickled off his nose. He looked up at the storm clouds tumbling one over another in a sky that grew darker as he walked along. Through the rain, he saw a lone farmer pitching hay in a roadside field. "Poor old cuss," he thought, and he called out, "If you got an extra pitchfork, I'll help you with that hay."

Anders pitched hay side by side with the farmer all afternoon, and at suppertime he found himself at the farmhouse table eating a home-cooked meal. The farm wife filled his plate again and again and remarked that his young frame needed some meat on it. He hadn't expected any pay, just helping the farmer out like that, so he was one happy guy when the farmer paid him forty cents an hour—the best wages he'd ever had. For the next few days, the farmer handed him off to neighbors who were also in the middle of haying, so for about a week, he worked happily for cash, meals, and a bed.

A bright late-August sun dried out the fields and the road as Anders picked up his suitcase and walked away from the farm toward the dam project. He arrived at noon, and by 2:00, to his amazement, he was on the job. Anders' work on the water supply dam meant picking up ninety-pound sacks of cement in ninety-degree temperatures and carrying them through clouds of cement dust and sandy grit that the wind picked up from the ground, swirled into the air, and thrust into his lungs. But it was a job, and in 1937, no able-bodied man turned down any job. Anyway, things might change for the better, thanks to God or good luck.

One day the cement mixer quit. After working around farm machinery all his life, Anders was pretty sure he knew, just by the sound of it, what was wrong with that Fairbanks-Morse engine on the mixer. He stuck his head in the engine and saw right away that the trip lever, the part that made the stationary engine fire up, had slipped down.

"OK," he told the boss, "I think I can fix this, but you better have everyone stand back, just in case something blows."

"Well, see what you can do, Andy. But watch yourself." The boss moved all fifty men on the crew out of harm's way and got even farther away himself. With nobody able to see how easy a job it was, Anders pushed the trip lever back and tightened the set-screw. Then he tapped a tool inside the mixer to make noise and to make the repair take a little longer. Finally, he started up the engine.

From then on, the boss wanted Anders right at hand. He gave him a safe, easy job, watching the run-off creek to make sure it didn't overflow. The engine kept breaking down, and each time Anders told the men to stand back, just in case. They always backed way off as he went through his secret fixing routine.

Even watching the run-off creek, Anders choked on the dusty air as he breathed the grit up into his sinuses. One Saturday he went into the town of Axeton and lined up a job at Nehring Lumber Company. But before he left the dam project, Anders took a worker he liked over to the cement mixer and showed him the trick of fixing the engine. Then Anders told the boss that he was quitting. "And Carl over there," he said, pointing out his friend. "You'd better never fire him, 'cause he's the only other guy around here who knows how to fix the mixer engine."

"Come on over here, Carl," the boss said, "I'm gonna need you to stand here and watch this run-off creek." Carl, who'd been hauling heavy sacks of cement, grinned as Anders walked away.

27

GETTING MARRIED AND PLAYING BALL

A beaded broach glittered at her neck, the weight of it pulling at the creamy fabric of her dress. Everything about her except the broach and the gathered detail of her sleeves seemed serene, unruffled. Her face was composed, and her honey blond hair lay in sleek waves placed firmly back from her wide, unlined forehead. Evelyn looked in the mirror and was amazed at the contrast between her calm exterior and her inner confusion. Tomorrow was her wedding day. How could that be? Had she really made a firm decision for this boy, this man about to become her husband?

Marrying Anders was no impulsive choice, certainly. Except for this time of dried up earth and jobs, they would have been married for years by now. She smiled as she thought of their Saturday evenings in summertime Brem. A block from home, she would hop into Andy's Model T, while her sister Mildred walked on to town with friends. Hours later, Mildred returned and waited until the Ford came round and Evelyn jumped out. Then the sisters walked back to the farmhouse where their mother met them at the front door each night with "Did you girls stick together?"

"Yes, Ma, we stuck together."

Evelyn frowned at herself, licking her fingers and wetting down a stray curl. Now the pastor would ask that question. Will you promise to stay together, through good times and bad? She would have to answer honestly this time, in front of God and the preacher. She turned from the mirror, slipped off her fawn-colored silk dress, and stepped into a brown tailored skirt.

There was the license to get. Mildred wouldn't be with them here in Spokane. No one from either side of the family could be at the ceremony, although they had all by now given their blessing. In these hard times, no one could afford train fare to come to a marriage. So Evelyn and Anders entered the courthouse on that Friday, just the two of them, to apply for their marriage license.

"Yes," said the clerk loudly as he took the application fee, "and where is your witness?" A long line of other applicants stood waiting behind Anders and Evelyn as they looked at each other, quite stricken. They knew no one in Spokane available to be their witness, nor had they realized they needed a witness to get a license. The clerk waited impatiently, and Anders stood as helpless and silent as his young bride.

"Hey, there!" shouted a voice three couples back in the line. "What are you two doing here? You're getting married, too? So are we! This is great! We'll all have to celebrate together! You need a witness? I'll be your witness!" The man's honest Irish eyes looked directly at the clerk. "I've known them all my life. Where do I sign?" And the stranger from Boston signed his name to the marriage license of Evelyn Victoria Gustavson and Anders Jens Nilsen, both from Brem, South Dakota. They had never seen the man before and would never see him again.

Evelyn's father Gustav had warned her against getting married on a Friday. A bad luck day, Friday. You wouldn't start anything new on a Friday. Gustav Gustavson wouldn't sign a business deal on a Friday. And you sure wouldn't want to start a marriage on a Friday. So Anders and Evelyn waited until the next day, Saturday, February 19, 1938.

Evelyn took Anders' hand and led him through Spokane and across the railroad tracks to the Lutheran church by the river. "You walk here alone?" asked Anders as they crossed the tracks. "I walk here at night. To the Sunday evening service."

Anders glanced sideways at this slender girl whose pretty face and silk dress concealed a strong-willed woman. She came from farm folk who had plowed the dirt of Småland in Sweden, braved the wide Atlantic, and homesteaded in Dakota. She would do well as a wife, working with him to make a life in Montana. He trembled at the cold and at his unreasonable good fortune as he kept a tight grip on her small hand.

Pastor Larson married them, with Mrs. Larson and the young intern pastor as witnesses. After the ceremony, Mrs. Larson invited them into her small dining room for a lunch of salmon salad sandwiches, sliced cucumbers in sweetened vinegar, and white cake with vanilla frosting. By each napkin she placed a tiny wedding bell made of a thimble trimmed with pink ribbon.

The afternoon slipped by as a time out of time—a trance in which they wandered about, hand in hand, laughing over nothing, the two of them alone even in the jostling crowds of downtown Spokane. Anders and Evelyn had dinner in a restaurant, a turkey dinner as a special treat. Except that the turkey slices were served half-raw. They didn't complain. Unwilling to disquiet the charmed circle of their contentment, they tried to eat the dinner but were perhaps too nervous to eat anyway. Evelyn watched her husband (her husband!) as he paid for the meal and, she noted, left too much for the tip. She took his arm, and they walked around the corner to a small hotel for their wedding night.

On Sunday, they caught the train to Axeton. Anders had to be at the lumber mill first thing Monday morning. As the train rattled through the mountain passes, he felt himself stronger, weightier than the single man he had been. He was married, responsible for a wife and for children, should they come soon.

But Evelyn knew that for them children would not come soon. During her years as a housekeeper and secretary for Dr. Emily Mattson in Spokane, she had learned ways of delaying the conception of a baby.

Dr. Mattson, who treated the ailments of overworked mothers and repaired women damaged in botched abortions, believed every woman should be given birth control information, though dispensing this knowledge was still illegal in many states. Nearly five years had passed since Evelyn's trip to the Chicago World's Fair, but she could still picture the jars holding partly-formed babies. She had listened to Dr. Mattson and learned from this woman, who was first her employer, then her doctor, and finally her friend.

Anders and Evelyn moved into a shabby little furnished house a few blocks from Axeton's main street. The rent was cheap, partly because no one could afford more and partly because the old man who owned the house liked the idea of a young couple living in his childhood home.

Anders came home from the mill each day and hammered a few nails into the loose boards on the rickety front steps. Evelyn spread a bright quilt on the bed and covered the kitchen table with a hand-hemmed dish towel embroidered with red roosters. In the evening sitting beside their Crosley radio, they listened to the news, to "Amos and Andy," and to President Roosevelt's fireside chats. When the weather was just right and Anders held his hand on the radio, they could listen to the baseball games of the Chicago Cubs, their favorite team. If a game was close, Evelyn couldn't stand the excitement, running from the living room to the bedroom, then sitting on the bed with the door closed. Every few minutes, she opened the door and called for the score. Finally, she crept back into the living room for the last inning, leaping to her feet if the Cubs won or slumping onto the floor if they lost. But for Anders, listening to baseball could never compare to playing the game.

Nehring Lumber Company sponsored the Axeton baseball team, and as soon as Anders heard about the team, he wanted to play. In these Depression times, he felt lucky to have a job at the Nehring mill making forty-five cents an hour, enough to cover the rent on a house. A decent job, a good wife. Anders' next goal seemed obvious to him: catching baseballs for the Axeton town team.

Growing up in South Dakota, Anders first caught for his high school team and then for the Brem town team in the South Dakota Lake Region League. He'd learned his best moves matched against the traveling exhibition teams that rolled through town. Playing these out-of-state teams, Anders met athletes unlike any living in his part of the country. The men on the House of David team glared out from behind full beards, and the words on the back of their pitcher's shirt commanded, "Thou Shalt Not Steal!" The Kansas City Monarchs of the Negro leagues threw harder, ran faster, and caught and batted as well or better than the players on the all-white major league teams.

The Monarchs exhibition team came into the Dakota farm areas and divided their twelve-member team in half, each group going to a different small town. The town teams handed over all gate receipts to the Monarchs, so by dividing the team, the

Monarchs doubled their take. To fill in the missing positions, their six players asked for a couple of local volunteers. Green, but eager to learn, Anders offered to catch for the Monarchs. Crouched behind the plate, he dissected plays, scrutinized signals, and memorized instructions from the patient Monarchs pitcher. Anders was just a fresh South Dakota country kid, but he knew he was witnessing greatness.

Now in Axeton, Anders approached the team manager. Confident he could catch anything thrown across home plate, Anders asked if he could catch for the team. "Sorry," said the manager, "We've got too many catchers. You can play outfield if you've got a decent batting average."

"I batted .350 my last season."

".350. Yeah—well, you'll have to prove that," snapped the manager.

For the opening game, the Rexford team manager imported a pitcher from Great Falls. With a powerful left-handed delivery, he smoked his fast ball across the plate. An early pitch smashed the outstretched fingers of Axeton's regular catcher. The back-up catcher stooped down, reached into the next sizzling pitch, swore in pain, and stomped away from the plate. The manager growled at Anders. "Want to give it a try?"

Anders squatted behind the plate, remembering the Monarchs pitcher's tip about catching a fast ball: never hold your fingers straight and rigid. Slightly bent fingers will fold, not break, if they collide with an inbound baseball. He held onto everything that Great Falls pitcher threw, and from then on Anders was catcher for the Axeton team.

Weekdays after work, the team played practice games at the local field in the shadow of the Cabinet Mountains. By evening, the air turned cold. Eyes on a fly ball, the players stumbled in the rough grass. Batters got no over-the-fence automatic homers.

The Axeton field had no fences, so outfielders could run after the ball and shoot it home.

On Sundays when a rival team came to Axeton, fifty to sixty local fans came to yell for the home team, shouting encouragement for their clumsy but wildly enthusiastic efforts. Evelyn came to every game, cheering for her own hometown hero. The Axeton team didn't win many games, but folks liked baseball. It was free entertainment out in the fresh air, with green trees and rugged mountains to admire if the game lagged.

When the mill bosses spread the scarce jobs around by going to a five-day, forty-hour work week, league games filled up those free Saturdays. Since all the teams had so far to drive, they usually played double headers, seven innings per game. The day's first game started shortly after 12:00 noon, and each game took about two-and-a-half hours to play. By 8:00 in the evening, the team would pile into jalopies for the long ride home.

Sandpoint, Kalispell, Whitefish, Rexford, and Banff. Two cars carried the team over twisted, rugged mountain roads to the other five towns in the league. The car Anders rode in held three other players: Marvin, a smart local kid who'd just graduated from high school; Harvey, who worked in the woods; and Sam, the team's fast-throwing first baseman, who during the week shined shoes in Mac's Barber Shop. In a newer car driven by the manager rode six other team members: three local men and three guys who'd just moved up to Axeton from South Carolina.

Whenever the Axeton players arrived in a town, they'd have a restaurant lunch, paid for by the team sponsor, Nehring Lumber Company. Anders soon noticed that Sam, the first baseman, didn't ever sit down in the restaurant and eat with the rest of the team. He'd get his lunch money from the manager and go off somewhere else to have his meal. "How come you never eat with us, Sam?" Anders asked one day.

"I know my place," answered Sam. "Those boys won't eat with me."

"Come on, Sam. They play ball with you. Why wouldn't they eat with you?"

"Listen, Andy. They play ball with me 'cause I'm a good ball player. But they won't ride in a car with me. You see how they're packed into that other car. And they sure won't eat with me, 'cause I'm colored."

So on each road trip, Anders, Harvey, Marvin, and Sam spread out in comfort in their car as it careened around the narrow, crooked roads carved out of the steep slopes of the Cabinet, Purcell, and Salish Mountains. One Saturday morning as they headed north toward Rexford along the Kootenai River, the car broke down. The four of them hitched a ride in a passing Ford, desperate to make the 12:00 game time. Sitting in the front seat, Anders noticed the driver's head nodding against the steering wheel. Tired or drunk, it was hard to tell, but this man clearly wasn't fit to drive. The players convinced the guy to sit in the back while Anders slid into the left seat and stepped on the gas pedal as hard as he dared.

A young man from the flat Midwest, driving a borrowed car, Anders held onto a crooked road that seemed only carelessly fastened to the mountain edge. Then a big Buick swung wide around a blind corner ahead. Anders pulled right, snagging two eighteen-inch guardrail posts, but the heavy Buick tagged the lightweight Ford's front fender and tire. The Ford jumped the guardrail and teetered over a sheer drop-off. Out of the right side-window, Anders looked down at the fields far below and at two tiny farmhands mowing hay with a toy-size combine. He jerked his head toward the road and saw Sam, outside the car, hanging onto the left front fender, using his weight to keep the delicately balanced car from tipping over the edge.

"How'd you get out there so fast?" Anders asked Sam later.

"I dove out the window, right on over your shoulder."

Anders could believe it, remembering all the times Sam had hustled with that same speed to steal a base or to put a runner out at first.

By the end of that season, Sam and Anders tied for the best batting average at .400. A local restaurant offered a chicken dinner with all the trimmings to Axeton's top batter each year. The manager took Anders aside.

"You know, Andy," he said. "I've been thinking. There's only one dinner. You get to go home every night to Evelyn and a home-cooked meal, but Sam doesn't. I'd sure like to give that dinner to him, if that's all right with you."

A funny mixed-up picture spun around in Anders' head just then. In it were hundreds of well-shined shoes, a Ford tilting over a mountain cliff, and a strong black arm snapping the ball from first base to home.

He nodded at the manager. "That'll be just fine with me."

Evelyn viewed this as a weakness, Anders' inclination to give things away. He would volunteer an afternoon's work to anyone who asked it, when the time could have been better spent on their own house or yard. Two drifters near the railroad station asked him for enough money for a meal, and he pulled out his wallet. Before she could stop him, he handed over a dollar and wished them good luck—scruffy men who would as soon rob you as look at you. When she scolded him, he became a bit gruff with her.

"You don't know how it feels to be flat broke—not a cent to your name."

So that was it. He'd been jobless, poor, and hungry, as she had not. But if they were to progress, bit by bit, to have their own house, a cushion of savings, and income enough for a family, it would take a firmer grasp on time and money than her husband seemed to have. She slipped her arm through his, and he patted her hand as they walked home, each having the sensation of leading the other.

28

LUTHERANS

From the point of view of the town's Catholics and Methodists, it was impossible to see why there should be two Lutheran churches in Axeton. The church buildings stood only a block apart, their gleaming spires aimed at the heavens, two white sanctuaries sitting heavy on the earth, like guard houses watching over the uncertain moral values and beliefs of the town.

To all appearances, the Lutheran churches worked in harmony, side by side. But it would have been more honest to say that the two congregations, each of them attached to a distinct national synodical division of Luther's holy army, observed an uneasy cease-fire. The central, though unspoken rule of the truce was that Good Shepherd Lutheran Church gathered in all newcomers of Scandinavian extraction, while Triumphant King Lutheran Church laid claim to all families of German ancestry.

Good Shepherd Lutheran Church became known for its fellowship hall potlucks, featuring Swedish meatballs, Norwegian cookies, and gallons of hot, strong coffee. Triumphant King Lutheran Church parties seemed more festive, perhaps because of the German custom of providing beer at official church celebrations. Catholics smiled and Methodists frowned as they observed these men, and not a few of the women, laughing and shouting during their church picnics, beer steins in hand.

Newlyweds Anders and Evelyn, hearing a knock on their door, invited Pastor Julleland into their tiny living room. "Won't you have coffee, Pastor," said Evelyn.

"No, no, please don't bother."

"But it's no bother. It's all made. We were just about to have some. And I have way too many cookies here for the two of us. Please help us eat them."

Evelyn vanished into the kitchen and brought out a tray of coffee cups and saucers, a coffee pot, and a plate heavy with sugar cookies. She placed them on the coffee table next to the couch where Pastor Julleland sat smiling.

"Oh my," he said. "I didn't expect all this. Now I can't resist having one cookie. But only one." He patted his round stomach, and shook his head as she pressed the plate of cookies nearly under his chin.

Evelyn frowned. "Well, I don't know what I'll do if you don't have a few more. I guess I'll just have to throw them out."

"Well, I wouldn't want that, they are so good. Maybe just a few."

After a dozen cookies and cup after cup of coffee, Pastor Julleland spoke of Good Shepherd—an active church, now sending aid to refugees in Europe. A growing church, with many young families. He would like to see them as part of it.

"Well, certainly," said Anders. "We'll be coming. I might not be able to stay to shake your hand afterwards though. I catch for Axeton's baseball team, and a game starts at noon every Sunday."

"I'll make you a deal." Pastor Julleland placed his cup gently back on its saucer and extended his hand to Anders. "You come to the church service, and I'll come and watch your baseball game."

"Done!" grinned Anders and shook the pastor's hand.

Just across the street from Evelyn and Anders lived a German family who, naturally, belonged to Triumphant King Lutheran. The six Ziegler children roiled around their yard and ran up and down the sidewalk, playing hopscotch and jumping rope. When Mrs. Ziegler waddled out to watch them, Evelyn, hanging work clothes on the line, left the last shirts in her basket and ran over to talk with her pregnant neighbor.

"How are you feeling today, Mrs. Ziegler?"

"Oh, ready to have this baby. The last month, you don't care much about what's to come. Only that you want to get it over with." She smiled wearily.

"I wonder sometimes." Evelyn hesitated, then lowered her voice. "I want children so badly. But—well, I wonder sometimes. Does it hurt—the birthing—very much?"

"Well, young Mrs. Nilsen, I won't lie. It hurts. But only for a short time. And then you go home with a beautiful baby. Many others, sick ones in the hospital, go through a very devil of pain, and they have nothing to show for it." Mrs. Ziegler spread her arms out as if to embrace all her screaming, giggling children. "Which one could I do without?"

A week later, Frieda Ziegler gave birth to a baby girl. The child cried weakly, seemed to choke and sputter, and died moments after she was born.

Hot dishes, cookies, pies, and cakes arrived at the family home, carried by friends from every church. Mrs. Griffith, a Methodist, watched over the smallest Ziegler children, and Mrs. McCullough, a Catholic, made school lunches for the older children. Triumphant King church women, close friends of Frieda Ziegler, came one day to sweep and scrub and wash every corner of her house, though they were sick at heart with knowledge of a deep pain within their congregation.

Walter Ziegler, father of the dead baby, sat in Pastor Krull's office, a heavy oak desk between them. The pastor's brow furrowed in genuine sadness as he said, "You know, Walter, it is not against you or your family. Neither is it something I would wish. But we must obey the synod teachings of our Triumphant King Lutheran Church. We have the promise of salvation through our baptism. But we do not know the fate our Father in heaven has for the unbaptized, even a tiny baby such as yours. Therefore, we cannot allow its burial within the churchyard beside those assuredly saved baptized believers."

A few hours later, Evelyn and Anders sat silently in their living room as their neighbor Walter told Pastor Julleland of this sorrow beyond sorrow. "And is it so, Pastor, that an unbaptized baby cannot be received in heaven—and that it cannot be buried in the safety of a churchyard?"

Pastor Julleland pressed his lips together and looked down at his hands. When he raised his eyes, Evelyn thought she saw a glittering there, but then a steadiness as he said, "Our God loves us more than a mother loves her child. God loves a baby even as it is knit together in its mother's womb. Your child is in God's arms. And your daughter's precious body will rest in our churchyard."

And so, the two Lutheran churches remained, just a block apart, like two parts of an old family Bible, one upholding the heavy burden of the Law, and the other offering the good news of the Gospel.

Some months later, Pastor Julleland called on the Ziegler family. The pastor looked with satisfaction at the rosy-cheeked children, who now filled up his Sunday school, and at the dedicated parents, who helped with every Sunday school project.

"I hope you are feeling at home in the church by now." Pastor Julleland shifted his gaze toward the kitchen. Mrs.

Ziegler seemed busy in there, though not so quick with coffee and cookies as his other church women. Still, he could smell something baking.

"Yes, and I thank you for the warm welcome you gave us, just when we needed it most." Walter Ziegler looked solemnly into the eyes of the pastor. "But there is one theological point I must have resolved, Pastor, and I would ask that our conversation together not leave this room."

"I will try to answer anything, to the best of my ability, and, of course, as your pastor, anything we speak of remains private, held in my heart."

"It is this, Herr Pastor. My wife and I would like to make a rather large donation to the church in the name of our baby, now in heaven. But before we do that, we would like you to join us in a glass of excellent German beer, if that would not violate your principles."

Pastor Julleland blinked and then laughed. "Ah, well! In the words of our spiritual father, Martin Luther, 'Let us drink beer!'" The moment these words left his mouth, Frieda Ziegler strode from the kitchen with a tray of three frosty glasses, a pitcher of beer, and a bowl of pretzels, crisp, brown, and hot from the oven.

29

BUILDING HOME

Uncle Erik's log cabin sat on the bank above Pearly Creek. Carrying off a pinch of soil each year for a thousand years, the little stream had carved itself a channel below the level of the wooded land above, so that visitors to the cabin half-slid, half-walked down the steep path to creekside. Once there, a fisherman found secure footing on the sand and rock edge of the stream, and a man equipped, as Anders was, with hip waders could stride right into the middle of the creek, stepping with some care out of respect for the rushing current and slippery rocks. A misstep could land a man smack on his backside in the swift water, gasping from the surprise and the cold of this snow-melt stream.

Anders waded up the creek, looking for a dark pool where trout lay, just waiting for his line and hook. "I'm on my way, boys," he crooned to the fish. "I'm comin' to get you." He turned and waved his fishing pole at Evelyn, sitting on a log beside the creek. She sat just where the sunlight met the shadow beneath the tall trees—fir, cedar, and aspen. She felt hidden, once Anders disappeared around a bend in the stream. The creek was infused with light, so that tan and copper rocks gleamed through the olive-green water. Other rocks, black spots on white stone, dappled as trout, resisted the push of the stream, making ripples and whipping up foam. Urged along by the melting snow and bubbling springs high in the mountains, the creek rushed down to join the Kootenai River. Around Evelyn lay a carpet of Solomon's seal, its sweet chartreuse leaves wind-shivered and silent in shadows cast by quaking aspen overhead.

A sound attracted Evelyn and she looked up. "Cheet cheet cheeteree." A yellow bird, brighter than a canary, but small as her ring finger, sang from the opposite bank over the roar of the stream. "Cheet cheet cheeteree," it called, hopping from branch to branch in the wind-tossed fir, singing to the yellow sun, or perhaps for the joy of being beautiful on this fine day. "Cheet cheet cheeteree." Evelyn smiled at its boldness, at its lack of modesty. Yet, she felt the same sweet assurance. "Yes," she whispered back to the bird. "We are both beautiful. We are both admired. We are both filled with life." She placed her hand on her stomach, hoping for some little movement, though she knew it was too soon for that. Only two months along, yet the doctor said a heart was beating in the tiny inch of this beginning of a baby. An inch—half the size of the singing yellow bird. "Yes, we are beautiful," she whispered again. "We are beautiful and filled with life."

In Axeton, the first trees cleared for milling were those that stood closest to Nehring Lumber Company. Crashing down, the giant trees fell, hills echoing, ground trembling from the smashing of timber against earth. Left behind were stumps—acres of stumps, square-mile sections of stumps, stretching across Axeton and into the foothills.

When Anders and Evelyn Nilsen bought a half-acre lot on the edge of town, the stumps confronted them like stubborn squatters on the land they now owned. How best to remove the stumps? They puzzled over that. Back in South Dakota, a farmer would dig around a stump, then attached a chain to a team of mules that pulled and sweated until finally the stump gave way. But South Dakota stumps were the few meager remains of willows. In Montana, ancient fir trees left stumps like broken columns of granite, heroic markers imbedded in the rocky ground.

Early one crisp, autumn Saturday, Anders sat on a stump and looked unhappily at twelve others, stuck here and there across his building site. Beyond the stumps on the lot west of his land, he saw a workman smoking a cigarette as he walked back and forth in front of his bulldozer. Anders called over, "Clearin' there today?"

"S'posed to be," called the man back, smoke drifting from his lungs into the cold air as he spoke. "Owner shoulda been here an hour ago."

"What are you charging these days for pullin' stumps?"

The man threw the stub of his cigarette into the dirt and rubbed it out with the toe of his boot. "Five bucks an hour." He threw the number out like a challenge, daring anyone to object to it.

Anders eyed the stumps, their roots stretched like talons gripping the rocks and dirt. "I might have that much right here," he said and patted the wallet in his back pocket. "Just hold on a minute. I'll get us some help."

On land to the east sat the cabin of Herman, a gyppo logger who dumped a load of logs at the mill from time to time. "Herman, you home?" Anders pounded on the cabin door. Herman opened the door and stood scowling. "Time to wake up, Herman. I've gotta job for you, with a bottle of beer at the end of it."

The three men attacked the stumps, Herman setting the choke, the driver heaving and dragging with his dozer, and Anders running from one stump to the next, pointing and shouting over the clattering of the engine and the ripping of roots from the soil. Finally, the driver cut the dozer engine, and in the silence, Anders looked around, his eyes making a final sweep over the lot. The stumps lay twisted in defeat, heaped in a pile for burning. He glanced down at his watch. Half an hour had passed. He grinned and walked to the dozer. "You know how to run that machine," he said and placed two one-dollar bills and a fifty-cent piece in the operator's hand.

"I was pretty much born to it," said the man, and he lit a cigarette, started up the engine, and guided the bulldozer back to the neighboring lot.

Anders turned to Herman, "Now, you old choke-setter, you've earned a bottle of something, and I don't mind having a taste myself, just to celebrate. Don't you be mentioning it to my wife though." And Herman, the bachelor logger, nodded and chuckled to himself, thinking how happy he was to be free of a woman. A woman, who in her soft and pretty way, would set a choke around your neck, telling you it was for your own good, keeping you, a hard-workin' man, from a sweet sip of brew you'd earned with your own salty sweat.

Now the half-acre lot lay open, a flat space surrounded by new sprouts of fir and spruce. Evelyn could imagine a little white house centered in the trees, square and neat, with a basement for winter storage of root vegetables—potatoes, carrots, and beets—and shelves for jars of fruit—pears, cherries, and peaches. She could see the fruit, lined up in rows of pints and quarts, glistening with sugary syrup, gleaming like rubies and pearls. These shiny urns would be her secret hoard against this Depression and the warring world.

A basement before all else. Anders and Evelyn borrowed Uncle Mathias' strange but strong little tractor and another machine called a "scoop" that the tractor pulled behind it. At first, Anders wanted to hire a workman to drive one of these two machines, while he drove the other. Evelyn wouldn't hear of the extravagance.

"I can drive a tractor. You don't grow up on a farm without knowing how to drive a tractor." She yanked on a pair of Anders' overalls and climbed onto the metal seat of the tractor. Her skeptical husband jumped aboard the second piece of equipment to operate the scoop, the big mechanical shovel that would carve out the basement.

The work at first was no harder than plowing a South Dakota field. The dirt in the northwest corner gave way easily, as Evelyn drove the tractor and pulled the mechanical scoop behind. Anders, riding on the second machine, swung the arm of the scoop to scrape up the soil with its ragged teeth. He pulled levers that lifted the arm up, swung it to the side, and deposited the dirt onto a berm forming beside the basement hole.

On the third day of digging, Evelyn heard a chugging in the engine and a grinding underneath. She cut the engine and yelled back to Anders.

"Andy, what's that noise? Is something wrong with the motor?"

"Just the dirt grinding," he yelled back. "Kinda rocky in this part. Montana scree."

From then on, every foot forward on the tractor was hard earned; every shovel full of rocks extracted its weight in human stubbornness. Often the grit and gravel jammed up the gears, so that everything stopped while Anders poked the stones out of the mechanical works. The digging proceeded by inches; at day's end the hole looked no bigger.

Yet, after a week, they could see progress. The hole was indeed many feet deeper. Standing on the edge, Evelyn felt a pleasantly dizzy sensation as she peered down into the earthy abyss. At the same time, she felt powerful, a five-foot-three giant of a woman who was literally carving out her own future.

Perhaps it was this heady mix of emotion that made her stop the tractor one evening just at the edge of the great basement hole. It might have been the overreaching confidence that allowed her to ignore the right rear tractor tire hanging precariously into space. Possibly it was the secret she alone knew that distracted her as the tractor began to wobble toward the drop-off. As Anders stared transfixed and horrified, Evelyn jumped down into the soft, caving dirt, just below the teetering tractor. The tractor trembled and shuddered above her.

"Run," Anders whispered, and then "Run!" shouting it out.

Evelyn scrambled away from the tractor to the middle of the basement hole. She stomped her feet wide apart into the dirt and lifted her face to her husband with a smile that said, "I am strong, I am yours, I am life!" The tractor, like a wild horse tamed by her fearless look, settled back into the soft soil of the bank above.

———

Both Anders and Evelyn knew very well that no one praised President Roosevelt—or any Democrat—in the presence of her father, Gustav Gustavson. Though not a man to swear without cause, he seemed unable to say "Democrat" without an emphatic "damn" in front of it, so that it became one explosive word: "Damndemocrat!" Certainly the Nilsen family in South Dakota deplored some New Deal policies as well, especially the slaughtering of cattle and bulldozing them into burial pits. The government compensated farmers for these cattle and claimed that the grisly policy helped to support the price of beef, but the sight of tons of wasted meat in a nation of hungry people was so abhorrent to Midwest farmers that they walked away from the carnage in disgust.

Yet other Roosevelt programs seemed to be helping folks, getting them fed and back to work, and as Evelyn and Anders considered building a house in Axeton, they heard of a plan coming out of Washington, D.C., offering ten-percent down government housing loans.

"We wouldn't have to tell Pa about this," said Evelyn, her eyes fixed on her folded hands.

"No need to do that," answered Anders. With persistence, he had finally won over Berit, Evelyn's mother, but her father still seemed unconvinced. The key to his father-in-law's complete approval would be Anders' ability to shelter and provide for Evelyn and any children to come. His competence as a provider was still an open question in the mind of Gus Gustavson. A sturdy house of their own would be a mark in Anders' favor, but they would most certainly not confess that it had been built with a loan from President Roosevelt's New Deal.

On Monday morning, Evelyn and Anders sat across the desk from the bank director. Both men wore suits, though Anders' shone from age and wear about the knees. Evelyn's navy and white polka-dot dress fell in ruffles just at her knees. The bank director liked this young couple on sight. What optimism! Abundant good cheer in an economic depression that seemed endless. So it was with regret that he said to them, "You've just begun your job, Mr. Nilsen. You can't expect to afford a house just starting out." Sadly, but firmly, he turned them down for the government-backed housing loan.

That might have been the end of it, but they both had in their bones the mettle of their homesteading grandparents. "What about the mill? All that lumber stacking up with no buyers. They must want to move it." Evelyn turned from the cookstove and thrust her hands deep into her apron pockets.

"Maybe." Anders' frown lifted itself into a grin. "Mr. Nehring slapped me on the back after the baseball game last week. Maybe he'll remember me, even without my catcher's mitt."

So it was that when Anders spoke, cap in hand, to J. B. Nehring, owner of the lumber company, the big boss agreed to give him lumber on credit as needed for the house. Limping along as it was in these bleak times, the lumber company still aimed to come out even, so the paymaster took twenty dollars a month from Anders' check as payment for the lumber.

From then on, good luck or Providence seemed to guide the construction of their solid little house. One day Anders spotted a boxcar of lumber on a side track by the loading platform. "Where's that one going?" he asked the loading boss.

"Going nowhere. Shame, too. Clear lumber, but the shop grooved it wrong and the customer sent it back."

"We've been buying grade-two lumber for our place." Anders looked with envy at the clear wood.

"If you want it, take it. Sell it to you for the grade-two price." Anders' boss marched away, glad to be done with it. Anders looked at the car of clear lumber, more lumber than they needed. But the whole load for seventy dollars! He pictured the fine wood everywhere in the house, every wall, every floor, all covered with clear wood, not a blemish in the lot.

Plumbing was another matter. The Sears and Roebuck catalog offered package deals for pipes and fixtures. Anders sent a plan—"plumbing schemata," Sears called it—and the pipes came cut and threaded, with tools and instructions for installation. The pipes arrived just as ordered, but because of a change in the house plans, one pipe needed rethreading. The Nehring Lumber Company shop had the only pipe threading equipment in Axeton.

"Lars, it'll take you five minutes to do it." But Lars, with four children and a wife to support, wasn't about to take the chance of using company time and equipment for rethreading Anders' pipe.

"Not risking my job. You want to do it, show up for the night shift, 3:00 early Sunday morning. Nobody's around then. You watch me on the machine and then do it yourself."

At 3:00 the next morning, Anders stepped up to the pipe threading machine, and Lars walked out of the shop for his break. Anders inserted the pipe into the threader and clamped down. Mingled with the scrape of the clamp came other sounds—of a door opening and of men's voices. He kept his head down, eyes on the pipe, but he could feel a bead of sweat emerge on his upper lip. One of the voices behind him belonged to J. B. Nehring. The company owner was showing his fishing and drinking buddies through the mill after a Saturday of hooking trout and a Saturday night of celebrating their catch.

"Right here's the threader," called out Nehring with pride. "New machine. Threads any pipe in minutes." He stopped and looked at Anders. "Didn't know you worked nights."

Anders met the big boss's gaze with the steady, innocent eyes of a prairie lad. "Oh yeah. Part of the time."

Nehring nodded and moved a bit unsteadily onto the next machine. "And over here is the steel cutter. Slices through steel up to an inch thick." A man in the group shouted, "The best machine shop in Montana, J. B.!" The bunch of them stumbled out into the night. For a week, Anders stiffened each time a fore-man walked toward him, expecting to be fired. Only after J. B. Nehring came to a baseball game the next Saturday to root for the team did Anders finally relax.

"Now, you say there's nothing good about beer, Evie." Anders lifted his coffee cup, clicking it against the cup in Evelyn's hand, as they sat together after the game in the kitchen of their rented house. "But I'll tell you this. If the boss hadn't had a few that night, I'd be out of a job."

Evelyn didn't reply. She put down her cup and pulled the Sears and Roebuck catalog in front of her, opening it to the page that displayed bathroom fixtures. The catalog offered a special deal if a customer bought all three fixtures together—the sink, the tub, and the toilet. Still, they couldn't afford that much money all at one time. Evelyn took out paper and pen, and in her careful school teacher penmanship wrote a letter:

To the Sears, Roebuck and Company Plumbing Fixtures Manager
Dear Sir:

Please note in your ledger that the Nilsens of Axeton, Montana, have ordered and taken delivery of considerable pipes and other materials from your establishment. Please further note that all bills concerning this transaction were paid promptly and in full, and that all tools provided on loan from your company for the installation of these pipes were returned in good condition.

With this record on our part, we now have a reasonable re-quest to make, which we have every expectation that your compa-ny will honor. We would like to buy a sink, a bathtub, and a toilet from Sears and Roebuck, knowing the excellent quality of your products and appreciating your offer of a discount on the price when all three items are purchased. We cannot at this time pro-vide the total amount of money, however, and make this proposal:

we will order all three of the items, but we will take delivery and make payment for one item at a time, beginning with the toilet. As finances allow, we will request delivery and send payment for the sink, and finally, the bathtub.

Please notify us of your decision at your earliest convenience.

Sincerely,

Mr. and Mrs. Anders Nilsen

Two weeks later, an envelope arrived from Sears and Roebuck. Evelyn opened it and read:

Dear Mr. and Mrs. Nilsen:

We are pleased to accommodate your proposal. Your toilet will be shipped upon receipt of payment, with sink and bathtub to follow when requested. Although we require full payment on the first two items, when the final item is shipped, your bill will be substantially reduced to reflect the purchase of all three items.

Appreciative of your continued patronage, we remain,

Sincerely yours,

William J. Parker, Manager

Sears, Roebuck and Company

Evelyn thrust the letter in Anders' face as soon as he came home from work. He raised his shaggy eyebrows in surprise as he read it.

"You bargain like a Gypsy, my little Swedish wife." He grabbed her around the waist and twirled her into a quick polka step.

"I saved you from building an outdoor privy!" she said.

"And saved yourself from being eaten by a big black bear some snowy night on your way to the privy."

"So you think I did a good thing, writing to them, Andy?"

"A very good thing, my *svenska flicka*." They fell together onto the worn and sagging couch, and he kissed her.

———

No one knew. No one knew, except the two of them, about the baby. And Dr. Miller, who called it a fetus. "The fetus is about four months along," he said in a voice filled with professional experience and scientific knowledge. Evelyn, as she whispered to it, touching her belly, called it "baby" from the first. "Are you warm, my baby?" she said each cold morning. "I love you, little baby," she murmured as she drifted into sleep at night.

Then one day there was a scarlet spot on her white panties and cramping in her stomach. They had no phone, so Anders rode his bicycle to the doctor's office, and the doctor drove to their house and put her to bed. "It may subside," he said, "or it may not. These things happen," he said. "The fetus may be malformed. Nature knows best."

When it was over, they told no one. She felt ashamed that she could not do what a woman is created to do. "She lost the baby," people would say, if they knew. So she wept in her husband's arms in a dark house with the curtains drawn. She felt his throat go tight, but his breathing stayed steady. When she looked up through her tears, his eyes were dry, staring at a distant point beyond the bedroom wall. His hand moved up her back to the nape of her neck, his fingers slipping through her hair, drawing her head more firmly against his chest.

Out among people she smiled and chatted, amazed at herself and amazed that shopkeepers still kept shop, that men still went to the mill, and that baseball games still filled the park with cheering crowds. It should all have come to a halt—all of it, in honor of this tiny lost baby.

Half a year later, Evelyn became pregnant again. This time she felt tentative, cautious, apprehensive. She waited until her prominent stomach announced the pregnancy to the neighborhood before writing to her mother about it. In the final month, the baby kicked and turned. She could feel its fist drag across her belly. One evening she placed Anders' hand on the baby's energetic swings.

"A baseball player," he grinned, and she smiled back.

Evelyn visited the hospital where two of her friends rested in adjoining rooms, one having given birth to a girl and one to a boy. The babies were adorable chubby red-faced little bundles, as alike as two tomatoes on a vine, said the nurse, picking up one from the nursery and depositing it in its mother's bed. With firm hands and brisk stride, she placed the second baby with its mother. "Whew," said the first mom, "this little guy needs a change," and she unwrapped her baby. "Oh," she said, "wrong baby. You gave me the girl!" The nurse and the two mothers laughed and remarked again at how much the babies looked alike. "Good thing their bottom halves are different," giggled the baby girl's mother, "or we'd never tell these two apart!"

Evelyn was horrified. On her walk back home, she stopped at the house of a nurse who took in one birthing mother at a time, and Evelyn arranged to have her baby there. A few weeks later, when the infant came forth with a mighty cry, Doctor Miller handed the baby girl to the nurse, who washed her, wrapped her snug in a cotton blanket, and laid her beside her mother. "You have a healthy daughter," called the nurse to Anders, who was pacing in the hallway. He came into the room and looked down at his wife's face, shining with sweat and triumph. "Wonderful," he said. "You—her—wonderful." The words trembled slightly, and he bent down to brush the tops of their heads with his lips.

Then he turned with a grin to shake hands with the doctor and to slap a cigar into his hand. "Thanks, Doc," he said. "Fine little girl, Andy. What's her name going to be?" Evelyn answered. "'Karen' after Andy's mother Kari. And 'Grace'—it means 'gift.'"

"That's it: Karen—Grace—Nilsen." Anders pronounced the name slowly and firmly, like a radio announcer intoning: "President—Franklin—Delano—Roosevelt."

The nurse kept mother and baby for ten days, pampering Evelyn with oven-fresh meals, long naps, and sweet-smelling lotions. "Best vacation I ever had," she said to the nurse as she left for home with Karen in her arms. "And I know this is my baby—my very own."

30

WAR

The radio crackled news of a Japanese attack.

"Where is Pearl Harbor?"

"Hawaiian Islands," answered Anders. "Shh!" He leaned down so that his forehead touched the wooden face of the radio. "What does it mean?"

"That's U.S. territory. I'd say we're at war." He looked at Evelyn and baby Karen, his eyes and mouth tight.

In the next days, a barrage of news and rumors ricocheted around the shops, the mill, and the homes of Axeton. "Jap subs on the coast!" said a worker with a brother in California. "They got a treaty—Japan, Germany, Italy," said another. "All us men are registered. The army'll call us up now."

A line of volunteers formed at the U.S. Army office, mostly young, unmarried men. Seventeen-year-olds begged their parents to sign permission waivers for them to enlist. Not a mother signed, though some fathers did, and recruiters took the word of other fuzzy-faced high school lads.

Men who hesitated felt a certain guilt. "Uncle Sam Wants You!" said the posters. Anders balanced the country's needs against his own fear and Evelyn's tearful pleas. "You're a husband, a father, Andy. In the name of God, don't volunteer!"

"I'll be drafted anyway."

"Maybe not. We could move to Seattle. They say men welding up bombers in the Boeing factory don't get drafted."

"I'm not running to Seattle, Evie. I won't volunteer, but I won't run."

And then, through Evelyn's prayers or by simple chance, the announcement came from the mill: Lumber is needed for a thousand government defense projects. This mill is classified as essential industry. All Nehring Lumber Mill workers are frozen on the job. Stay and the draft board won't touch you. Leave your job, and you're on your way to war.

Evelyn's oldest brother, Will, already in the army, wrote letters from Fort Lewis as he waited for orders. Henry worked at a government job in Washington, D.C., and Herbert was sent as a civilian for cleanup and reconstruction work in Hawaii. Her youngest brother, Russell, joined the navy and shipped out with the Pacific fleet.

Uncle Mathias and Aunt Inga's daughter, Betty, married a young recruit named Donald, who enlisted with her brother, Norm. "We'll watch each other's back," said her husband as the two men dearest to her waved from the window of the train. Betty stood watching until the caboose disappeared around a curve in the track. From their honeymoon cottage in Axeton, she moved back to her childhood bedroom in the log farmhouse.

Names of casualties were printed in the newspaper in alphabetical order, and every day the eyes of mothers and fathers, sisters and brothers, relatives and friends searched the list, praying not to see the name of a loved one. Civilian sacrifices seemed small by comparison, so those left in Axeton tried not to complain about rationing. Now every man had a job, many women, too, but wages couldn't buy goods in short supply. The war effort came first, and those at home made do. Mothers traded ration cards—sugar for children's shoes. Young doctors shipped out with the troops along with medical supplies; old doctors scurried from one house to another, with little time or medicine. In their stead, a mother counted on her neighbors' folk remedies and her own whispered prayers.

———

The two little ones played on a blue and white quilt, crawling and scooting from one pieced square to another, sometimes straying beyond the scalloped edge. One mother, without missing a word of her friend's conversation, would then reach down to redirect the child from the cold floor to the warmth of the quilt. David, almost two years old, showed great patience with Karen, eighteen months. She adored him and grabbed him by the ears to kiss him on the eyes and nose. Then she rested her head on her favorite quilt patch, embroidered with a mommy duck swimming with her two white ducklings. Karen kissed the ducks on their bright orange beaks.

"This time of year it's so hard to keep the house warm." Gertrude poured another cup of coffee for Evelyn and passed her coffee cake.

"No, no, I couldn't. I've got to get this weight off. Those months in maternity smocks, I just ate and ate."

"You look fine, Evie. Men like a little meat on a woman. One more piece, so I won't think you don't like my baking." Gertrude pushed the pink china plate of cinnamon-topped cake right under her friend's nose.

"Well, just one more. They smell so good. But you shouldn't have wasted your sugar ration on me."

"I'm not wasting it on you. You're the excuse. I'm doing it this morning for me. And here I go with another slice!" Gertrude plunked a slab of cake down on her own plate, nibbled off a corner, and took a swig of coffee to wash it down.

Now David toddled off the blanket again. Evelyn lifted him up, settled him next to her own little Karen, and patted the wisp of brown hair that lay against his forehead.

"I think he's a little warm. What do you think, Trudy?" It was the only touchy point between these new mothers, for one to suggest anything about the care of the other's child.

Gertrude undid the top button of David's sweater and looked out the kitchen window. The October snow fell gently, tiny flakes seeming to have no weight at all as they drifted down to the frozen earth. "I say you can't keep them warm enough in this kind of weather."

"Well, you're probably right." Evelyn looked again at David, whose cheeks seemed unusually pink. Then he coughed.

"That's the other thing," Gertrude picked up David and held him on her lap. "He's got this cough. It's not often. But I do like to keep him warm." David coughed again.

At week's end, David's cough came night and day. In another week, Karen began coughing. Not much at first. She had a runny nose, so it might have been just a cold. By November, the cough came more often and sank deep into her little chest. The doctor arrived at the house, listened to Karen's breathing, handed Evelyn a honey syrup, and told her to keep the toddler indoors.

Evelyn stepped between the doctor and the door. "She hasn't been out for weeks, and she's getting worse."

The doctor seemed offended. "In my professional medical opinion, this has the look of whooping cough. I have given you the best kind of syrup we have in wartime, and all we can do in these cases is to wait."

During the day, between coughing spells, Karen played contentedly with her toys and books. Then another choking, gasping fit came, with nothing to do but to cradle her until it stopped. Evelyn and Anders moved her crib into their room, rubbed her chest with a vaporous salve, and took turns at night when the number of coughing attacks increased to fifteen, even twenty times, before morning light.

On the night of November 10, a Tuesday night, Karen gave a rapid burst of coughs and then, with a high, gasping wheeze, strained to pull air back into her lungs.

Evelyn, holding her, called out to Anders, who sat upright, turned on the light and leaned across the bed. "What is it?"

"She can't breathe. She's not breathing."

The parents watched in horror as Karen's face took on a bluish cast and her body went limp.

Crying in desperation, Evelyn held her out to Anders. His rough carpenter hands received the little body, pressed it to his shoulder, and released it again to the softness of the bed. Karen gasped, her in-breath sounding a faint, high-pitched whistle. She sucked in another breath and opened her eyes. She looked up at her mother and father and reached out a little hand to each of them.

By the first week in December, both David and Karen ran about and chattered incessantly to each other. Their mothers sat again at Gertrude's kitchen table, watching the little ones play. "Don't look like they could have been sick," remarked Gertrude, stirring heavy yellow cream into her black coffee.

"They can't even remember, not like us—we'll never forget those nights. Still, they're alive and well now."

"You have to wonder, from all the pain and heartache, why it is we have children," said Gertrude.

"Yes, and why we keep on having more." Evelyn smiled as she patted her stomach.

"Gad, Evie, I thought you were just eating too much of my cake. How on earth did you and Andy have time to do that, in the middle of all this trouble?"

"Just crazy, I guess," said Evelyn.

31

SILLY OLD GOOSE

By her second birthday, Karen knew all the nursery rhymes in her red and yellow Mother Goose book. Evelyn bit her tongue more than once to keep from bragging to other mothers whose toddlers spoke only a scattering of words. Karen snuggled into her mother's lap and looked at the pictures of Little Bo Peep and Old King Cole, as she reeled off the verses one after another. Her favorite—and the one she considered as funny as funny could be—pictured a frantic white bird surrounded by a cloud of feathers.

"Once there was a silly old goose
Who cackled so much all her feathers came loose."

Here Karen pointed to the feathers swirling around in the picture, and she dissolved into uncontrollable giggles. After catching her breath, Karen finished the poem.

"'My goodness,' she cried as she looked all around,
'It's only July, and there's snow on the ground!'"

Karen looked up at her mother to share the joke, and they smiled at each other.

"Silly old goose!" said Evelyn.

"Silly old goose!" echoed Karen.

Evelyn put down the book and held Karen by her shoulders at arm's length. "Look at me."

There was something about Karen's eyes. The left one wandered a bit before focusing on Evelyn. It happened at dinner time, too, as the child's eyes tried to center in on her spoon and plate. Back in Brem, a boy in school had an eye like that. He wasn't quite normal in other ways. He couldn't learn in class and was finally sent away somewhere.

For that long week, as she waited for an appointment with Doctor Miller, Evelyn couldn't sleep. She listened as the clock struck each hour and spent the fifty-nine minutes between each chime inventing sad scenarios for her daughter. Perhaps it was a brain tumor pressing against the eye. Maybe a disease of some sort that would spread and create mental retardation in this bright little child. Blindness was a possibility. Evelyn, who had longed so for a baby, had not foreseen this heartache, this extreme sensitivity to anything that might harm her little girl. If only she could wrap the child in blankets of fluffy cotton, protecting her from every pain.

Anders took another view of bringing up his daughter. He assumed that, like his farm-raised sisters, Karen would be athletic and healthy. He first rolled a ball to her and then tossed it into her waiting hands. She fumbled the catch, but threw the ball back, right to him. "A pitcher!" he said.

Anders rode a bicycle to the lumber mill each work day, and as soon as the closing whistle sounded, he hopped on his bike and rode the mile back home. By the time he reached the corner of their block, Karen spied him from the front porch and ran to meet him. He scooped her up into the bike's wire basket, and she rode home clinging to the handlebars, screaming with delight. "She'll be fine," he said to Evelyn on the day of the doctor appointment.

Doctor Miller examined her and suggested glasses. If that didn't do it, a routine surgery in Spokane might be in order.

"The problem most certainly can be fixed," he said kindly, seeing the dark circles under Evelyn's eyes. "I'll give you a rule to live by. If something won't be a problem a year from now, it's not a problem worth worrying about."

Both parents took great care to admire Karen's little gold-rimmed glasses, so she wore them with pride. When she looked at storybooks, her mother slipped a bit of paper between the lens of her glasses and her right eye, forcing the lazy left eye to work. By the end of May, the focus of Karen's eyes converged straight and true on her picture book, the jelly toast on her breakfast plate, or the tiny hand of her new baby sister.

———————

Evelyn peered out the bedroom window, nestling baby Clara against her breast. With her free hand, she directed two-year-old Karen's head to the springtime scene outside. "Look, the little brown bird on the honeysuckle vine. See? Just above the orange flowers. It's singing to us."

Karen pressed her face against the window glass, pushing her little glasses up to the bridge of her nose and clouding the chilly window with her warm breath. Evelyn used the edge of the baby's blanket to wipe the window clear again.

"That's a mommy bird, and she's building a nest in the bushes there. We can watch her. She'll put eggs in it—and after a while we'll see some baby birds."

Karen's eyes went wide. "Mommy bird? Baby bird?"

"Yes, remember the mommy deer and baby deer that came in the yard? Birds have babies, too."

And I have babies. Evelyn shifted Clara to her other breast, and the little head, covered with reddish fuzz, emitted hungry, slurping noises. Karen snuggled against them both, watching as the little sparrow gathered bits of grass and twigs for its nest—and listening as it paused to whistle again and again its pretty song.

Through late spring and early summer Evelyn and little Karen peeked through the window at the song sparrow's nest. It was so close to the house that they could see tiny beaks reaching up for bugs that the mother bird scratched from the dirt using a hopping motion, both feet at once.

Then something strange happened. The mother bird left her little ones and began building another nest in a bush just a skip and a flutter away from her babies. Her song changed, and maybe it held a command, because the father bird swooped in and began feeding the chicks she had left behind.

By the end of the week, the new nest was finished; and in a day more, four blue-green eggs lay in the feathery circle. The song sparrow sat on the nest, hustling off only for a quick bite of bugs and a joyful song from the honeysuckle vine.

"Maybe she's singing to her babies inside the eggs. I used to sing to you when you were in my tummy." Karen smiled, spread out her arms, and raised her shoulders in her particular gesture of wonderment.

A day later, something even more peculiar happened. A new egg appeared in the song sparrow's nest, bigger than the other three and different in color—white with brown specks. The song sparrow didn't seem to notice the extra egg, and she spread her wings and nestled her feathery breast over all of them. When the birds hatched, she fed the big, awkward chick with as much devotion as her little ones.

For once, Evelyn was a mystified as Karen. Over Sunday dinner in the log farmhouse beyond Pearly Creek, she turned to Uncle Mathias and Aunt Inga. "You've lived here in Montana for onto twenty years. Have you ever seen anything like what's going on in our back yard?" And she described the song sparrow's two nests and the large, strange egg in the second nest.

"*Vel*, now," said Mathias, happy to pass wisdom on to these young folks. "*Vel*, now, you see, you could learn a lot from these birds. The *fuglereir*—the bird nest of the song sparrow—that little bird that sings so pretty—she makes a second nest and moves on so that her lazy husband has to feed the first brood. Pretty smart. But then you have an even more *flink* bird, the clever one we call the cow bird. She makes no nest at all of her own but sneaks her eggs into a neighbor's nest. Most times, it works. Her neighbor lady bird hatches and feeds the cow bird's baby until it's ready to fly. Then all the cow birds, the whole fam-damnly, fly off to the *varme* south, leaving the poor little song sparrow here in cold Mont*awna*."

The next day, they watched the song sparrow feed her chicks—the three small ones and the fourth chick, twice as big as the others. Evelyn and Karen listened again to the song sparrow as she paused in her mothering to sing her joyful song. Evelyn wondered, does she know what is ahead for her family? Will she be ready? Their own house was unfinished inside. Bare two-by-four beams held batts of insulation, and plumbing pipes poked into the bathroom, still unconnected to the tub and sink. And yet, the house was sturdy and warm, ready for the coldest Montana weather.

A melody from Evelyn's childhood flitted around in her head. "Listen, Karen," she said. "Here's a song about a bird."

"The north wind doth blow,
And we shall have snow,
And what will the birdy do then, the poor thing.
She'll fly to the barn, just to keep herself warm,
and tuck her head under her wing, the poor thing."

"Mathias barn? Inga barn?" asked Karen.

"Yes, maybe our little bird will fly this winter into Uncle Mathias' big log barn and keep herself as snug and warm as you, little girl!" And Evelyn wrapped an arm around her daughter and listened again to the hope-filled tune of the song sparrow.

32

Lost

With determined strides, Evelyn pushed the baby buggy. She hurried the buggy and Karen, scampering along beside her, down the unpaved road toward their house. So focused was Evelyn on her goal that she scarcely glanced at the distant Cabinet Mountains, their craggy peaks still shimmering with snow in the July sunshine.

In the buggy, along with Karen's strawberry-blond baby sister, was a small ham for lunch. Anders, with an hour's break from loading boxcars at the lumber mill, rode home on his bicycle every day to toss down a stack of sandwiches made with Evelyn's home-baked bread. Very soon now the noon whistle at the mill would signal the lunch break for the working men. Evelyn grabbed Karen's hand and pushed the buggy even faster. Karen planted her little feet and forced her mother to stop.

"What is it?"

"David?" Karen answered with a plea.

Karen, just a few months more than two years old, went almost every day to play with David, who lived across the street. Evelyn watched her little girl cross the gravel road and wave back from the gate in front of David's house. The lumber company whistle screeched as Evelyn shouldered open the front door, one arm wrapped around the baby, the other around the ham.

Karen waited for a moment, watching the door close. Then, looking down at the road through her little round glasses, she spied a very interesting rock and began to kick at it. The rock rolled away from her, and she stepped up to it and kicked it again—and then again. Kick, walk, kick, walk—she concentrated on the rhythm of it, the smooth round stone rolling obediently at the impact of her white leather shoe. Kick, walk, kick, walk. The summer sun warmed her white-blond curls, and she paused to look at its glare. Dark branches framed the sunlight. Then she looked around her. She was in the midst of trees. She was lost.

In that place, Axeton, Montana, and at that time, 1943, a small child was vulnerable to particular dangers and safe from others. Far north in western Montana, surrounded by forest and mountains, the little town had a population of a thousand loggers, farmers, and trappers, with as many or more elk, deer, mink, and bear at its borders. Pearly Creek ran through the town, and swift little branches of it, a few feet wide with grassy edges, rippled through back yards and gardens. Trout wriggled along Pearly Creek, and any fisherman with a mite of skill could go out before breakfast and fill his family's table with a mess of fish in an hour's time. The main channel though, after snow-melt, could carry even a big man away, and mothers watched their children on picnics, sometimes even tying a rope around the middle of an unpredictable child to keep the babe a safe distance from the rushing water.

So, lost in the woods at the age of two, Karen was in danger from the river and the bear and from the vast, untrackable forest. She was not, though, in danger from any person, man or woman, who might happen upon her. At the core of this community was a solid belief that whatever might come—the depression or the war, injury or death, good times or terrible—in the soul of this town was a firm belief that people here would help you get through whatever trouble there was.

Karen stood small and alone where the road ended, beyond the town's houses on the edge of the deep woods. She looked into the dark forest and up at the yellow sun. She looked down at a tiny ladybug on her arm, and then at her white stockings and shoes. She could hear the chirping of grasshoppers and the distant roar of the creek. She sat down in the crisp dry grass and looked up the empty road for a long time. She covered her face with her hands, pushing her little gold-rimmed glasses tightly against her nose. The sun felt hot on her head and neck.

"Well, what are you doing here, all alone!" Karen heard a voice above her. She opened her eyes and looked up at a tall woman in a blue dress. The woman seemed to be part of the bright blue sky, except for her shiny, brown hair which was caught up in the white web of a hairnet. Karen stood up and brushed the dirt off her dress and stockings.

"Whose little girl are you?" said the woman. "What's your name?"

Karen tried to say her name, "Karen Grace Nilsen," but she couldn't say her "r's" or "l's" clearly.

"Well, never mind. We'll get you home."

The woman lifted Karen up onto her hip and carried her back to where the houses began. The woman's house was the one closest to the woods, the last on the phone line. The criss-cross of Axeton's roads ended at the telephone pole in front of her house. Still holding Karen, she phoned her boss, the lumber company lawyer. "Strangest thing," she said. "I went walking and found a little blond-haired girl sitting in the woods. She must be lost. But how she got there, I don't know. I'll be late to work. I have to find out where she lives. Her parents must be frantic."

Before long, a black car with a big man in it pulled up in front of the house. "It's my boss," said the lady in the white hairnet, her brown eyes looking directly into Karen's. "He's going to help me find your mother and father."

The three drove all around Axeton, looking at houses and talking to people. "Is this your street?" the man and woman kept asking. "Can you say your name again—slowly?" Many times the man stopped his car and asked someone who was walking, "Do you know whose little girl this is?" Finally, a man in overalls and a plaid red shirt smiled and nodded. "Her dad's Anders Nilsen. Works at the mill." He pointed to a house up the way. "There," he said. "She lives there!"

Then everyone was shouting and laughing and crying all at once. Evelyn, Anders, and the neighbors, who had been looking everywhere, rushed to the car as it pulled up. The man driving the car jumped out, lifted Karen from the seat, and held her high over his head while he turned around and around in a circle, so she was spinning high above everyone, higher than her mother, higher than her father, higher than her house, higher than the trees, higher than the sun!

Next to their house was a pasture surrounded by a fence built to corral a neighbor's frisky young horse. In spring and early summer the pony, hoping for an apple or carrot, wandered over to the fence to visit with Evelyn and the little girls. It occurred to Evelyn that the grassy pasture would easily support another animal, so with the neighbor's permission, she added a cow to the meadow. Milk from the cow brought in a bit of money, which Evelyn secreted away in a little wooden box hidden in a bureau beneath her cotton panties and her white silk wedding slip. During the day, as she cooked meals and bathed the girls, Evelyn considered what might be done with her small stash of coins and dollar bills. Something that would last. Something beyond the reach of their tight budget. Finally, she saw it in the home of their widower friend Hugo. An upright piano.

"Do you play the piano, Hugo?"

"*Nei*—not me. I have a tin ear, you know. Frida used to play, and quite well, too. Now I just use it for holding up the old family pictures."

"Would you sell it to me? I'd pay a fair price." She inherited her father's business sense, toes to fingertips, and she knew what the piano was worth.

"Take it. It's no good to me, and no one to pass it on to when I'm in the ground."

Tempting as it was, this offer of a free piano, Evelyn had a moral streak. What she did not want done to her, she would not do to another. Fairness, not greed, was the Gustavson family code of business.

"I'll tell you what, Hugo. I have a little money from selling milk to the neighbors. Add to that my cleaning of this dusty little cabin of yours once a week, and after two months, I'll collect the piano. But only if you will come over then to hear me play a tune for you."

On the first Saturday evening in October, Hugo accepted an invitation to have a pork chop dinner and a sing-along with Anders and Evelyn. After the first song, *"Du Gamla, Du Fria,"* about the beauty of Sweden, Hugo mercifully silenced his low monotone and listened with a smile as Evelyn played his old

piano and harmonized with Anders to "Oh, Suzanna," and
"Daisy, Daisy, Give Me Your Answer, Do!"

Her clear soprano and his rich baritone blended in close-
woven harmony, seeming to Evelyn like interlaced strands tying
Anders to her, as a willful pony might be firmly tethered with
braided leather and guided down a sensible path. For Anders
reminded her at times of a young horse, distracted by a passing
butterfly or startled by a hooting owl, not knowing which road
to take. He could work—work so hard that no amount of food
could put meat on his skinny frame. But baseball or hunting or
fishing or talking to a complete stranger—any of these could
draw him away from useful tasks for the better part of a day.
What would her father Gustav think of that, if he knew of it?

And then there was beer, which she suspected he drank
when it was offered to him by one of his uncles or hunting pals.
She had never seen him unsteady on his feet; neither had she
smelled it on his breath. All she knew was that anyone in the
Nilsen family who touched alcohol sooner or later became a
drunk—look at his brother Rolf.

Whenever she mentioned the dangers of alcohol to him, he
changed the subject. He had the devil's own way of teasing her,
making her laugh, and gathering her into his arms. That ended
any serious talk they might have had. So it went.

33

PICNIC

In the springtime of 1945, a newsreel announcer said the war might be over soon. Hitler and his Nazi troops were on the run. The world could be settling down to something normal again. Cousin Betty had a baby boy, born into her mother Inga's hands in the log farmhouse. Betty sent the happy news in a letter, hoping it would get to Germany and her husband, Donald, gone now three years except for short visits home on leave.

Medicines were still in short supply. Her baby got the croup and coughed in wracking hacks. Then its tiny body shrank into itself with pathetic whimpers. Finally—silence. Within a week, two telegrams came to the log farmhouse. The first announced the death in action of her brother; the second said her husband had been killed near Berlin. Folks said they didn't see how Betty could go on living, but somehow she did.

Then, first in Europe and finally in the Pacific, the war was over. No one called it a war to end all wars as they had said of World War I. When the news of this war's end crackled across the nation, people filled the streets and cities and went mad with joy. Afterward, the same people sat in movie theaters, stunned by newsreel footage of bombed-out London and Cologne and of the dead and near-dead of Auschwitz and Buchenwald. The world after this war was desperately in need of repair.

———

Uncle Will was a soldier in Germany. In the picture he sent to Axeton, he was standing very straight in his uniform, and a big dog with a long nose was sitting beside him. Karen said that it must be fun, being in the war with a dog. Her daddy said war is never fun and the dog was not for playing. The dog had a job, too.

Uncle Herbert didn't have a uniform. During the war, he worked fixing broken boats on a faraway island, and when he came to Axeton, he wore a green shirt covered with big yellow flowers. He brought Karen a dried grass skirt that made a rustling sound when she moved, and a stiff-feeling brown and tan sun top that tied around her neck and middle. She wouldn't take it off for three days, and she did the hula dance that Uncle Herbert taught her. She learned that "hula" means you move your hands from one side to the other and wiggle your hips. Young Uncle Russell was wearing his navy uniform when he got off the train with Uncle Herbert. Karen saw that he was tall—even taller than her daddy.

"Do you have any little girls?" asked Karen. Uncle Russell said, no, they had to find ladies crazy enough to marry them first. The uncles played croquet out in the yard with Karen and Clara, and then Uncle Herbert picked Karen up and said to Uncle Russell, "This one's no good, I think I'll throw her away," and he threw her up in the air, and Uncle Russell caught her. They did the same to Clara, and then to Karen again, and the little girls screamed and couldn't stop laughing until Mommy made the uncles quit and come in to dinner. After a week, the uncles had to get back on the train and go to Oregon to live there with Grandma and Grandpa Gustavson.

Daddy and Mommy brought the girls home from the train station and tucked them into bed. Mommy read them a story, and then they said nighttime prayers—three prayers. "Our Father, who art in heaven" was the longest, and Daddy said it in Norwegian after the girls said it in English. "Now I lay me down to sleep" was next, and then one, not exactly a prayer, more of a poem.

> "Pretty stars, overhead
> Looking down on my bed.
> Can they be God's kind eyes
> Watching me from the skies?"

The poem ends in a question, but the girls didn't ask it like a question, with their voices going up high; Karen and Clara, even with her two-year-old lisp, said it flat and strong with voices that said, this is really true. Their parents said it softly with their eyes closed.

As soon as the soldiers didn't need all the trains anymore, Oregon Grandma Gustavson came for a visit. Mommy said that Grandpa Gustavson couldn't be pulled away from the houses he rented out to people in Oregon. Karen had a picture in her mind of Oregon Grandma grabbing Oregon Grandpa by the belt, trying to pull him away from his little houses, like the ones in the Monopoly game, and finally giving up. To keep her company on the train, Oregon Grandma brought Janice, Karen's almost grown-up cousin.

With Oregon Grandma in the house, Karen had to sit quietly on the couch and play with her doll. Grandma asked Karen, did she sew yet, and Karen shook her head. Grandma Gustavson said maybe she would learn pretty soon. Karen nodded and looked at her doll and then at her daddy.

"Tell you what," said Daddy, "we'll go on a picnic."

Karen pushed her doll off her lap and onto the couch. "And fishing?"

"Of course, fishing."

"Me?"

"Yes, you're old enough now, I think."

"Clara?"

"No, she's still too little. Maybe next summer for her."

Karen felt her ribs lift up and her back straighten. Inside her head a voice whispered, "I am old enough."

They all piled into a car that her daddy borrowed from Hugo, the old man who lived down the street. Karen sat on Janice's lap and bounced around as the car rolled over the roughly paved road out of town and then down a rock and gravel road to Pearly Creek. Karen watched as her daddy spread out the blankets, and her mommy and Grandma Gustavson laid out the picnic food—lots of it.

Karen sat on the log in a short, print cotton dress, her white cotton panties and bare legs pressed against the scratchy wool blanket stretched over the fallen tree trunk. Through her little gold-rimmed glasses, she gazed transfixed at her thirteen-year-old cousin, Janice. Janice had on long pants, although the two little sisters and the grown-up women at this picnic all wore dresses. Mommy sat on the edge of the cotton cloth spread on the ground, her legs tucked sideways under her short polka dot skirt. Oregon Grandma wore her second-best housedress with swirls of yellow flowers stamped on brown. A leather belt held up Daddy's pants. His striped shirt stayed tucked in as he stretched out on the blanket, but his brown hair pushed its way from under the front of his white cap. Baby sister Clara leaned against his leg and fussed, her little red face wanting its first bite of picnic cake.

But it was Janice who held Karen's eyes. Janice was visiting from that faraway place called Oregon, where it rained, mostly, and hardly ever snowed. It was near an ocean, with big waves, and big, big water, bigger even than Flathead Lake. Janice ran fast and played baseball and could hit a ball high, high over Daddy's head. And she looked eye to eye and really listened when Karen told her about Toby, the squirrel who lived in the backyard tree, and about Franny, the dog who lived next door. Daddy, Janice, and Karen dug worms together for fishing; they would fish as soon as everyone finished the picnic. Janice wasn't afraid of worms. Karen wasn't either, but Daddy promised to put the hook into the squirmy worm for her.

Then it was time! Mommy and Grandma put the food away in the big basket while Daddy moved the fishing poles down to Pearly Creek. Mommy kept saying, tie a rope around her, meaning that he should tie a rope to Karen's middle and the other end of it to a tree, as she stood by the edge of the creek.

"It's one-foot deep and just trickling along," said Daddy.

"Tie a rope around her," said Mommy, and so he did.

Janice and Daddy waded into the creek, their rubber boots stopping the water and making it swirl and bubble. Karen stood on a flat rock, holding her fishing pole and being very quiet, even though the branch of a bush behind her tickled her back. Then she felt a jerk and the tip of her pole dipped toward the water.

"Daddy!"

"Hang on! I'm coming!" Daddy waded back toward her, careful not to tangle his pole with Janice's. He laid his bamboo pole alongside the creek and put his hand around Karen's hand on her bobbing pole.

"OK, good, now you slowly reel him in."

Karen pinched the knob on the reel and made little circles, drawing in the line. The trout splashed across the surface of the water, its scales shining brighter than the rippling creek. Daddy kept his left hand on hers and with his right hand reached a net under the fish.

"There, honey! You caught him! You caught a fish!"

Karen watched as Daddy dipped his hand in the creek, gentled the fish out of the net, carefully removed the hook from its lip, and stuck his thumb in the fish's mouth. In a quick motion, he snapped the head backwards and the trout was still. Karen turned her head away.

"It's what we have to do, honey. It's so the fish won't suffer, won't hurt anymore."

Karen looked up at Daddy again, and now he had to look away from her eyes. She took his hand and looked at the fish in it.

"I did catch it myself, didn't I? Janice, I caughted a fish!"

Janice knelt down beside her on the rocks and looked at her fish.

"You are a good little fisherman, Karen. I hope I can learn to be as good at fishing as you are."

Janice said that. And Janice is thirteen and hits a ball really high—really high, over Daddy's head.

Soon the sun hid behind the high hills and the trees, and Mommy made them all put on sweaters. Daddy built a fire, dragging little branches and big chunks of wood, and pretty soon the fire jumped up and around. Karen's back was still cold, but her front was hot as anything. Then Oregon Grandma reached in her pocket and took out something silver. She put it up to her mouth and made a tune that came swirling across the fire. Nobody said anything. They all looked deep into the fire.

After she played, Grandma put the silver thing in her lap and sang the words to the song: "Oh the moon shines tonight on pretty Redwing." It was a sad song about an Indian maiden, and in the flickering red coals, they could almost see the girl crying. After Oregon Grandma went back home, Karen heard that song over and over in her head.

34

TRAIN RIDE TO SOUTH DAKOTA

When Karen was six years old and little sister Clara was four, their mother took the girls on a train from Axeton to visit their South Dakota grandma—their daddy's mother, whose name was Kari, almost the same as Karen, but you said it "Kahri."

The two sisters watched as a brown man in a dark suit with gray stripes carried their bags onto the Northern Pacific train. "What kind of man is that?" whispered Clara to her mother.

"He's a porter, a Negro, like Sam who plays baseball," said Mommy. "Very polite people," she said, as Clara and Karen climbed up into the train car and onto the fuzzy sofa bench across from their mother.

A woman came into the car, dressed in a long black robe tied with a rope. Stiff white cloth made a circle around her face, and something hid her hair. She shuffled and rustled and wriggled like a fluffy black hen into a seat five rows ahead of them. Now they could see only the black cloth that covered her head and shoulders.

"A nun," said Mommy, "and you shouldn't stare. She's Roman Catholic. She's given her life to their church, to help the priest. He's like our pastor. She will never marry."

"Just help the priest?" Karen asked.

"Maybe help a priest in a church like St. Mary's in Boise. Or teach in a Catholic school. There's a St. Francis school, near Grandma Gustavson's house in Oregon. Or she might be a nurse in a Catholic hospital like Sacred Heart in Spokane. And try to remember, don't stare."

The girls were allowed to walk up and down the aisle of their train car. "Talk quietly and don't bother anyone." Karen and Clara nodded solemnly to their mother.

They walked slowly up the aisle, touching the backs of the seats to keep their balance as the train began to rock from side to side. Following Mommy's rule, they did not stare at the nun, but only peeked at her face and robe, looked at each other, and then, fast as they could, made their eyes look straight ahead. On the way back, the girls sneaked a look at the nun again, and then looked hard at the water cooler at the end of the car. They did this over and over, walking back and forth by the nun six times. On their seventh peek, Karen was shocked to see the nun looking right back at her. "Hello," said the nun.

"Hello."

"Where are you girls going?"

"Back to our seats." Karen grabbed Clara's hand.

"No, I mean, are you traveling to visit someone?"

Karen felt her face turn red because she hadn't understood what the nun meant. "We're going to see our South Dakota grandma," said little Clara. She hopped back and forth and talked high and squeaky as a chickadee.

"What a wonderful thing to do. You must be very good girls. Would you like some candy?" The nun held in her hand a bar of five flat, square gumdrops, each a different color—pink, yellow, green, red, and black—all in a row.

Clara looked at her big sister and waited to see what she would do. Taking candy from a stranger was strictly forbidden. But, since they had been talking to the nun, she was not really a stranger. Also, if she worked at St. Mary's church or St. Francis' school, or at Sacred Heart hospital—

Suddenly Clara's little hand flitted by Karen and snatched a gumdrop from the nun's hand. "Thank you," she bubbled out through the pink, sugary candy already in her mouth.

The nun turned to Karen. At that moment, it seemed better to eat the quivery, green gumdrop, that might be filled with poison, than to be directly rude to an adult. Karen took the gumdrop, thanked the nun, moved the candy toward her mouth, and popped it in. It was rough with sugar granules; it was chewy and sweet. Karen smiled at the nun, and she smiled back.

Her name was Sister Mary Francis. So she was a sister, like Clara and Karen; and her name, Mary Francis, probably meant she worked at both St. Mary's church and at St. Francis' school. During the train ride, the girls visited her often, for her smile and for her bottomless bag of candy.

By the second day on the train, their mommy let them go one car ahead and one car behind. The car behind theirs was the caboose.

"Obey the conductor," said Mommy, "and be very safe."

The conductor had gray hair, blue eyes, and pale cheeks. He wore a dark blue uniform with gold braid on his sleeves and more gold braid above the shiny bill of his hat. He told all the children at the back of the caboose that they could stand looking out the open door, but that they must not set one foot across the doorstep onto the open balcony of the train.

After he left, Karen wiggled her way through the cluster of six or seven bigger children and got herself just beyond the doorway, where she stopped, still able to grab both sides of the metal door frame. She could see the Montana miles of tracks come together at a point far away. She felt the cool wind rushing by the train. She felt brave and wild. Then she felt the conductor's hand clamp onto her shoulder.

"I told you kids to stay inside. It's not safe out there."

All the kids stepped back, and the conductor pushed Karen to a place at the back of the bunch.

Clara and Karen looked at each other, scared. Not only had Karen disobeyed the conductor, she had done something unsafe. She didn't need to make her little sister promise not to tell their mother. If Karen, the older sister, lost Mommy's trust, they would both be kept in their seats for the flat, long, hundreds of miles left of Montana and South Dakota.

"How was the caboose?" asked Mommy when they sat back down beside her.

Clara, who normally replied to questions with paragraphs—this chatterbox, who usually spit out sentences so fast that grown-ups couldn't understand a word—looked at Mommy sideways through reddish-blond eyelashes.

"Good," she said, and stared out the window, very interested in the hot, dry, yellow prairie.

She was skinny, this South Dakota grandma, with a sharp chin. Her chin looked like the point of the cake server that she pushed under each slice of cake. She put a little piece of cake on Karen's plate. It was white, with white frosting, but Karen knew to say thank you to her. In South Dakota they didn't know, maybe, that children like chocolate best.

This grandma looked right at Karen, who saw that they both wore round, gold-rimmed glasses. It seemed funny to Karen that an old lady would have matching glasses with someone six years old. Karen didn't laugh, though, because grandmothers are not giggly people like sisters or aunts. You have to behave yourself around grandmothers. If you are going to visit a grandmother, you'd better wear a Sunday school dress and black patent-leather shoes and sit quietly on the couch until it's time to go home.

The South Dakota grandma sat down at the table right beside Karen, across from Daddy and Uncle Johan. Daddy looked tired because he drove by himself after work all night from Axeton in his new second-hand car. This house was Uncle Johan's and Aunt Leona's, with their little girl, Mary and the South Dakota grandma, too, all of them together.

This grandma turned her head and with it her pointed chin and nose. "So you are little Karen," she said. She said it "Kahren,"—like "car in"—like if Daddy was putting a car in the garage. "Did you know that Kari is also my name?" She said it "Kahri."

Karen nodded her head.

"And did you know that our name has been in the family a long time, back in Norway?"

Karen shook her head sideways. She didn't know that.

This grandma sipped her coffee and pointed over at Uncle Johan, who looked just like Daddy but had little wrinkles around his eyes. "Did you know this is my biggest boy?"

"And this is my littlest boy." She smiled at Daddy, and he smiled back.

Karen nodded again and smiled, too, because it was very funny to think of Daddy as a little boy. The South Dakota grandma caught her smiling, and for a minute they all smiled together. Karen couldn't believe it. Smiling with a grandma!

"Do you like to bake, little Karen," she said, waving her hand toward the cake.

"Cookies," Karen said. It was the first word she had said out loud to this grandma, and her voice came out in a whisper.

"So maybe your *mor* and *far* will leave you here, and we can bake together."

A picture from a storybook came into Karen's head of a pointy-nosed witch and a boy and a girl that were almost baked in the oven.

"Sure, *mor*," said Daddy, "if it's not too much for you. We'll visit Bensons for the afternoon. They have a boy about Mary's and Clara's age, so the little girls can play with him." He said this quick and excited like he was happy to leave his oldest girl behind. He probably didn't remember the witch story. Karen tried to signal him with her eyes. Usually that worked with Daddy, but this time it didn't. Uncle Johan pushed open the screen door and walked out with Aunt Leona and Mary. Mommy walked out right after them and then Daddy, carrying Clara in his arms.

Karen looked again at this grandma. Her white hair was pulled straight back behind her head, even the top part, so her forehead went way back, farther than Karen could see from down below. She wore a long black dress with long black sleeves, even though it was summer and very hot. The front of her dress hung straight down, not poufed out like Mommy's front, soft as a pillow. This grandma looked like a tree in winter, her arms like spiky branches and her hands prickly twigs.

"So," Grandma said, very quietly, like a secret, "we will make very special cookies."

She opened a drawer and took out a blue and yellow apron. She slipped it over Karen's head and arms and tied it around her middle. It went around Karen twice and covered her shoes. "Just right," said Grandma, and it sounded like "Yust right." Her voice was round and soft, like a song bouncing off her pointy chin.

She went to her cupboard and lifted out flour and sugar. She brought eggs, butter, and cream from her icebox. She put everything on the table where Karen could see it. She put her hands around Karen's middle and said, "Jump!" It sounded like "Yump!" Together they got Karen standing on a wooden chair, so she was almost as tall as Grandma.

When Karen baked cookies at home, Mommy did some things, like cracking the eggs, and Karen did others, like stirring. Today with Grandma, Karen did everything. She broke the eggs into the big bowl, and Grandma laughed; and when an eggshell fell in with the egg, she said, "*Ingenting*—it's nothing." She took a spoon from a drawer and scooped out the shell and dumped it in the sink. Karen poured in a cup of sugar, lots of flour, butter, cream, and two spoonfuls of good-smelling vanilla and almond flavoring. She remembered not to say, "I like chocolate better." They made two balls of dough, squishing them a few times before rolling them round and putting them in the ice box.

Then they made a new bowlful of dough, this time with melted butter, cream, and seeds that they smashed until the seeds were tiny. This was runnier stuff, easy to stir. Grandma brought out an iron thing that opened like the waffle iron at home. It was smaller with handles, and Grandma put it on the cookstove to get it hot. She dropped butter onto it and let Karen spoon the cookie goo onto the iron. She closed it and put it back on the stove, for just a minute, and then turned it on the other side for another minute. When she opened the iron and popped the cookie out, it had a beautiful design pressed into it. "*Krumkaker,*" she said.

After they were finished with the *krumkaker,* and Karen got to eat the first one as soon as it cooled, Grandma took the icebox dough out and put it on the table. Together they made little balls and put them in straight rows on a cookie sheet. On top of each ball they stuck a tiny bit of almond and a tiny bit of red cherry. Very pretty. Karen counted them as she stuck in the decorations, and there were thirty-six. Grandma called her *flink,* said she was clever to know her numbers so well. Karen said right back to Grandma that she was *flink* to know how to make these pretty cookies. Grandma took Karen's face in her hands. They were warm from the *krumkaker* iron and from putting cookies into the oven. She made a funny face, and they giggled together. Karen couldn't think what was happening—giggling with a grandmother!

———

By 8:00, the children were asleep, Karen, Clara, and Mary in one bed, tangled together like a pile of puppies. Johan excused himself soon after, saying that morning milking would come early. As she followed him, Leona added, "Sleep as long as you like. We'll have breakfast later, all together."

Evelyn slipped off next, tired from the long day of visiting. Then it was just Anders and Kari, a son with his mother, sitting together on the couch. He smiled at her and took her hand. Very well did she remember that boyish smile, almost irresistible, no matter what mischief he had been about.

"And so...what will you do, now that this terrible war is finished?"

"I don't know, *mor*. Axeton's still a good place for me, I guess. Lots of hunting and fishing. Baseball, too, I can still hit and catch a ball." That grin again. She turned from its brightness.

"And what does Evelyn think?"

"Oh, well, she's always ready to take us off to Oregon. Her father, Gustav..." Anders didn't need to say more than that. Everyone in Brem and the surrounding farms still spoke of that ambitious farmer and sharp businessman. "Moneybags!" some called him. "Hear he's a big landlord in Oregon now," others muttered.

"And would there be a job for you there? A place to live for your family?"

"Yeah, Gustav would arrange all that. Said he'd give us a duplex, us and Evelyn's sister. Maybe a building lot in town close to the university. Might be a carpenter job open at the U. They all think college is important for the girls. I don't know. Maybe a man could do some fishing around there. It'd be the end of hunting probably, and baseball, for sure." He shook his head, as he considered the loss.

Kari sat in silence. She would not speak her thoughts unless he asked. Minutes passed.

"What's on your mind, *mor*." Another minute went by.

"*Vel*..." She took a breath. "*Vel*, my son, it is this. We have been through a terrible time here on the farm, heat and dust without end. Then prices so low on crops that Johan plowed them under. Your brother Rolf..." Kari paused and then began again. "Now the world is wounded and sick almost unto death from this war. It may be time for you to put away childish things. You might look to Johan, your oldest brother, and strive to be a man like him, living for the sake of your family, as you cross over the ten years between you."

Anders looked down at his hands, gnarled by mill work and bent by the impact of flying baseballs.

"I have said too much." Kari's voice grew tender.

"No, *mor*, I think you said just enough—and said it well." He held her close for a moment, released her, and walked up the stairs to his bed.

35

THEY ALL RODE HOME

In the morning when the girls woke up, they stuffed their mouths with Aunt Leona's pancakes. Karen could feel her tummy pouf out as she pushed the last forkful onto her tongue. Daddy and Mommy packed up their bags and loaded them into the trunk of the car.

South Dakota Grandma took Karen and Clara to a corner of the living room. "Your cousin Mary lives here with me, you know, and someday will have the few nice things I have. But you two should have something as well." She unwrapped a ceramic doll with red-blond hair and dimpled cheeks. "This baby kewpie doll looks just like you, little one," and she handed the doll to Clara. "And you, my very own namesake, give this to your mother for safekeeping until you wear it on your wedding day." She placed a gold bracelet in Karen's hand and closed her fingers over the filigree.

Mommy took a picture of Karen, Clara, and Mary standing around their grandma as she sat in a straight-back chair. Karen watched as Daddy put his face next to Grandma's and whispered something into her ear. Then he held his hand out to Uncle Johan, who wrapped both of his wide hands around the palm and fingers of his younger brother. The two men looked at each other without a word, and then, with a quick shake, released their grip and finished loading the suitcases.

The girls settled into the back seat of their new used car for the long ride ahead, all the way from the eastern edge of South Dakota to Axeton in the northwest corner of Montana. The July sun shimmered in distant puddles of water on the two-lane concrete roadway—shiny mirages that disappeared as the car rolled closer. The temperature climbed to ninety-five degrees midday on the eastern plains of Montana. With the Chevy windows closed, the air in the car was stifling. With the car windows open, a dry, hot wind blew their hair straight and their cheeks red.

Karen and Clara played in the back seat on a soft, level platform built up with boxes and pillows and covered with a quilt. The Chevy coupe had no doors in back, so the girls had a snug little play area. They stripped down to their underpants, and each time a car zipped by, going the other direction on the two-lane highway, they shrieked and giggled and ducked down flat on the quilt, out of sight. Then Karen peeked up over the back of the front seat.

"OK. No cars coming," and the girls sat up again to pretend they were cowgirls riding horses across the prairie.

As their Chevy passed the signs spread a few yards apart on fence posts beside the road, Daddy read them the Burma-Shave slogans. He said the rhymes in little bursts of words:

"I use it, too—
The bald man said—
It keeps my face—
Just like my head—
Burma Shave"

Four-year-old Clara didn't understand some of the jokes, but Karen at six did. She carefully explained the funny rhymes to her little sister and tried to read the short words herself before their daddy said them.

At noon they stopped at a café for lunch. The girls pulled on their shirts, shorts, and canvas shoes, crawled into the front seat, and scrambled out of the car. "This will be our main meal," said Mommy, "so eat everything on your plate." Mommy and Daddy looked carefully at the menu, as they always did, and then ordered hot turkey sandwiches, as they always did. For Karen and Clara, they cut one hot turkey sandwich in half and used an extra plate for Clara's part. It was hard to divide because even though the menu called it a sandwich, it was really two pieces of white bread with mashed potatoes and gravy in between, and gravy with cut-up turkey poured over everything. "Tastes great," Daddy said about a hot turkey sandwich, "and really fills a guy up." Daddy never looked filled up. He was as skinny as South Dakota Grandma.

The waitress was wearing a short white dress with spots on it. She brought coffee, and milk in little bottles with paper lids for Karen and Clara. She lifted the lid off Clara's little milk bottle, poured the milk into a glass, and put it in front of Clara's plate. "Thank you," said Clara. The waitress tipped the second milk bottle toward Karen's glass, and the paper lid fell into the glass with milk pouring in after it. "Oh, darn," said the waitress. She waited until the lid floated to the top of the milk, and then she reached in with her thumb and middle finger to pull it out. Her fingernails were painted bright red. "There!" she said and dropped the milky lid onto the table.

Karen looked at Daddy, who was looking back at her. He was not smiling, and he lifted his eyebrows just a little. She did not drink the milk. When they got back into the car, he said, "Good girl," and gave her a wink.

Clara and Karen napped then, tummies full and energy sapped by the heat. Evelyn glanced at the back seat bed, comforted by the sight of her sprawling, sleeping daughters and by the thought: Once they go to sleep you know they are really safe.

———————

His mother's words weighed on Anders' heart. Through the years of his boyhood she had criticized him so little. Any correction, any discipline was left to his father, and when Jens died, Kari became yet softer toward her adult children, thanking them for help on the farm and blessing them on their way when they left. Now, it seemed to Anders, she was giving last words of advice, words his father might have said if he had lived.

Loved by his mother, captivated by his wife, and enchanted by his daughters, Anders felt himself swaddled by women, wrapped in a quilt of their soft, domestic ways.

He yearned for the freedom of tramping the Dakota prairie, flushing out a pheasant, and bringing it down with one shot. He longed to defy the elements, trudging through Montana snow in cold so harsh it froze breath on a man's beard—or in summer, fishing along Pearly Creek, making a turn, and facing a moose crowned with towering antlers. He wanted to feel the thunk of a baseball hitting his catcher's mitt and the whack of a bat sending a ball over the fence.

And yet—his mother's words rang true to him, that it was time for him to give up childish ways. His body was telling him as well—knees that complained as he crouched behind home plate, fingers and toes half frozen in winter as he hunted or loaded lumber into boxcars, and a back that laid him flat for days after he dragged home a deer.

He thought of boys in Axeton and Brem who never became men, who never grew up but spent their lives drunk every Saturday night—men who drifted from one job to another, from one woman to another, never sticking to anything or anyone. He thought of his brother Rolf. "Look to your oldest brother," his mother had said. Look to Johan.

When the next Oregon letter came from Berit saying that Gustav had made the final payment on city lots near the university, Anders spoke first.

"Generous of your pa. Maybe a good chance for us."

"You think so?"

Anders could hear the surprise in Evelyn's voice and answered, "Probably time for us to make the move. Gets mighty cold around here in winter."

"In a town that big—you wouldn't be playing baseball there."

"Have to watch those college boys play, I guess. I'd give 'em a few suggestions."

"Yell at the ump, you mean. I'd have to go with you to calm you down."

He grabbed her hand across the table and held it. "Me yell? I'd have to settle you down. You get more excited than I do, watching a game!"

"There'd be fishing—trout in the McKenzie river."

"I'll catch those little fish, mama. You fry 'em in a pan."

"And who will eat them?" They smiled together at the thought of their two little girls crunching away on crispy trout.

36

GOING HOME

The sky was still dark when the phone rang. From her little bed, snuggled under warm blankets against the nighttime chill, she heard the phone ring—two short jingles, the signal that the call coming through on the party line was meant for their house. Then Karen heard her father's footsteps padding down the stairs to the phone in the kitchen. She heard her mother's footsteps a minute later.

"Hello," said Daddy loudly, in his telephone voice. "Yes," he said, and she heard the scrape on the floor as he pulled a chair from the kitchen table and a creaking as he sat on it. "Yes," he said again. "No, you don't need to call them. I'll tell the others. I'll be there." He paused for a moment. He was no longer using his telephone voice, but his soft voice, the one he used when he tucked her in at night. "I'll be there by Saturday morning." She heard the chair scrape again as he stood up and a click as he settled the earpiece of the phone into the prongs of the telephone on the kitchen wall.

She crept out of bed to the stairway and peeked through the railing into the kitchen. Mommy had both hands on Daddy's face, holding his head so he looked right at her. "Your mother lived a good life," she said. "Kari was a good woman. She lived a good, long life, and she had a peaceful death. We can't ask for more than that."

He shook his head slightly and sat down at the table. "No, we can't ask for more than that."

Karen understood that they were talking about South Dakota Grandma. Karen remembered just how she looked in her farmhouse, very old in a long, dark dress. Her hair was thin and wrapped around the back of her head. Her hands were tiny for a grown-up and looked like they would crackle if you touched them. When she took your hand in hers, you could feel the bones of her fingers and could count them as she talked to you. Her words sounded funny, just a little, but happy and bouncy, with an up and down music in her talk. Karen remembered that trilly voice and remembered the papery touch as Grandma put the gold bracelet into her hand back in South Dakota.

Grandma had given Clara a little doll, not to play with, but to put on a shelf and look at. The doll was hard and smooth, painted so her shoulders and hands and feet were light pink, like skin, and her hair the color of cinnamon. Her mouth was painted in the shape of a bow, the edges of it pushing out against her dimples. Her eyes were looking up at something so that her painted eyelashes almost touched her little eyebrows. Karen noticed the doll's eyes especially, because the light blue in them matched exactly the blue in her grandma's eyes. She thought at first that the doll might have been made when Grandma was a little girl, to look like her. The girls kept the doll in the room they shared, on the bookshelf next to their bed, so they could see it when the family said in bedtime prayers, "And bless Grandma in South Dakota." Karen always said "in South Dakota" and then "in Oregon" because God heard about lots of grandmothers and might get mixed up about the ones she meant.

Karen moved down the stairway, a step at a time, hanging onto the railing and watching her mother and father. Daddy's face was very still, and he kept looking at Mommy. Then he turned toward the window. The sky was getting light.

"I could drive today and most of the night and be in Brem by morning."

Mommy moved toward the coffee pot. "I sure hate to have you driving all night." She filled the coffee pot with water, put it on the stove, and turned on the burner. She took some coffee from the green coffee can and put four big spoonfuls in the top part of the pot. Karen could smell the coffee as it started to bubble. Then maybe she made a noise, or they saw her move because they both looked at her at the same time.

"Come here, Sunshine." Daddy was using his soft voice. She ran to him, and he lifted her into his lap. "You heard?"

She nodded. "South Dakota Grandma?"

"Yes, South Dakota Grandma. She died last night. Now she's up in heaven."

Karen nodded again. Every night, just after they prayed "Our Father who art in heaven," they said, "Now I lay me down to sleep, I pray the Lord my soul to keep. If I should die before I wake, I pray the Lord my soul to take."

She smiled, surprised that Daddy thought he had to say that Grandma in South Dakota was now Grandma in heaven. Karen knew that already, from the prayer.

She hugged him so that he would know she understood. She thought of the rest of the prayer: "If I should live 'til other days, I pray the Lord to guide my ways." Then she smiled at Mommy to let her know that she didn't have to worry about Daddy's driving. God would guide his car all the way to South Dakota and back.

———

Their trim, two-story white house sat back on the deep town lot, front door opening directly west. From her east-facing kitchen, Evelyn spied the first glimmer of the rising sun filtered through the dark green needles of fir trees. In the early morning, between the time Anders pushed off on his bicycle for the mill and the moment she heard the girls babbling and giggling in their bedroom, Evelyn gazed over her coffee cup, through the evergreen branches at the snow-topped mountains in the distance.

With the house up for sale, she tried to stamp this sight into her memory. Then as she placed dishes in the kitchen cupboards or sheets on the beds, she wondered: this house—our first house—the house of our own skill and labor—will I remember this? She wanted to record every detail. The thought of a stranger moving into her house was too much to consider, and she put it out of her mind.

The house must be sold, of course, before they could move to Oregon. But the logic of her head could not soothe the pain in her heart. She did not speak of it to Anders. The two of them talked only of practicalities: renting a cheap place here in Axeton to live in after they sold the house; shipping the piano to Oregon and selling the rest of the furniture; quitting the mill job; tuning up the car for the trip through the mountains and across the dry lands to a college town in the green Willamette Valley.

Anders packed up his catcher's mitt but gave away his Axeton team uniform.

"Hey, don't disgrace my number, Butch," he said as he handed the new team member his uniform, carefully washed, pressed and folded. The high school kid looked with admiration at the town team veteran.

"I'll do my best, Mr. Nilsen."

"I'm counting on you." Anders grinned at the boy, turned and walked away. Jeeze! The new catcher called him Mr. Nilsen. Anders' knees seemed to creak under him.

Every familiar activity—walking in the woods with Evelyn, hunting above Mathias and Inga's farm, catching trout in Pearly Creek—took on importance as the summer wore on. Would this be the last time?

At the annual church picnic, Evelyn's good friend Gertrude settled the dilemma of the house sale. "Wally and me—we've been thinking. Would you feel right about selling your house to us? We're tired of paying rent—and we've been saving every month. When you'd come back to visit, you could stay with us, Evie, in the house you and Andy built."

And that was it. Though it was painful enough as they moved out of their home and into a shabby rented cabin, Evelyn could bear to hand over her scrubbed and polished house to Trudy.

———

They walked down the path to the lake, just the two of them. Part of the way, the path was wide enough so that Anders could take Karen's hand, and they walked together. In some places the edge of the path pushed in at her, scratchy with berry bushes, and she ran ahead.

"Not too fast, Pumpkin." She heard her father's voice calling to her. "Your old dad can't keep up." Karen knew that wasn't true, 'cause she'd seen him play baseball with the other grown-up men, running really fast, trying to run faster than the ball. Baseball was something like tag, and Daddy was very good at it.

The lake was big and smooth, unless the wind was blow-ing, and today it wasn't. Daddy sat down on the rock they called "chair rock" because it was the right size for two grown-ups to sit on. It was too high for Karen, but Daddy picked her up by her middle and lifted her onto the rock beside him. They didn't say anything, either of them. It was very quiet. The lake sat still and blue as the sky. Great tall green trees all around the lake pointed up to the sun.

Daddy looked at his feet. He reached down, and his fingers rustled around in the speckled stones by his shoes. He picked up one and then another. He looked carefully at each stone before he handed it to Karen. One, two, three, four, five, six, seven. She couldn't hold them all in her little hands, so Daddy scooped them up from her and walked to the edge of the lake. She slid down off chair rock and followed him.

Daddy squatted down, just like when he played catcher in baseball, and his eyes were even with her eyes.

"You know we're moving to Oregon," he said.

"Yes."

"What do you think about that?"

"Is everybody of us going? Mommy and Clara, too?"

"Of course. We always stick together. You know that."

"Will we have a house again?'

"Grandpa Gustavson bought us a duplex. That means two houses in one. For awhile we'll live there, in half the duplex, until I get a job. Then we'll build a house."

She didn't like the way Daddy said all this. His eyes looked a little sideways in the middle of it, and his voice sounded too soft.

"Why do we have to go?" she asked.

Daddy didn't say anything for a minute. He looked out across the lake. Karen heard the stones scratch together in his hand. "You know it's very cold here in winter, when I load the boxcars. Remember I was sick last Christmas? And there's a big university in Oregon. I might be able to get a carpenter job, building housing for the soldiers coming back to college. Mommy thinks you and Clara could go to college there someday."

Daddy smiled then and looked right at her. "Want to learn something new?'

Karen nodded.

Daddy put the stones in his pocket, all except one. He stood up straight and tall, a skinny shadow against the sun. He pulled his left arm way back to the side, and then he snapped it to the front and let go of the stone. It looked like it would go far, far away, he threw it so hard, but the stone splashed into the lake close by, and then splashed again and again across the water.

"You like that?"

"Teach me?"

"OK—you do it like this." And Daddy taught her how to skip a stone across the lake. "My mother—your South Dakota Grandma Kari—showed me how to do that. She said it would make me lucky."

"Did it?"

"Sure did. Couldn't be luckier than having Mommy for my wife and you and Clara for my little girls, could I?"

Daddy and Karen skipped all the stones across the water. After a few tries, she could make three skips easy. On his very last throw, Daddy made the stone skip seven times—a very lucky number. Then they ran back up the path, and Daddy ran really fast. He almost won.

ACKNOWLEDGMENTS

I am grateful for the generosity of those who helped me as I wrote *Skipping Stones*. Although it is a work of fiction, which freed me to imagine conversations and thoughts of characters, the kernel of many stories within the novel came to me through the years from family members whose parents were immigrants from Norway and Sweden.

First and foremost, love and gratitude for my father, Ludvik Reinertson. Dad moved into a story with a grin and a shake of his head, seeming scarcely able to believe his own account of his boyhood—playing baseball, guiding horse and sleigh into blizzards, and staring through campfires, bedazzled by dancing Gypsies. He held us entranced. Thanks as well to my mother, Florence Carlson Reinertson, who though she had heard Dad's stories many times, never corrected his evolving versions.

Great-uncle Jens Reinertson wrote of his shipboard crossing of the Atlantic to America as a boy. Uncle Harry Carlson typed out his memories of life on the South Dakota farm for the benefit of his son, grandchildren, nieces, and nephews. Many descriptions of farming in *Skipping Stones* are based on his clear and clever writings. I quote his phrase in describing the harvest work horses, as ranging from "good sense to hammerhead but... patient and faithful for all of their years." I simply could not think of better words. Thanks to Aunt Ragna Reinertson Burt for writing of her immigrant family's traditional Norwegian Christmas celebrations and of her other memories.

Relatives and friends still living in Scandinavia became a precious resource in sharpening descriptions of life in Norway in the late 1800s and in correcting my use of Norwegian and Swedish language in the novel. Norwegian cousin Klaus Egge worked patiently to make sense of my attempts at using Norwegian phrases in early chapters as Kari travels from Norway to America and as she creates her life in Dakota. At my request, Klaus used Nynorsk, the language of Western Norway, Kari's birthplace. He chose words that were in use in the late 1800s. Heartfelt thanks to him for his careful and accurate work; any mistakes in the final printed version are entirely mine. Thanks to Finnish cousin Pernilla Holmgård, who kindly supplied Swedish phrases.

Norwegian cousin Reidar Bjørnerheim read my first chapter and gently corrected the likely route and the time it would take for Kari's journey from Nordfjord to Bergen. Friend and professional language translator James Skurdall and his Norwegian wife, Anne-Guri, drew for me a clear picture of living conditions for farming families in 1880s Norway. They saved me from using a departure song not written until the 1900s for Kari's late 1800s sailing, and they suggested an older, more appropriate farewell song.

To Circle of Stones, talented writers and caring friends, who gather twice a month to listen, receive, and reflect back each writer's words: You made this happen. Suzanne Schlicke and Sally Windecker, thanks for your careful reading. For encouragement, skilled editing, and printing expertise, my gratitude to daughter Karen Koll; and for personal and technical support, my thanks to son Rob Koll.

Finally, I give deepest appreciation for Bill, my husband and dearest love, who took seriously my need to write and who brought tea and cookies to me each morning at 11:00 on my writing days; and for our present and future: Karen, Matthew, Robert, Melissa, Alison, Alfie, Christian, and Theodore.

PUBLISHED SOURCES

Resources for *Skipping Stones:*

Ken Burns, *The Dust Bowl, A Film By Ken Burns* (PBS: Public Broadcasting Service, 2012)

Otis M. Carrington, *Windmills of Holland, Operetta in Two Acts* (Myers & Carrington, 1913)

Day County Historical Research Committee, *History of Day County* (Aberdeen, South Dakota: North Plains Press, 1981)

Cheryl R. Ganz, *The 1933 Chicago World's Fair, A Century of Progress* (Urbana and Chicago: University of Illinois Press, 2008)

Robert Kenner, producer, *The American Experience, Influenza 1918* (PBS: Public Broadcasting Service, 1998)

Kristine Leander, Ed. *Family Sagas, Stories of Scandinavian Immigrants* (Seattle: Scandinavian Language Institute, 1997)

Paul Maccabee, *John Dillinger Slept Here, A Crooks' Tour of Crime and Corruption in St. Paul, 1920-1926* (St. Paul: Minnesota Historical Society Press, 1995)

Stan Tekiela, *Birds of Montana, Field Guide* (Cambridge, Minnesota: Adventure Publications, Inc. 2004)

Sno-Isle Regional Library System Information Request regarding Walter Liggett, resulting in newspaper clippings such as *New York Times*, **December 10, 1935**.

READING GROUP QUESTIONS

1. As the novel begins, Kari leaves her home in Norway, knowing she might never return. What influences her to do this? What poignant moments indicate the pain of this departure for Kari and her family? Why do you think emotions are so restrained in this culture?

2. How do women help Kari, both on her journey and as she settles in the Dakota town of Brem?

3. In contrast to the mountains of Norway, the flat prairie of Dakota disheartens Kari. How do her feelings about the prairie change over time?

4. How do romance and practicality intertwine as Kari and Jens meet and marry?

5. Kari's son Anders emerges as a main character, even in childhood. What incidents show a special relationship between this mother and her youngest son? As they relate to each other, what is said—and what is not said?

6. What is the importance of baseball in the novel?

7. Whether in good or hard times, the Nilsens find room for recreation, relaxation, and celebration. How does their Norwegian past mix with their American present in these activities?

8. Members of the Gustavson family work—and then work some more. Why are they so driven? What are the positive and negative results for this family?

9. How does World War I change attitudes about preserving language and heritage of the old country or becoming more American?

10. In large families, the oldest sibling sometimes plays a guiding role for younger children. In the Nilsen family, how does Johan do this for Anders and others? In the Gustavson family, what is Wilhelm's role?

11. Scandinavians in this story brush up against other cultures in America. Recall incidents involving (using the terminology of that time) Gypsies, Indians, Irish, Greeks, Negroes, and Germans. What are the roots of friction between Norwegians and Swedes in the story?

12. Why is persistence important in the lives of Kari and Jens; Berit and Gustav; Anders and Evelyn?

13. Historical events from 1880 to 1945 intrude into the lives of individuals in *Skipping Stones*. Discuss the effects on the main characters of the Homestead Act; Indian wars; World War I; 1918 influenza epidemic; voting rights for

women; Dust Bowl and Great Depression; prohibition of liquor; World War II.

14. Anders travels from his drought-stricken farm to crime-ridden Minneapolis and then to Aunt Inga's and Uncle Mathias' log farmhouse in Montana. How do these experiences and places change him? How does living in Montana reconnect Anders with his Norwegian heritage?

15. Anders Nilsen and Evelyn Gustavson are different in personality and upbringing. What are the weaknesses and strengths of each? Is the push-and-pull of these differences harmful or helpful to their marriage? To their creation of home?

16. Struggles of birth and death are depicted in *Skipping Stones*. What sources of strength sustain women and men in this story?

17. Is religious faith important in the lives of these people? Are there doubts? What about luck? What positive and negative aspects of church are portrayed?

18. Through rhythm and tone, *Skipping Stones* at times slips into a child's voice. When does this happen? Is it effective?

19. Leaving home and creating home are major themes of *Skipping Stones*. What are the practical and emotional aspects of this for Kari and Jens; Gustav and Berit;

Evelyn and Anders? Why is leaving and rebuilding home an overarching American theme?

20. Characters in the novel are deeply affected by their natural surroundings: shape of mountain and plain, surge of sea and river, and power of sun and storm. How important do you think these will be to Anders, Evelyn, and their daughters as they move to a small city in Oregon? How important are natural surroundings to people today? What has changed? What is still the same?

21. How does this story inform and raise questions for the reader about the competing values of independence and community; patriotism and ethnic roots; frugality and generosity; youth and maturity?

CPSIA information can be obtained at www.ICGtesting.com
Printed in the USA
LVOW07s1219130915

453974LV00002B/298/P